MURDER
ON THE
MED

MURDER ON THE MED

A Kat Lawson Mystery

Nancy Cole Silverman

First published by Level Best Books 2024

Copyright © 2024 by Nancy Cole Silverman

All rights reserved. No part of this publication may be reproduced, stored or transmitted in any form or by any means, electronic, mechanical, photocopying, recording, scanning, or otherwise without written permission from the publisher. It is illegal to copy this book, post it to a website, or distribute it by any other means without permission.

This novel is entirely a work of fiction. The names, characters and incidents portrayed in it are the work of the author's imagination. Any resemblance to actual persons, living or dead, events or localities is entirely coincidental.

Nancy Cole Silverman asserts the moral right to be identified as the author of this work.

Author Photo Credit: Craig Sotres Photography

First edition

ISBN: 978-1-68512-652-0

Cover art by Level Best Designs

This book was professionally typeset on Reedsy. Find out more at reedsy.com

To my mother, whose wit, beauty, and wisdom were the inspiration for Kat Lawson. Thank you, Mom.

Praise for Murder on the Med

"A fun romp on the high seas with an unexpected twist."—Libby Klein, author of the Poppy McAllister Mysteries

"Silverman delivers another stylish, addictive page-turner that will have eager readers cruising from chapter to chapter." —Ellen Byron, Agatha Award Winner and *USA Today* bestselling author

Chapter One

Gulf of Naples - Italy

July 2000

"Overboard! Are you telling me the woman fell off the ship? And nobody did *anything*?"

I was sitting in the Athena's English Garden Cafe with the Churchill sisters, Irene and Ida, elderly Brits, who occupied one of the hundred and sixty-five luxurious condominiums aboard a renovated ocean liner. It was nearly four p.m., and we were enjoying high tea with white linen napkins and a four-tiered tray of finger sandwiches, cakes, chocolates, and scones when Irene, the more talkative of the two, casually mentioned she believed Dede Drummerhausen—whose condo my publisher had arranged for me to sublet while covering the ship's tour of the Amalfi coast—had disappeared.

"I doubt anyone was around to see. And even so, what could anyone do?" Irene dabbed her upper lip with the edge of her napkin. "I suppose if someone had seen, they might have thrown her a life preserver. But even a strong swimmer would have had trouble reaching it. Poor soul. She liked to stroll the deck alone at night. Likely, she fell overboard, and well, there you have it—she's gone, nobody on board wants to believe us, and there's not a thing anyone can do about it."

I took the scone I was about to take a bite of and rested it on the saucer with the teacup in my hand. I couldn't believe what I was hearing.

"But you didn't actually *see it*, right?"

"Well, of course not. Nobody did. But my sister and I know for a fact that Dede didn't get off the ship in Naples. We had plans to meet for breakfast when we docked, and Dede never showed up." Ida plopped a sugar cube in her tea and stirred it slowly. "And now, you're here, staying in Dede's apartment and writing your little travel feature. I don't imagine we'll know what happened to Dede until we dock in Positano, where, if she's still alive, she's scheduled to rejoin us. And, where I assume you'll take leave of us?"

"That's the plan," I said. Convinced the old ladies might be drinking something stronger than tea, I placed my cup and saucer on the table and tried to keep my hands from shaking. This was my first full day aboard *Athena*, and I had yet to get my sea legs. Whether it was Irene's casual description of her shipmate's fate or the pitch and roll of the ship, my stomach felt like it was about to follow.

Ida snatched a scone from the tray. "Believe me, if Dede had been aboard, she would have shown up for breakfast. Trust me, Dear. The woman never missed a meal. You only needed to look at her to know."

"Large boned, she liked to say." Irene studied me from over the rim of her teacup.

"More like well-padded." Ida swanned her neck in her sister's direction.

"Not that it slowed her down." Irene dipped a lemon biscuit into her tea. "Woman never met a pool or a piece of cake she didn't dive into. Took a swim every afternoon in the pool and afterward would waltz around in her robe and flip-flops, her red hair dripping wet, with a croissant or chocolate in her hand. Never a thought about how she looked. All very American. Present company excluded, of course. No offense."

"None taken." I smiled, albeit a bit disingenuously. While appearing well-meaning, the sisters were undoubtedly a bit batty, if not tipsy.

My name is Kat Lawson. I'm a reporter turned undercover operative for the F.B.I. working for a travel pub as a feature writer. My assignment with *Journey International* was to cover the *Athena*, a former Russian troop tanker abandoned in a shipyard in Bremen, Germany, in 1991 when the Soviet

CHAPTER ONE

Union collapsed. A group of international investors led by a young South African named Neil Webster, with family money and connections to the diamond trade, saw an opportunity. They bought the ship, brought her out of dry dock, redesigned her from the bowels to the bridge as a kind of condos at sea for seniors seeking to sail into their sunset years, and christened her *Athena*. My publisher, Sophie Brill, thought it might make for a fascinating story and rewarded me with the assignment for my previous undercover work. This trip was a chance for me to relax and regroup. After all, how much trouble can one find aboard a 600-foot yacht with a bunch of senior citizens in the middle of the Mediterranean?

* * *

I left the café, anxious to get some fresh salt air and my sea legs beneath me. If I were still back home in Phoenix, I would have been on an early morning run. But with the nine-hour time difference and the fact I had arrived late and slept even later, I figured a walk along the Sun Deck would be just the thing to help me adjust to the time change. The view of the Bay of Naples as we pulled from the harbor and the city behind her looked chaotic with its urban sprawl of high rises and busy port. A sharp contrast to the calm blue Mediterranean waters ahead of us.

"Ms. Lawson?" I stopped to see who had called my name, and the ship yawed sharply. I reached for the rail, but too late. Like a drunken sailor, I slipped. But not before a strong pair of hands broke my fall.

"You okay?"

I grabbed the rail and straightened myself. "I'm fine. Thank you."

Standing in front of me was the ship's Captain. With one hand on the visor of his wheeled hat, he did a quick salute, then stepped back and introduced himself. Tall, blond, and in the instant it took for our eyes to meet...*trouble*. The kind of trouble that happens when you don't go looking for it and suddenly can't stop thinking about it or hoping to run into it again. Trouble that after two marriages and a couple of false starts, I had sworn off of—or at least—thought I had.

"Allow me to introduce myself. I'm Captain Byard McKay. I'm still kind of new here. The previous captain was McKey, so people on board call me Captain or Captain Byard. Makes it easier. You can call me whatever you like. We're an informal group. 'Least between the residents and crew." The captain extended his hand.

"And you can call me Kat."

"Sorry we didn't get a chance to talk last night when you came on board. I couldn't leave the Bridge. I trust you're settled?"

Trouble had a sexy British accent. "You're English?"

"Nae. A Scotsman." Even worse. His accent was intoxicating. "But you're not the first American to confuse the accent. *Athena*'s an international bunch. But don't worry, the crew all speak English. First mate's German. The doctor's a Swede. The chef is French. And below deck, we have an entire United Nations."

"And the residents?"

"They're from all over as well. Got one from Russia. A couple from Germany. England. France. America. We like to think of ourselves as Citizens of the World. Some residents have been aboard so long they think of *Athena* as their own private country."

"Excuse me, Captain?"

Interrupting us was a short, stocky, pale-skinned man dressed in navy pants and a white shirt with black shoulder epaulets sporting a single gold bar.

"Sully." The Captain addressed him with a nod of his head.

Sully did a quick salute. "Sorry to interrupt, Sir. Just wanted you to know, that little matter we addressed last night?" Sully tilted his head in the direction of the Naples' port. "It's all taken care of."

"Good to know." The Captain cleared his throat. "You can fill me in on the details later. Meanwhile, Ms. Lawson, this is our Head of Security, Chief Henry O'Sullivan."

"You can call me Sully. Most do." The Chief extended his hand. He had a firm, if not slightly clammy, handshake. "You're the American in Dede Drummerhausen's cabin. Writing a travel feature, I understand."

CHAPTER ONE

"I see news travels fast."

"Ay. For a big ship, *Athena*'s mighty small." The Chief pulled a pack of Marlboro Golds from his pocket. "Mind if I smoke?"

I shook my head.

The Chief put a cigarette in his mouth, covered the tip with the palm of his hand, and lit it. "Not much happens aboard that everyone doesn't know about."

"Including someone falling overboard?" It seemed like the appropriate time to ask. If the Churchill sisters were correct in their belief that Dede Drummerhausen had fallen overboard and not walked off the ship as she was expected to do in Naples, then who better to ask than the head of security?

"Ugh! You must have been talking to the Churchill sisters, Ida and Irene? Sorry to say, but those two old biddies? Nice ladies, but I wouldn't put much credence into what they say. They're a bit daft, and—"

"Charming." The captain interrupted. "I believe the word you're looking for, Chief, is charming. Isn't that right?"

The Chief took a drag on his cigarette, locked eyes with the Captain, and exhaled a ring of smoke from the side of his mouth. "Sounds about right."

The Captain rested a hand on the railing. "I wouldn't want you to think any of our residents are crazy. Most of those onboard are older, and like people in any retirement community, some have a few quirky habits, but I'm sure you'll find them all quite harmless. Just people enjoying their senior years at sea."

Humph. The Chief took another drag on his cigarette. "You might want to warn her about Marco."

"Marco?"

"Ay." The Chief raised a brow. "His name is Nicholas Marcopoulos. Goes by Marco. You'll know him when you see him. Full head of white hair. Mid-seventies. Greek. Maybe Italian. Not sure which. But you'll recognize him. Walks with a bit of limp and, when he's dressed, wears a yachtsman's hat."

"When he's *dressed*?" My eyes went from the Chief back to the Captain. "Is there something you're trying to tell me?"

5

"Uh-huh." The Captain cleared his throat. "Go on, Sully. Tell her. She might as well hear it now. No point in holding back."

"Marco's been aboard for a long time now. Suffers from dementia and tends to be a kleptomaniac. We've found things in his suite that don't belong to him. During the day, he's not much of a problem. But at night, I'll warn you, he likes to sleepwalk. Been known to wander the deck wearing nothing more than his hat on his head."

"You mean he wanders around naked?" The words tumbled from my mouth. I didn't know whether to laugh or be concerned.

"Don't worry. He's harmless. Maybe naked as the day he was born, but we keep an eye out for him. But if you hear any midnight reports about the Moon over Med. You'll know it's Marco."

Chapter Two

I left Captain Byard and Chief O'Sullivan on the Sun Deck to discuss whatever matter Sully had taken care of the night before and hadn't wanted to discuss in my presence. Whatever their concerns, including their warning about Marco's late-night moonwalks or the Churchill sisters' insistence that Dede Drummerhausen had gone overboard, I was convinced from the captain's response that I had little to worry about. And with the warm weather and the briny smell of sea salt, I wasn't about to let it bother me. After all, I was on a beautiful yacht in the middle of the Mediterranean and on vacation with a handsome Captain. How bad could things get? I did a quick lap around the Sun Deck, took one final view of Naples and the sparkling blue Mediterranean Sea at her shore, and returned to my cabin.

The rich live differently. My cabin, or Dede's condo, was on the twelfth floor or four floors above the Promenade Deck, where I had entered the ship and came with a maid and cabin steward for butler services. My steward's name was Finn, who, like his name, had come from Finland and had welcomed me aboard the night before. Finn looked to be in his early thirties, with white-blonde hair, luscious long lashes, blue eyes, and a gracious and very accommodating manner. In addition to helping me find Dede's cabin, Finn had placed a welcome basket in the living room, loaded with fruit, candies, a chilled bottle of champagne, and put chocolates by my bedside table.

Not counting the outside deck, which ran the entire length of the apartment with floor-to-ceiling sliding glass doors, the cabin was at least 2,000 square feet. Two master suites complete with jacuzzi tubs, large walk-in closets, a spacious living room with a big screen TV, a formal dining room, a fully stocked bar, and a dine-in kitchen. I could get used to this. After my divorce, I downsized. Not necessarily by choice, but what at the time had been a matter of what was affordable, and what was affordable, was a small studio apartment above my grandmother's garage. Barebones as it gets.

I got as far as the living room when I heard a noise from the kitchen. Someone had closed a cabinet door, and I could hear water running.

"Hello? Anyone here?" I knew it couldn't be Finn. I'd seen him enter one of the other cabins when I came down the hall. Instinctively, I reached for the bottle of champagne from the ice bucket on the dining table and held it by its neck, like a weapon, above my head. "Hello?"

Seconds later, a man appeared from the kitchen, wiping his hands with a dishtowel.

"Oh!" He stopped abruptly, surprised to see me. "You must be Kat Lawson. I wasn't expecting you."

I lowered the champagne bottle and held it against my chest. "And you are?"

"A friend of Dede's." The stranger tossed the dishtowel onto the dining room table and offered me his hand. He was tall, with greying blond hair, silver-rimmed glasses, and slim. I pegged him to be about my age, or maybe slightly older—mid to late forties, and based upon the ease with which he navigated the apartment, non-threatening. "I apologize if I've frightened you. Finn, your butler, let me in. I assume you've met?"

I nodded.

"I forgot that this was the week Dede had agreed to sublet her cabin. You must be the journalist."

"Yes, I am." I put the champagne bottle back on the dining table.

"I stopped by to restock Dede's spice shelf. She and I enjoy cooking and experimenting with different spices when I'm on board. Her late husband Walter and I used to consider ourselves food aficionados. But you mustn't worry. I won't let myself in again. I promise."

"You have a key?"

"No, I don't need one, I—"

CHAPTER TWO

"Own the ship." I stepped back and stared at my intruder, impeccably dressed in his white slacks and light blue collared polo shirt, as another more formal, professional picture came to mind, along with his bio. Neil Webster. Head of one of London's most successful investment funds and heir to a South African diamond mine estimated to be worth more than five billion dollars. "You're Neil Webster, *the* Neil Webster. I didn't think you'd be on board."

"I'm not ordinarily, but I wanted to be this week. My Aunt Ida is celebrating her birthday Saturday, and I didn't want to miss the celebration."

"Ida Churchill?"

"You know her?"

"I had High Tea with the Churchill sisters this afternoon. Ida and Irene."

"Yes. Lovely ladies. They're like family to me. I met Ida and her sister Irene years ago when I attended Eaton College for boys in London. When they retired, I suggested they take up residence on board the *Athena* rather than live a solitary life in soggy old England. I gave them a suite, and they've been aboard since the first day."

"That was very kind of you."

"It was the least I could do. The Churchill sisters were very good to me. Right after I started Eton, my mum and dad were killed in a plane accident in South Africa. My only living relative, my uncle, had no interest in taking me in and was content to have me away at school. Neither Ida nor Irene had any family of their own. The war had taken away any chance either would ever marry. They were spinster schoolteachers who took me under their wing, and we adopted one another. I think of them as my aunties. They're like family."

"And now, here you are. Ready to help celebrate Ida's birthday."

"I am. However, selfishly, I wanted the time away from work. London's been hectic, and *Athena* and the Med have always been my Happy Place. One day, maybe I'll be able to retire and spend my days sailing into the sunset like every other resident on board. But don't worry, if it's any consolation to you, I won't disturb you again." Neil reached for the dishtowel he had tossed on the table and folded it neatly across his arm. "Unless, of course, I can ask you to have dinner with me one night?"

I couldn't believe my luck. A Mediterranean cruise. A handsome captain. And now, a dinner invite with one of the most successful and sought-after investment gurus on the planet. "I'd love to."

"Good. However, I'll warn you, my dinner invitation isn't for an interview, at least not about me. *Forbes, The Wall Street Journal, Barrons,* and *Fortune* have been after me for years for a story, and I prefer to keep my personal life out of the news. So, if you promise not to grill me about my company or ask for any investment advice, I'd welcome the opportunity to chat with you about *Athena*. So why not? It'll give me a chance to get to know you better."

I bit back a smile. I didn't think for a minute that Neil's idea of getting to know me better was any type of come-on. From what little I knew about the man, he had never been married, nor did he have a reputation as a playboy. In fact, I was certain Neil wasn't interested in me as a woman, or any woman at all, for that matter. But as far as an interview with Neil Webster went, I was plenty interested. And, if I was careful, I'd walk away not only with a story about *Athena* but Neil Webster as well, and every financial publisher in the Western World would be knocking on my door for the inside scoop on one of the world's wealthiest men.

"Sounds fair enough. But, on one condition."

"And what might that be?"

"You said you're a food aficionado. You like to cook. Make dinner for me. Something I can write about for my magazine. And if I like what I eat, with your permission, I'll include something about your culinary skills." I held my hand up to wave off any objection. "Nothing about your business, I promise. Just something a little folksy my readers will enjoy."

Neil smirked. I was making headway.

"Alright, you're on. My apartment. Wednesday night." Neil brushed past me to the front door and stopped. "Come hungry. But remember, no questions about my business or my personal life. It's off limits."

"No problem." I closed and locked the door behind me and did a celebratory fist bump. If I could get Neil Webster to cook dinner for me, I could convince him to give me an interview.

Chapter Three

I was still thinking about Neil and how I would tell Sophie he had agreed to cook one of his special meals for me when I noticed a small black crocheted handbag on the table next to the door. I had missed it when I came in the night before. The apartment had been dark, and the door had hidden the small table behind it when open. But now, in the light of day, with the door closed, there it was, a woman's handbag abandoned, as though forgotten.

I couldn't imagine the bag belonged to Dede. What woman would go off and leave her purse behind when going into a foreign country? Unless, of course—I was already kicking myself for the thought—she had gone overboard like Ida believed—either accidentally or otherwise.

Captain Byard and Chief O'Sullivan thought Ida and Irene were lovely old ladies, but a bit daffy and known to amuse themselves with conspiracy theories. Consequently, I refused to entertain any thought of Dede's demise. There had to be a more obvious explanation. Perhaps Dede had changed out her purse at the last minute, or maybe the bag belonged to one of Dede's lady friends who had come to visit and forgotten it as she hurried out the door.

I should have left it at that. But I couldn't let go of the idea that a woman wouldn't leave her handbag behind any more than I could unsee the bag on the table. It was as though it were calling me. I debated whether I was within my rights to look inside. If this wasn't Dede's bag but some other passenger's, I'd be doing them a favor by learning the owner's identity and returning it.

The bag won out.

I moved it to the dining room table so I could better look at what was inside and found a thin, medium-sized red wallet, a small, grey flip phone, keys, lipstick, and a palm-sized English-to-Italian dictionary. I opened the wallet, hopeful I would find another woman's I.D. Instead, staring back at me was a Colorado driver's license with Dede Drummerhausen's photo prominently displayed on the left side. Round face, short curly red hair. Beneath her picture, her address, and her date of birth. June 2, 1933. Eye color: Green. Height: Five foot five. Weight: 165.

I placed the wallet on the table and stepped back. *Okay, Dede Drummerhausen, where are you?*

As a journalist, I had reported from enough crime scenes to know there were always clues left behind. I'll never forget my first homicide. A young couple had gone to park beneath the stars, been dragged from their car, and shot point blank beneath a Palo Verde tree. When I arrived, the bodies had been removed, but the Inspector was still combing the scene for evidence. I asked what he was looking for, and he pointed to scuff marks in the sand and fibers from a pink ribbon hanging from the tree. He taught me to read the scene. The young girl had tried to run but to no avail. From that day on, I knew no matter the crime, there were always clues. One just had to learn how to look for them. I scanned the living room for signs of an argument or a disturbed mind.

Dede's quarters included maid service, which presented a problem. Aside from my unmade bed in the guest room, everything appeared to have been swept clean. On the surface, I could see nothing out of the ordinary. No signs of a struggle or disarray. The living room, or great room, a combination living-dining area, with its cream-colored walls and overstuffed furnishings, included a couch, coffee table, two oversized swivel chairs, and a formal dining table, all set against a wall of floor-to-ceiling sliding glass doors that lead outside to the deck, The kitchen, with its stainless steel appliances and highly polished aluminum counters, didn't have so much as a smudge. Everything, from the books on the coffee table to silver-framed pictures on the buffet, including several of Dede, one with her sitting in a golf cart with

CHAPTER THREE

a man who I assumed might be her husband and another of her holding a bottle of Champagne and christening *Athena*, suggested a very organized and comfortable lifestyle.

I was about to stuff Dede's wallet back into her bag when I heard a tapping on the cabin door, followed by a man's voice. "Knock. Knock. It's your butler, Ms. Lawson."

I still couldn't get used to the idea of a butler and gathered Dede's bag into my arms as though it were my own. Finn entered the apartment, cabin keys in one hand, dry cleaning in the other.

"Sorry to disturb you. I've Ms. Drummerhausen's dry cleaning. I'll just be a moment." Finn disappeared into Dede's bedroom. I put Dede's bag back on the table and followed Finn as far as the bedroom door.

"Finn?"

"Yes, ma'am?"

"I apologize. We didn't get much of a chance to chat last night. I was so tired when I came in. I haven't even unpacked." I nodded in the direction of the guest bedroom, where my small rolie and backpack remained untouched on the floor. "I wanted to thank you. Particularly for the welcome basket."

"I'm glad you liked it. If you need anything, just ring the operator. Use the house phone. There's one in the kitchen, the bedroom, and by the front door. Ms. Drummerhausen may be gone, but you're here, and her quarters are my responsibility."

"I appreciate that. However, I did have a question."

"Yes." Finn leaned casually against the closet door, the dry cleaning folded over his arm.

"I'm curious. Do you know what time Ms. Drummerhausen left yesterday?" I was hopeful Finn might have seen Dede leave and put an end to any suspicions I had concerning the Churchill sisters' worries about Dede's whereabouts.

"I've no idea." Finn retreated into Dede's closet and hung up the dry cleaning. "I was busy with Professor Braun and his wife, Greta. They live across the hall. Nice people. I'm sure you'll meet them." Then poking his head out of the closet, he asked. "Anything else?"

"No, that's quite alright."

"Oh, I forgot to tell you last night, there's a mini-safe in your closet for valuables." Finn pointed in the direction of the guest room. "The instructions are printed on the outside. Just key in whatever code you like." Finn paused outside the closet door and scanned the room as though he were taking inventory. Satisfied everything appeared to be in its place, he ran his hand across the bureau, rubbed his thumb and index finger together, and then slipped past me in the doorway. I followed Finn to the living room, where he stopped in front of the glass doors. The late afternoon sun was streaking through, and the room had begun to heat up. "I can close the verticals if you like."

"No need," I said. "I'm sure I can do it."

I wondered if Finn had paused in front of the glass doors because of the heat or if he had noticed Dede's black bag on the dining table. Whatever his concern, he appeared satisfied I could handle the blinds on my own and moved toward the front door.

"Will you be going for cocktails at six? The residents usually gather in the bar every night at about that time."

"Not tonight. I was planning on unpacking and reviewing my notes for tomorrow."

"Very well, then. I'll leave you be. Good night."

I waited until Finn closed the door, returned to the dining room table, and stuffed Dede's wallet, phone, and keys back into her bag. I was about to put the small dictionary into the side pocket when I felt something hard and round beneath the lining. It felt like a loose coin. I took everything out again, turned Dede's bag inside out, and looked for a hole in the lining through which any loose change might have fallen. But there was none. Instead, I could see where the lining had been cut and carefully resewn.

I pulled at the thread until it gave way to a small opening in the bottom of the purse. A mini plastic bag like I had used to carry a small pair of earrings was hidden beneath the lining. But inside wasn't a pair of earrings, but a gold coin, about the size of a nickel. On one side was a head-and-shoulders profile of a man. And on the reverse was a skullcap between two daggers

CHAPTER THREE

with six letters beneath the images, all in caps and evenly spaced in two groups of three letters each. I read them aloud. E.I.D. M.A.R.

With the plastic baggie in my hand, I walked out onto the balcony and held the small bag up to the light. The gold coin inside caught the last rays of the late afternoon sun as the light danced across the Mediterranean's blue waters. Whatever the coin was, it had to be valuable. Why else would it be hidden inside of Dede's bag? It made no sense. If Dede knew it was there, she wouldn't have left it—not voluntarily, anyway. And if Dede didn't know anything about it, then who did?

I palmed the coin and returned to the dining room table, where I picked up Dede's bag. *Whatever this odd, unusual-looking gold coin was, it wasn't my business. There had to be some reason why Dede had hidden the coin inside her bag, just like there had to be some sensical reason why Dede had missed breakfast the morning the Churchill sisters thought she had gone missing.* But still…I paused and looked at the coin in the palm of my hand. While it seemed authentically old, how could I know for sure? Maybe it was just some lucky talisman Dede had hidden inside her bag for good luck. What I did know was that I was on a cruise around the Amalfi Coast on a first-class ship and that I had landed an exclusive interview with Neil Webster. Whatever this coin was, it didn't belong to me. I slipped the gold coin back beneath the bag's lining and returned the bag to the table behind the front door. If someone were to come looking for the bag and found it without the gold coin hidden beneath the lining, they might suspect, since I was staying in Dede's suite, that I had something to do with its disappearance. And then, who knows what trouble that might bring?

My mind was racing like a pinball machine. Why might Dede have left her bag behind the door or failed to show up at breakfast with the Churchill sisters? I returned to the dining table and uncorked a bottle of red wine from the gift basket Finn had left for me. It was almost nine p.m. Whatever had happened to Dede, whether she had gotten off the *Athena* on her own accord—or not—I couldn't let go of the idea that something was wrong. Call it a reporter's sixth sense, but things didn't feel right despite *Athena's* serene surroundings. I took a sip of wine and was about to take my glass and the bottle out to the balcony when the apartment phone rang. It was Captain Byard.

Chapter Four

"Good evening, Kat. It seems our late departure from Naples this afternoon has created a small change in our itinerary and an unusual opportunity. Something that I think you might find interesting. We'll be sailing past Mount Vesuvius around ten p.m. I thought you might like to join us on the bridge. The view from here's spectacular, and if you like, I could give a tour of the ship afterward."

I twirled the stem of the wine glass in my hand. I could think of nothing better than spending a beautiful, star-studded evening in the company of the ship's handsome Captain. But, tempting as the offer was, after finding what looked like an ancient gold coin hidden inside Dede's bag and thinking she might or might not be missing, I decided to put the brakes on the idea of a shipboard romance, at least for the moment. If Captain Byard was wrong about Dede and she hadn't gotten off the ship of her own accord, or even worse, if he was lying to cover up some sinister event, I thought it best to keep things professional. At least until I had a better understanding of Dede's disappearance and the gold coin I had found in her bag. Still, I did have a story to write, and I needed a tour of the ship. I accepted Byard's offer, promised myself I wouldn't get caught up in his charms, and told him I'd meet him on the bridge at ten, then returned to the guest bedroom to unpack.

It didn't take me but a few minutes to get organized. I travel light. I'm not much of a clothes hound. No point in dragging heavy bags halfway around the world. And, since this was a warm weather cruise, everything I thought I'd need fit in my backpack and a small rollie. A half dozen t-shirts, shorts, pants, tennis shoes, sandals, a swimsuit, a simple black shift, and a long-sleeved hooded sweatshirt. I considered wearing the dress, but it seemed inappropriate if I had to climb stairs. Instead, I opted for a pair of slinky black palazzo pants and a white t-shirt, then wiggled into a pair of black flats and pulled my hair into a ponytail. Lastly, I took my camera from my backpack, strung it around my neck, checked the mirror, and added a bit of mascara and lip gloss. I may have had my doubts about the captain, but I still wanted to make a good impression—just in case.

***

Finn had included a map of the ship with the gift basket, and I checked it quickly for directions. The Bridge was on the Sun Deck or the Lido Deck, at the front of the ship or the bow, opposite the Ivy Café where I had High Tea with the Churchill sisters that afternoon. The map showed three sets of elevators. One at the ship's bow. One mid-ship, closest to Dede's apartment, and another at the far end of the hall, closer to the stern. I elected to take the elevator mid-ship and punched the button to the Lido Deck three floors up. When the doors opened, the ship's yellow party lights illuminated an empty outdoor play area, easily the size of a football field. The bar was closed, the pool and jacuzzi were empty, and the deck chairs were all neatly folded and pulled beneath the sun awning. Directly ahead of me, towards the bow, was the Bridge, a large windowed structure that ran the entire width of the ship with two winged room-like areas off the port and starboard sides. A crew member sat outside a door marked *Crew Only* and, seeing me, opened the door and escorted me inside.

Inside, the Bridge was illuminated with red lights, and for a moment, I felt like I was standing on a movie set for the Star Trek Enterprise. It looked almost futuristic. Three oversized swivel chairs faced a panel of tall, expansive windows that looked out over the front of the ship to the sea beyond and into the inky black night sky. Beneath the windows were a series of computer screens, and centered between them, a small wheel, the size one might see on a toy car. Not at all what I expected for a ship the size of *Athena*.

Captain Byard stood up as I entered the room. "Welcome to the Bridge, Kat."

Maybe it was the ship's movement or the haze from the red lights that engulfed the room, but looking at the Captain, I suddenly felt faint. I stepped back and braced myself against the wall.

"Are you okay?"

"I'll be fine." I put my hand to my head. "It's the movement of the ship. I'm still getting used to it."

But it wasn't the movement of the ship that caused my knees to go weak, but a feeling of déjà vu. A flashback to a life long gone. I hadn't noticed the similarity before. Perhaps because the captain was wearing a hat, and the sun was in my eyes, but now, seeing him on the Bridge in the low light, the resemblance was uncanny, and it all came crashing back to me. The shadow of the young Air Force pilot I had married in college…and buried in an empty coffin. To Eric. Gone too soon to a senseless Vietnamese war—but never forgotten.

"Here. Take a seat." Captain Byard offered me his chair.

I sat down and tried to dismiss the striking similarity. It was going to be hard enough to focus on the task at hand and not relax in his company. But not until I knew Captain Byard wasn't hiding the truth about Dede Drummerhausen and her whereabouts or if he might have any idea about the gold coin I had found inside the bag she'd left behind did I dare to let my guard down.

Captain Byard introduced me to his first mate, Captain Rob, also known as the Officer of the Watch, who, along with his counterparts, manned the bridge twenty-four hours a day. Then went on to tell me more about the Bridge.

"From here, we have a clear view of the surrounding area." Captain Byard pointed to the window. "That's Mount Vesuvius straight ahead. And on the bulkhead below, these rounded radar screens give us *Athena's* position, approaching vessels, maps of the ocean floor, and the coastline."

I glanced at the blips on the green computer screens, like glowing orbs. I had no idea what they meant.

"The Bridge is the heart of the ship, the safest place to be. We keep all our important papers in the safe up here. Ship's registration. Maps. Crew passports. Emergency cash. The windows are fortified for heavy-duty storms and, for security reasons, bulletproof."

"Bulletproof?" I snapped a couple of pictures of the deck and Athena's crew, then held my camera to my side. "Are we expecting trouble, Captain?"

"Nothing you need worry about."

I took a quick picture of the captain.

He offered me his hand. "Come, I promised you a tour."

Chapter Five

C aptain Byard explained we would spend the evening cruising slowly along the Italian coastline before we dropped anchor at Procida the following day. Procida was a short thirty-minute cruise away, but due to our late departure and traffic in the harbor around the island, *Athena* would wait until morning to arrive. Meanwhile, we had a spectacular view of Naples, with its twinkling city lights behind us and the red glow of Mount Vesuvius directly ahead.

"Looks like she's still active."

"She is. The last big explosion was March of forty-four. But the one most people know about that wiped out Pompeii was seventy-nine AD. She'll blow again someday. In fact, she's the only active volcano in all of Europe."

I stared at the quiet scene across the bay, then snapped a couple of shots with my camera. The crescent-shaped mountain ridge was draped in misty-white clouds, making it impossible to see anything but the faint orange glow in the moonlight. If nothing else, I hoped I might get an artsy shot.

"The eruption that destroyed Pompeii and Herculaneum was over in fifteen minutes. The ash and the clouds were so thick you wouldn't have seen anything from here. Archaeologists are still finding evidence of what was once an active trade port."

I took one last look through the binoculars and followed Captain Byard outside to the deck and back to the elevator I had taken from Dede's floor to the Bridge. Beneath the moonlight, steps ahead of me in his white jacket, the captain cut a handsome figure—*so like Eric*. He paused when we got to the elevator doors and pointed one last time at the orange glow in the sky. When the doors opened, Byard stepped inside, pushed the button to the Promenade deck, and stepped back.

"I thought we'd start in the reception area on the Promenade Deck. It doubles as *Athena's* Grand Lobby. You came in so late last night you may not have had much chance to see it."

The elevator doors closed, and I noticed the captain studying my reflection in the mirrored glass. I smiled quickly, awkwardly. Byard looked ahead, but not before he returned my smile with what I suspected was an involuntary wink. I pretended not to notice and looked down at my camera.

"The elevator stopped, and the mirrored glass doors slid open onto the Promenade's two-story lobby. I was stunned. Byard was right. I had been too tired when I arrived last night to notice its sweeping staircase, the crystal chandelier, or the stunning gold and ivory statue in the center courtyard."

"How did I miss that?" I pointed to the statue.

"You didn't. But now you know why we left the dock late last night." Byard gestured to the statue. "This is the Goddess Athena. Known as the Greek goddess of wisdom and warfare. We picked her up in Naples yesterday. We're transporting her to Alexandria."

The statue was enormous, at least fourteen feet high, and centered in a shallow reflecting pool, surrounded by a waterfall of crystal beads. She loomed over the lobby like a reigning queen.

"Is she real?" I walked beneath the gold and ivory statue and took several shots of her. On her head, she wore a gold helmet, and in one hand, she held a giant spear. In the other, a shield.

"You're asking the wrong person. However, there are some onboard who do know about Greek and Roman antiquities. Your neighbor, Professor Braun, for one. He and his wife, Greta, live across the hall from Dede. He can answer your questions. As for me, I'm still new here. I can tell you anything you want to know about the ship. But when it comes to art, I haven't a clue."

After walking through the Grand Lobby and a labyrinth of connected hallways lined with boutiques, restaurants, and gift stores, Byard led me out onto the Promenade Deck, where we strolled beneath a full moon and the sound of waves crashing against *Athena's* hull.

CHAPTER FIVE

Byard explained *Athena* was twice the length of an American football field, had 165 luxury condos, three hundred and fifty-five residents with an average age of sixty-two, and a crew of a hundred and twenty-five.

"*Athena* caters to a very exclusive clientele. Most of the cabins have one and two bedrooms. Some are fancier than others—like Ms. Drummerhausen's—and a few studios in between. The residences are on the top five floors above the Promenade Deck and beneath the Lido or the Sun Deck."

"And the cost?" I asked. "How expensive is the average apartment?"

"Entry-level would be about one point five million for a small studio."

"And for a cabin like Dede's?"

"My guess would be at least two and a half to three million. Plus, yearly association dues and a guaranteed wealth analysis of five million dollars."

"That's some serious money."

"For some, *Athena's* their last home. But for a few, a suite aboard is nothing more than a second or third home. Right now, many of our regulars are away on summer vacation."

"And the crew? They come and go as well?" I could get all the statistics I wanted about Athena from the brochure Finn had left in my gift basket. But I hoped that if I could keep Byard talking about the crew and maybe himself, he might reveal more than he had initially told me.

"There's not much turnover. Most have been on the ship since Mr. Webster bought her in ninety-one. His people are very loyal."

"And you? You said you're still new here. How long have you been aboard?"

"A little less than a year. Why?"

I sensed an uneasiness in Byard's response. A resistance like a brick wall. Something in his past he didn't want to talk about.

"Just curious." I ran my hand through my hair and looked down at my feet. I didn't want to meet his eyes. "So, where were you? Off in the South Pacific or somewhere like it?"

"No. I was working odd jobs in South Hampton." Byard rubbed the back of his neck.

"Really?" I felt I had scratched the surface of something he didn't want to talk about.

"Why do I get the feeling you're trying to interview me?"

"Would that be so bad?"

"Not if you promise not to quote me."

"Okay."

"Because Neil wouldn't be happy with me if he thought I were talking about it."

Byard stopped at the railing and wrapped his fingers around the metal bar. "I suppose it's a matter of record. Nothing you couldn't find out if you wanted. Neil hired me because there had been an accident with the last Captain."

I gripped the rail and looked out at the water. "What happened?"

"He fell overboard. He drowned."

"Drowned?"

"When Athena pulled into South Hampton, Neil needed a Captain. A sober Captain. He asked around and found me at an AA meeting. I hadn't had a drink in three years. Before that, I'd been fired from my previous position for being drunk and disorderly. When Neil offered me the job, he warned me he'd fire me on the spot if he ever heard or saw me with a drink. The accident with Captain McKey isn't something Neil would like me to be talking about. So, if you could keep that between us, I'd appreciate it."

I tapped the railing with the palm of my hand. If Byard was sober and in the program, my hunch was that he lived a clean life. If he knew Dede had fallen overboard, he wasn't about to cover it up and risk losing his job. And, based upon the Churchill sister's somewhat looney reputation, I could see why he might think they were unnecessarily concerned about Dede and believe that she had gotten off Athena in Naples, as expected.

"I wouldn't worry about what happened before. My job here is to report on Athena's cruise around the Amalfi Coast. I don't see how your past is part of that."

"I can assure you, it's not. But it is getting late, and I would like to show you below deck."

I took several more pictures, and we walked back to the elevator. Byard pushed the button for the Marina Deck directly below. When the doors

CHAPTER FIVE

opened, he stepped out and whirled around with his hands above his head.

"And this, Kat, is the play deck. Complete with pool, jacuzzi, gymnasium, and ocean-tight platform doors." Byard pointed to Athena's sidewalls. "When we drop anchor and open them, they provide our residents with a private beachfront playground."

The space was immense. Wide and open, with every kind of workout gear I'd ever seen: ellipticals, treadmills, weight machines, yoga mats, and big-screen TVs everywhere. But what caught my attention was the Olympic-size pool and a set of large metal rings hanging from the ceiling. A small, pixie-sized woman had laced her body between them with multicolored scarves and stood ready to dive.

"Who is that?" I focused my camera on the woman and took a quick shot of her standing inside one of the rings.

"That…" Byard put his finger to his lips and whispered, "is our resident aerialist, Madame Camile Garnier. Madame once worked for a traveling circus."

I stared as Camile adjusted the silk ties about her body, then dropped headfirst in a death-defying spiral, stopping only inches above the pool. Then, righting herself, pirouetted like a ballet dancer en pointe, delicately walking above the water before wrapping herself again in the security of the scarf and climbing the silk ties like a rope back to her original position high above the pool.

"No way that woman's sixty-two."

"She's not. Camile is Inspector Leon Garnier's much younger second wife. They're from Paris. The Inspector's retired. Perhaps you've heard of him? He's quite famous. He's solved a number of very high-profile crimes in Europe."

I shook my head, my eyes still on Camile as she adjusted the silk scarves and prepared for a second dive.

"We really should go. Camile enjoys working out alone in the evenings when no one is around."

I glanced across to the end of the pool, where a well-tanned, middle-aged man sat with his eyes locked on Camile.

"And is that the Inspector?" I doubted it even as I asked.

Byard dropped his head and grinned. "No. That's Carlo, Skipper for *Athena's* toy boat."

"Toy boat?"

"*The Muse*. You may not have noticed when you came on board. She's a much smaller craft. She follows us wherever we go and carries those toys our residents like to have with them."

"Like what?"

"Ski jets. Parasailing equipment. And what we don't have, we helicopter in. There's a helipad on the Sun Deck directly on top of the bistro."

"You are a floating city," I said.

Byard motioned for me to follow. "Come. We should move on. There's one other person I'd like to introduce you to before it gets too late."

I followed Byard toward the end of the gym. A young woman, who looked to be barely out of her teens, was arranging free weights. She stopped as we approached and placed her hands on her hips.

"Well, Cap'n Byard. What brings you eh-round this evening?"

"I have someone special I'd like you to meet. Kat Lawson, this is Elli, our fitness instructor. She's here with us from California while our regular spa manager is on vacation."

Elli had the California look. Tall, blonde, and tan with a tight body to match, but not the accent. To my ears, the girl sounded like a Brit.

"Kat's a travel reporter, Elli. Treat her well. We don't need any bad press."

"I'm sure you've nothing to worry about." I offered Elli my hand.

The girl responded with a firm, youthful shake. "Welcome aboard. Let me know if you want to use the spa or the gym. I'm usually here from nine to five. Better yet, I'll send up an invite for a free massage."

"That'd be nice." I rolled my shoulders. "I'm still suffering from jet lag."

"You're in Dede's suite, right?"

I raised a brow. Clearly, everyone on board was aware of my presence and where I was staying. "Yeah. I am."

"Getting tired?" Byard folded his arm across his chest. "We could go on if you like, or call it a night. It's up to you."

CHAPTER FIVE

I yawned involuntarily, then caught myself and covered my mouth. "Sorry about that."

"Don't be. There's not much more on this deck besides the resident's storage cages."

"No, seriously, I would like to see it all. I need pictures, you know."

"Then, perhaps you might like to join me for dinner one night. Afterward, I could show you the crew quarters, the engine room, the engineer's cabin, the chain locker, where we store the anchor, and the war room."

"The war room?"

"It's actually a small arsenal. For security purposes. It's not a common occurrence, but there have been incidents with pirates in various parts of the world."

"Pirates?" The thought hadn't even occurred to me.

"Not so much where we're sailing now, but *Athena's* a classy ship with a wealthy clientele. It's always wise to be prepared. However, if we needed to, *Athena* could outrun any ship that would cause her trouble. I wouldn't worry about it."

Chapter Six

I thanked Byard for the tour, and sensing he was as committed to truth as he was to his sobriety, I dismissed the idea that he had anything to do with Dede's questionable disappearance and returned to Dede's apartment. I was too exhausted to even think the idea of pirates might be a problem. By the time my head hit the pillow, I had blocked out any thoughts that the gold coin might be anything more than a talisman Dede had hidden in her bag and allowed Athena's swift sail to lull me into a deep sleep.

The following morning, a thin stream of yellow sunlight eked through the bedroom blinds and woke me, along with the squawking sounds of seagulls outside my window. I got up and opened the drapes to a picture-perfect view of Procida beyond my deck. Like a post-impressionist painting, the sunlight danced on the Med's bluer-than-blue water surrounded by a pastel-colored harbor of houses stacked like boxes, one on top of the other—pinks, blues, and yellows—rising from the sea and cluttering the mountainside.

I slid the window open, the briny smell of sea air refreshed me. *Coffee*. I need something strong and black and padded barefoot toward the kitchen.

I stopped halfway down the hall. Beneath the front door, Finn had slipped a copy of *Athena's Daily Call*, a two-page newsletter. I picked it up and, taking it to the kitchen with me, skimmed the headlines. Little more than a summary of the world events, along with a more extended section entitled *Onboard Tid Bits:* The Commissary was having a two-for-one sale on wine. Movie Night included a showing of *You've Got Mail*. A gray-scale box marked *Celebrations* announced today was Nicholas Marcopoulos' seventy-ninth birthday. I knew from the picture this older-looking, grey-haired gent,

CHAPTER SIX

wearing a yachtsman's hat, had to be Marcos, Athena's resident sleepwalker Chief Sully, and Captain Byard had warned me about. Considering his age and the fact he was a known kleptomaniac and naked sleepwalker, I wondered how many more birthdays someone like Marco might celebrate on board. In a separate column was information about today's *Port of Call*. The forecast showed a high of 86 Fahrenheit, 30 Celsius, and described Procida as the Secret Island in the Bay of Naples. The smallest of the three Poet Islands—Ischia, Procida, and Capri—Procida was best known for her warmer waters. An italicized note indicated that those wishing to go ashore should disembark on the Marina Deck. *Athena* would be using a local tender, a small boat from the island, to shuttle us back and forth throughout the day.

Taking my coffee with me, I grabbed a banana and a couple of grapes from the gift basket in the living room, then went out on the balcony to enjoy the view. It wasn't yet ten o'clock, but already I could hear the voices of those preparing to disembark on the Marina Deck below me. I watched as a small motorboat approached and then leaned over the railing for a better view. Several crew members, including Captain Byard, dressed in nautical whites, were helping to guide the boat up next to *Athena's* open portal so that her residents might tender ashore.

I watched as the last of *Athena's* residents who were going ashore boarded the tender. I was about to back away from the railing when Byard looked up and waved.

"You plan on going ashore?"

"Soon as I finish my coffee." I lifted my cup and smiled.

"Take a good pair of walking shoes. The view of the bay from the top of the hill's beautiful, but it's a bit of a climb."

"Won't be a problem," I said.

I had read up on the island. I knew the narrow cobblestone streets and steep climb up to the walled medieval village of Terra Murata might be a challenge for some, particularly *Athena's* older residents. But I wasn't concerned. I looked forward to the hike and stretching my legs after the long flight.

"Dinner tonight?" Byard cocked his head and flashed a sexy grin in my direction. It didn't take much to read his mind, nor could I say we were on different pages. I had already begun to fantasize about what it might be like to spend a week on board in the captain's company. But in the light of day, I decided to slow it down a bit. Not that I wanted to.

"Sounds good." I waved a friendly goodbye.

* * *

It was easy to see why Procida was considered one of Italy's most beautiful seaside villages. Dozens of small fishing boats buoyed in the harbor while the morning light shimmered like crystals on the Med's deep blue water. Everywhere was a rainbow of color. Quayside, the Marina Grande, a narrow coastal road marked where the water met the shoreline and was crowded with small shops. Outdoor tables were piled high in front of their open doors with the day's catch, fresh octopus, and large silver fish in crates of ice.

My plan was to walk along the Marina Grande and take in the sights of the harbor and the tiered bungalows above the busy shops before heading up the hill to the Piazza D'Armi in the village of Terra Murata. There, I planned to visit the Abbey of San Michele Arcangelo and the Piazza Dei Martiri before heading down to the small harbor of Corricella on the other side of the island. I estimated the entire walk to be no more than about one-and-a-half miles and would give me a good feel for the island and its history.

It wouldn't have mattered which street I chose to head up to Terra Murata. Each was as inviting as the next, cluttered with shops nestled beneath residences with wrought iron balconies, some bursting with colorful flower boxes, others with bed linens perched over their railings, while below, a chorus of happy voices greeted each other. Ciao! Salve! Buongiorno!

The view from Terra Murata, with its grey stone fortified walls, had been built in the early 1500s for the island's governors and, despite the heat, was worth the climb. Behind its walls, the Palazzo d'Avalos was home to four museums, including the Royal Palace. It was later converted into a prison citadel and remained so until it was closed in 1988. I snapped several dozen

CHAPTER SIX

pictures and scribbled as many notes on my notepad, then hurried on to the Abbey of San Michele, famous for its Renaissance art collection.

Satisfied I had taken all the pictures and notes I needed, I stuffed my notebook back into my backpack and was about to leave Terra Murata and head down to the Marina di Corricella when I noticed a poster advertising antique coins and jewelry next to a souvenir shop outside the Abbey. I'm not much for souvenir shopping, but the sign had several pictures that caught my eye, including a gold pendant necklace that looked remarkably like the gold coin I had found in Dede's bag.

Curious I might find some answer as to what the coin was all about, I entered the shop, a musty narrow space, no more than three aisles wide and twelve feet deep. The shelves were crammed with religious paraphernalia, waxed candles, rosaries, and prayer books. In the back of the store, an old man sat hunched on a stool behind an antique brass cash register, reading a newspaper.

"Buongiorno, signorina." The old man folded his paper and shuffled from behind the counter. "How may I help you?"

I pointed to the sign outside. "I was wondering about the coins you have advertised. Do you have any I might see?"

The old man adjusted his glasses. "Are you a collector?"

"No, I'm a travel writer. I was hoping you might know something about the necklace with the coin. It's very unusual."

"Yes, it is. But unfortunately, a buyer was here a few minutes ago and bought all I had left of my coins, including a copy of that very necklace. Lovely piece. However, if you're interested, I have something similar in silver I could show you. Give me a minute." Without waiting for an answer, the old man hobbled back behind the counter and a black curtain that separated the shop from a small office. A few minutes later, he returned with a slim brown leather box and placed it on the counter. "Here. Have a look."

I dropped my backpack on the floor and looked closely at several pieces of gold and silver jewelry inside the box. All high-end costume pieces are designed for tourists, made from copies of old Roman coins, and crafted into rings and bracelets with matching earrings. But the most stunning of all was a solitary silver coin pendant necklace, very much like that on the poster. Other than being silver and much bigger than the coin I had found in Dede's bag, it was an exact match. I picked up the pendant and held it in my hand.

"How much?"

"Twelve hundred US dollars."

I handed the necklace back. "I'm afraid that's too rich for my taste."

"Too bad." The old man held the necklace up to the light. "For a pretty lady, it would look very nice around your slim neck."

I smiled and shook my head. Flattery wasn't going to make a difference. "Maybe if it were real, I might consider it."

The old man placed the necklace back in the box and laughed. "If it was real, I could retire a wealthy man. Do you have any idea what this coin represents?"

I shook my head.

"The original coin was minted both in silver and gold. In silver, there are maybe a hundred such coins. But in gold, only three are known to exist. It's called the Ides of March coin. You see the letters E.I.D. M.A.R." The old man placed the pendant in the palm of his hand and pointed to the letters. The same letters I had seen on the coin hidden in Dede's bag. "This coin was issued by Marcus Junius Brutus in 43... 42 BC. It's called the Brutus Coin. On the reverse side are two daggers, and beneath them is what the Romans called a liberty cap, a hat Roman slaves wore to announce their freedom." With his fingers shaking, he turned the coin over. "It commemorates the assassination of Caesar."

The old man had my attention. If the gold coin hidden in Dede's bag was real, it might explain why she had disappeared. I could ill-afford such a piece of costume jewelry, but I wanted to know more about the Ides of March Coin, and I wasn't going to leave until I did.

"So, what might a gold EID MAR coin be worth if you were to find one?"

"I doubt there are any more. But if you were to find one, you'd be a fortunate lady." The old man closed the box and hugged it to his chest. "Earlier this year, a gold EID MAR coin was sold at a London auction for

CHAPTER SIX

more than four million dollars."

Chapter Seven

Four-million dollars! I bid the shopkeeper goodbye and took the narrow stone steps outside the old fortress wall two at a time, following the view down the hill to the small fishing village of Marina di Corricella. After talking with the old shopkeeper, I couldn't shake the thought of Dede or the gold coin I had found in her bag.

What woman in her right mind would hide a 4-million-dollar gold coin in her purse and leave it behind? And if Dede hadn't been aware of the coin inside her bag or its value, then whoever had hidden the coin had to be looking for it—particularly if Dede hadn't arrived in Naples. And if she wasn't in Naples, then where was she? The bottom of the bay?

I paused when I got down the hill to catch my breath and take in the view. How could I be harboring such dark thoughts on such a beautiful day? I had no proof Dede had come to an uncertain end or if the coin I had found hidden in her bag was even real. Perhaps it was, as I initially thought, a lucky charm, a copy of the coin I had seen in the shop that Dede had hidden in her purse for good luck. My grandmother carried a silver dollar she had won at a bingo game in Las Vegas. The coin had been minted in 1902, the year of her birth, and although it wasn't worth a lot, she believed it brought her good fortune. I didn't know Dede. For all I knew, she might have done something similar.

"Ms. Lawson? Over here."

I scanned the cove until I saw a short, thickset, balding man standing next to a blue umbrella table in front of a small seaside café. Seated at the table next to him was an equally round, very pale-skinned older woman wearing

CHAPTER SEVEN

a large sun visor, her shocking white hair sticking out from the top like a bird's nest. I recognized both as residents I had seen Byard helping to board the tender earlier that morning. With his hat in his hand, the man waved to me.

"Over here. Come, please."

As I approached the table, the man extended his hand.

"Ms. Lawson, allow me to introduce myself. I am Herr Professor Braun, and this is my wife, Greta. We recognize you from the ship. "Please…" The professor gestured to an empty seat at the table. I noticed a gold signet ring on his pinky finger. "Join us. We've ordered a bottle of limoncello. It's refreshing for a hot day."

I dropped my backpack beside the empty chair and sat down. The Professor signaled the waiter to bring an additional glass while Greta, in a heavy German accent, explained that she and her husband Horst had the cabin across the hall from me on the ship.

"We are neighbors. I saw you at tea yesterday. I hope you are settled. Ja?"

"Yes," I said.

"And you are an American journalist?"

"I am. I'm doing a story about *Athena's* Seniors at Sea."

The waiter arrived, placed an ice-chilled limoncello bottle on the table, and then filled our glasses.

The Professor waited until the glasses were full, then picked his up. "Prost."

I tipped my glass to the Professor and his wife, then sipped sweet slivers of icy-cold, frozen lemon liqueur down my throat. Maybe it was the heat or the alcohol, but I don't recall tasting anything so ice-chilling delicious on a hot day. And potent. I could feel the buzz before I put my drink down.

"Good, no?" Greta placed her hand to her throat, her meaty fingers gently massaging a gold pendant necklace around her neck.

"Umm…yes. Very." However, it wasn't the drink alone that had my attention, but the gold pendant around Greta's neck. "That's a beautiful necklace. May I ask where you got it?"

"My Horst, he buys for me for our anniversary. Here. Up by the Abbey." Greta lifted the pendant from her neck with her thumb and index finger so

I could see it better. "Twenty-five years today."

"Congratulations." The necklace was stunning and looked exactly like the silver pendant the shopkeeper had shown me earlier, only in gold.

Greta patted her husband's wrist. "He is a good man. I think I keep him, maybe for another twenty-five."

We all laughed.

The Professor smiled and wiped his lips with a napkin. "And if it were real, Meine Liebe, you would keep me another twenty-five lifetimes." Then, kissing his wife's hand, he added. "Ms. Lawson, are you familiar with Roman coins?"

"No, not at all," I wasn't about to tell the professor I had a pretty good idea where the necklace had come from or that less than ten minutes ago, I had met with the same shopkeeper who had told me he had sold the gold pendant necklace to a collector who had bought the shopkeeper's remaining inventory of old coins. I was more curious about what the professor might say and feigned ignorance.

"This necklace, while very nice, is nothing more than a high-priced piece of costume jewelry. A copy of the EID MAR or The Ides of March Coin, also known as The Brutus Coin. It's very rare and impossibly expensive. But…if it makes my wife happy, why not? Once she knew about the coin, she had to have it."

Professor Braun explained he was a retired history professor from the University of Munich. "My specialty was the ancient world. When I retired, Greta and I bought a suite aboard the *Athena*, and I've made it our business to visit this area as often as possible. I find it fascinating. My favorite part of the world. In fact, we're here now because I've convinced our board of directors to retrace the old Silk Road from Western Europe to North Africa across the Mediterranean."

"You're the reason Athena's doing an Amalfi Coast Tour?"

"I am. Our board meets every year, and we decide where we'd like to sail. It's all mapped out in advance. Unfortunately, we've had to change our itinerary slightly since we got a late start out of Naples, and we'll be spending an extra day here in the Poet Islands, but they're all so rich with

CHAPTER SEVEN

history, it really doesn't matter. If you're interested, I'm lecturing tonight in the theater. Come by, and I can explain more about the area and share our findings. Eight p.m."

We visited for another half hour before the Professor said he had to excuse himself and snapped his fingers for the waiter to return with the bill. Then, reaching beneath the table, he picked up a black backpack, like my own, but with a yellow tag attached. "Would you like a ride back to the ship?"

"No thanks, I have more sightseeing to do. But thank you for the invitation to tonight's lecture. I'll be there."

I waited at the table while Professor Braun paid the bill, then hailed a taxi. The arriving car, if one could even call it that, was impossibly small, nothing more than an open-topped, motorized tricycle. Big enough to whiz through Procida's narrow streets with a driver and a single passenger with ease, but with two people the size of the Professor and his wife and their overstuffed backpack, I feared one bump, and they'd pop out like Pillsbury Doughboys.

But the Professor and his wife appeared not to be concerned and stuffed themselves onto the small trike-like backseat with the Professor holding tight to the outside seat rail and Greta on him. I waved goodbye and watched as the trike-bike turned on two wheels and sped away.

I had a lot to think about as I returned to the ship. Was the gold coin I had found hidden inside Dede's bag a copy, like that around Greta's neck? Or was it real? And if it were, just what was I supposed to do with it? And on top of that, just how could a retired history professor and his wife afford a luxury cabin aboard *Athena*? There had to be a logical explanation. Greta may have come from money. She had a very old-world, aristocratic look to her. But the idea that the Professor had visited the same small shop where I had been early that morning and bought the old shopkeeper's remaining coins had me wondering if Professor Braun was somehow tied to the Brutus coin I had seen in Dede's bag?

I hurried back to the dock. I wanted to return to my room as quickly as possible, take the coin I had put back inside Dede's bag, and hide it inside my room safe. Any other time, I would have called Sophie, my editor and FBI handler. I wanted to tell her about the four-million-dollar Brutus coin,

Dede's disappearance, the drowning of *Athena*'s previous Captain, and my suspicion regarding the Professor and his backpack full of antique coins. But this was to be a pleasure cruise, a reward for my earlier assignments, and like me, Sophie was on vacation. I was on my own. I couldn't go to the police. I had no proof Dede might have drowned or if the coin I had found hidden in her bag was authentic. All I knew was that I had stumbled into a situation and feared I was beginning to know things I shouldn't and didn't dare tell anyone.

Chapter Eight

"Yoo-hoo! Kat. Ms. Lawson. Up here." The Churchill sisters hugged each other and waved enthusiastically, like I was some arriving dignitary they couldn't wait to meet. "Might we see you for a moment? Meet us in the lobby. It's most urgent."

Curious about what might be urgent, I immediately went from the Marina portal, where I entered the ship and took the elevator to the Promenade Lobby. There, standing beneath the Athena statue, were the Churchill sisters. Irene, the taller of the two, had her hand to her mouth and had stooped to whisper in her sister's ear. Upon seeing me, she dropped her hand, and the two toddled toward me.

"We're so glad you're back on board." Ida took my arm, linking it through her own, and pulled me aside. "We've news."

I had no doubt the urgent matter the sisters wanted to discuss was Dede, but what could these two amateur sleuths have discovered that I didn't already know and dare not say?

"What's happened?"

Ida continued. "Well, after you left our tea yesterday, it occurred to us we might be able to find proof that Dede was missing—"

"And," Irene interrupted. "We decided to call Dede's cell phone, but—"

"She didn't answer." Ida finished her sister's sentence, patting my hand as she spoke.

"And you think that means what?" I asked. I had a vision of Dede's cell phone in the bottom of her bag ringing aimlessly inside my cabin.

"Well, what else could it mean? If Dede had been able to answer, she would have picked up. She's obviously in trouble. Don't you think?" Irene sounded miffed.

I didn't know what to think, only that I didn't want to let on that I was concerned Dede Drummerhausen might have come to an unsavory end. But still, I clung to the hope that she could have left the ship voluntarily.

"Explain something to me. Captain Byard and Chief Sully don't seem terribly concerned Dede might be missing. In fact, when I spoke with them about it, they appeared to be satisfied Dede had departed as expected Sunday morning."

"Of course, they would." Ida clenched her jaw. "Captain Byard and the Chief think we're nothing but a couple of crazy old loons. I'm sure they told you as much."

I squelched a smile. No need to go down that road.

"But they must have seen Dede's name on some manifest when she went ashore. Surely there's a record of her leaving?"

"That's just it." Ida shook a finger at me. "There's not."

"Why not?" I couldn't imagine there wasn't an accounting somewhere, but when I came aboard, only Finn met me, and he hadn't asked for my I.D.

"If this were a tourist ship, there would be all kinds of protocols. But *Athena* isn't a cruise ship. We're a permanent residence, and we operate like a commercial vessel. The residents and crew are all covered by the ship's manifest, and when we're in port and want to leave, all we do is flash our shipboard I.D." Irene dangled her lanyard with her picture I.D. in front of me. "With this, we can come and go as we like."

"I see. So, once the gangway was in place, Dede could have walked off—"

"Or," Ida jutted in again, "she was pushed overboard the night before."

"But who would do such a thing, and for what reason?" I could think of a four-million-dollar reason if the coin hidden in the bottom of Dede's bag was authentic. The coin may have cost Dede her life, and if I weren't careful and said too much, it might very well cost me my own life as well.

"We've no idea. But don't take our word for it. Join us for dinner tonight. Irene and I are dining with Monsieur Inspector Garnier. He's a retired private investigator and very respected."

CHAPTER EIGHT

"And his wife, of course. You mustn't forget Camile, Ida."

"How could I forget Camile? Poor thing, she's skinny as a rail. Speedwalks every morning on the Promenade Deck. You may have seen her around. Wears her hair in a bun so tight her brows arch like a draw bridge." Ida drew her brows back with her hands. "Like this. Can you imagine?"

"The aerialist," I said. "Yes, I saw her last night. Captain Byard gave me a tour of the ship. She was working out on the rings above the pool."

Irene took her sister's hands from her brow. "You'll have to forgive my sister. She tends to be a bit dramatic. But I'm sure, aside from the fact the woman eats like a bird, you'll enjoy meeting them. They're a lovely couple. Very friendly for Parisians. Please join us. We've made reservations at Romano's. Eight p.m."

Chapter Nine

I spotted Marco in the hallway as I returned to my cabin. Fortunately, the sun had yet to set, and *Athena's* resident sleepwalking kleptomaniac was very much awake and fully dressed. He nodded politely and tapped the top of his yachtsman's hat as we passed. I wished him a happy birthday, not wanting to be rude, and then hurried toward the cabin door with my keys.

Once inside, I checked to see if Dede's bag was still behind the door. I had an uneasy feeling Marco had been lurking in the hallway and that I had interrupted an attempted theft. Relieved to see the bag where I had left it on top of the entry table, I picked it up and immediately felt for the coin. Feeling it solidly within the lining, I took the bag to the dining table, where I emptied it, placing Dede's wallet and phone on the table. Then, I reached inside, felt for the hole in the lining where I had reinserted the small plastic bag with a coin inside, and pulled them out.

The coin was smaller and thicker than the flashy EID MAR gold pendant Greta wore around her neck. It looked worn and rubbed with age. Not at all like some highly polished souvenir charm Dede might have stuffed into her bag for good luck.

I closed my hand around the bagged coin. How had I gotten myself into the middle of such a mess? This was supposed to be a vacation, and now I feared I had stumbled upon a murder and a possible high-stakes smuggling operation. What was I supposed to do? Part of me wanted to return the coin to the bag and have nothing to do with it. And the other part of me, the part that knew better, wouldn't let go of the idea that I was on to a really big

CHAPTER NINE

story, and if I didn't cover it, I'd regret it. *Damnit.*

Rather than slide the bagged coin back inside Dede's bag, I went to the safe in the guest room, where I peeled back the safe's carpeted lining and, with the EID MAR coin safely inside the plastic bag, slid it beneath the padding then smoothed the lining back in place. If someone were to come searching for the coin and suspected I had hidden it inside, even if they could unlock the safe, it would appear empty. Satisfied I had done what I could, I shut the safe's door and locked it, using Dede's condo number 1-2-2-1 as the entry code. I then returned to the living room and took Dede's black bag from the dining table, and this time, rather than leave it on top of the entry table in plain sight, I placed the bag inside the top drawer. But before I had a chance to close the drawer, the apartment phone rang. Startled, I looked over my shoulder to make sure I was alone, then slammed the drawer shut and reached for the wall phone.

"Hello?"

"Kat, it's Byard. We on for dinner tonight?"

I clutched the phone to my ear. I would have liked nothing better than dinner with the captain, followed by a late-night stroll along the deck. But after meeting with the Professor and his wife this afternoon and learning that the coin hidden inside Dede's bag might be worth four million dollars, I was torn. I sensed a story. Not the story I'd been assigned to, but something sinister. Something to do with the Professor, Dede, and the Brutus Coin, and perhaps the unexplained drowning of the previous captain. The only way to find out what was going on would be to get to know as many of the residents aboard *Athena* as I could without being obvious. And broken dinner date or not, that's exactly what I would do.

"Rain check?" I apologized and told Byard the Churchill sisters had insisted I dine with them. "They have reservations at Romanos with Inspector Garnier and his wife."

"Let me guess, they have more to tell you about Dede."

I dismissed Byard's remark with a laugh. "It's a nice gesture, and I really can't refuse."

"I'm sure you couldn't. Nor should you. Enjoy." Byard hung up. I wasn't sure if he felt slighted that I had accepted another dinner invite or if his response was merely a polite way of maintaining a professional distance.

I looked out the bedroom's glass doors at Procida's port. I could feel the vibrations of Athena's heavy anchor as it was pulled from the deep waters beneath us. The lights of Terra Murata slowly began to fade as we began to move. Feeling like I had my sea legs, I showered, washed my hair, dressed, slipped into the simple black shift I had brought for dinner, and grabbed my camera.

* * *

As I locked the door to Dede's suite behind me, I noticed Finn in front of Braun's cabin door. He was dressed in his butler's attire, a three-piece grey pinstriped suit with white gloves. He held a passkey in one hand and a vase with a bouquet of white lilies in the other.

"Lovely, aren't they? They're the national symbol of Italy. Very fragrant with a light scent of sandalwood." Finn tipped the vase in my direction so I might smell them. "They're a surprise for the Professor's wife. It's their anniversary."

"So, I've heard." I explained how I had met the Professor and his wife while visiting the island that afternoon and shared a bottle of limoncello. "It was very nice."

"I'm happy to hear you're enjoying your trip." Finn palmed the passkey to the Professor's suite. "Will you be going for dinner now?"

"Yes," I said.

"And will you be attending tonight's lecture afterward?"

"Possibly. I haven't decided yet." I was unaccustomed to anyone monitoring my comings and goings. And now that I had learned the gold coin I had found inside Dede's bag might be worth four million dollars, I was uncomfortable with the idea of anyone entering my suite without my knowledge.

"Will you require a turndown? Dede always liked her pillows fluffed."

"No, thank you, Finn. I'll be fine on my own. Have a good night."

CHAPTER NINE

I left Finn at the door to the Professor's suite and took the elevator midship to the fourteenth floor where the Churchill sisters had made reservations at Romano's.

* * *

Romano's was warm with candlelight; the tables were set with white linen tablecloths, a string quartet played in the corner, while the subtle rich smells of roasted garlic and tomatoes wafted throughout. I allowed my eyes to adjust to the lower light while I waited inside the etched glass doors for the maître d.

"Ms. Lawson. Welcome. The Churchill sisters are already seated. Allow me to show you to your table."

The maître d escorted me to a window table set for five with sterling silver, crystal goblets, and a small bouquet of flowers in a glass vase with a small candle. Irene stood as I approached. She was dressed in a long yellow caftan and clasped her hands together as I took the empty seat beside Ida.

"Ida and I are happy you decided to join us. I hope your day was satisfactory."

"It was more than satisfactory. I feel as though I've gone back in history more than four hundred years. Terra Murata was fascinating." I placed my napkin in my lap. "And thank you for asking me for dinner. I'm looking forward to getting to know more of the passengers. I met Professor Braun and his wife Irene while in Procida this afternoon. Interesting couple."

"*Humph!* "Ida unfolded her napkin and slapped it on her lap. "I suppose if one can call *pompous* interesting. You ask me, the Professor is boorish and overbearing."

"Shush." Irene put a finger to her lips, then pointed to the door. "The Inspector and Camile have arrived. We mustn't be talking about the Professor like that. You'll get yourself in trouble. You know better."

Irene stood up and gestured to the two empty seats at the table. The Inspector, a solid, stern-looking man wearing a navy jacket with a neck scarf, and his wife, Camile, in a sparkling gold lame jumpsuit, cut an imposing figure as they crossed the room. Heads turned, followed by a low murmur. I stood as they approached while Ida remained seated, her fingers wrapped around the stem of her empty wine glass.

"Thank you for joining us tonight." With a hand on the Inspector's shoulder, Irene air-kissed each side of his face, then did the same to Camile. "I'm most anxious for you to meet our guest, Ms. Kat Lawson."

I offered the Inspector my hand. He took the tips of my fingers, held them slightly longer than I felt necessary, and stared at me through his steel-framed glasses. "Ah, yes. The reporter. I've heard rumors of your arrival."

"All good, I hope." I dropped his hand, then turned to Camile. Her back was to me, her hand in the air. She had hailed the waiter.

"Garcon!" Camile snapped her fingers.

The Inspector, aware of his wife's impatience, pointed to the waiter. "Champagne, please. For everyone." Then, looking across the table at me, he added. "After all, we are here to celebrate new friendships, no?"

"Absolutely." I smoothed the napkin on my lap, thankful Camile's impatience with the waiter had taken her husband's attention off me. But not long enough.

"So, Ms. Lawson, I was surprised when I heard a reporter was aboard and planning to write a feature about us. Seniors at Sea, something about our sailing into the sunset, is that correct?"

"Yes. I—" I began to explain my assignment when Irene interrupted.

"Please, Kat, stop!" With both hands on the table, Irene shot me a look that only a retired schoolmarm knew how to give. Had she a ruler, I would have expected her to slap my knuckles. I stopped mid-sentence. Irene continued. "You can talk about what you do later, Kat. But I've asked you to meet the Inspector tonight because, as you know, Ida and I believe something awful happened to our friend, Dede. And we have high hopes that somehow you and the Inspector might be able to work together to find her."

The Inspector jerked his head. "I'm sorry. Are you saying you think something has happened to Ms. Drummerhausen?"

"She's missing, Inspector. Perhaps fallen overboard. We don't know for

CHAPTER NINE

sure. Captain Byard and Chief Sully think we're imagining things. But we're not, and we thought, with your experience and Kat's investigative reporting skills, that the two of you could help."

This was not at all what I expected. I sat back and folded my hands in my lap. I didn't want any undue attention. I needed to remain low-key, keep my head down, and maintain my presence as nothing more than a travel writer. Certainly not as an investigator.

"Champagne?" The waiter returned, balancing a tray with five tall glasses. Bowing politely, he served the Inspector and his wife.

The Inspector paused until we had all been served, then picked up his glass and, tipping it to Irene and Ida, said, "To investigations." Then, clicking his glass to mine, added, "And new acquaintances."

I smiled.

"And you, Ms. Lawson. You're a reporter. Strange, we've never had a reporter on board before. We're not a tourist vessel. Most of our residents enjoy their privacy. But I am curious. Do you have any suspicions?"

"Me?" This was not the time to brag about my checkered past as an investigative reporter. If there was anything at all to the coin I had found in Dede's bag, and the growing feeling I had that something had happened to her and maybe the previous captain, I wasn't about to say. "I'm afraid I'm still getting my sea legs."

The Inspector put his glass down. "Alright, Irene, tell us what you think happened? I haven't heard a word. Camile and I only returned to the ship last night. We left two weeks ago to visit our home in Paris, then flew to Rome to spend a few days with friends before coming aboard again in Naples."

"Then you really don't know?" Irene put both hands around the stem of her drink and pulled it closer to her.

"About Dede?" The inspector shook his head. "Irene, I'm sorry, but this is the first I've heard of it. I thought you invited Camile and me to join you because you wanted us to meet Ms. Lawson."

"Inspector! Please, stop." Ida swilled the last of her champagne, swallowing what was left in one gulp, then slammed her glass on the table. "What my sister is trying to say is that we believe Dede Drummerhausen may have been murdered."

"Murdered?" Camile put her glass down and looked at her husband. The color drained from her face. "Why would you think that?"

"Because Dede was supposed to get off the ship in Naples when we docked Friday morning. But we've no proof she did." Ida raised her empty champagne glass above her head and, catching the waiter's eye, wiggled the glass for a refill.

"You mean, no one saw her." The Inspector leaned back from the table and crossed his arms.

"Which, of course, doesn't mean anything." Irene took her sister's hand from the stem of the champagne glass and whispered to her sharply. "You've had enough for one night, Dear." Then, looking back to the Inspector, Irene completed her thought. "We even tried to call Dede's cell phone today, but she didn't answer. We know she liked to go for late walks at night, and we're concerned she might have fallen—"

"Let's not mince words." Ida jerked her hand from her sister's. "We think someone pushed her overboard."

The Inspector furrowed his brow and twisted his mouth. A pensive, if not patronizing look. Like Captain Byard and Chief O'Sullivan, the Inspector didn't appear surprised by the sisters' concern but was willing to politely humor his elderly shipmates.

"Ladies, I'm sure there's a logical explanation. We all know how much Dede enjoyed traveling and taking the occasional cooking class while ashore. I'm sure she was entrenched in one when you called. But I promise I will look into it tomorrow if it makes you happy."

Camile took the menu in front of her and, hiding her face behind it, announced she was thinking of the Brodetto.

"Wise choice, Mon amour." The inspector explained that everything on the menu was superb. Romano's Chef Louie had studied under Massimo Bottura, an Italian restaurateur with three Michelin stars. Neil had hired Chef Louie away with the promise of his own restaurant and suite aboard Athena. "In fact, the chef sometimes gives cooking classes on board. Something, Ms. Lawson, you might like to check out. I'm sure there'll be one this week."

CHAPTER NINE

Irene put her menu down. "He's right. Dede loves Chef Louie's classes. She never missed one."

"Well, there you have it. Perhaps Chef Louie suggested a class for Dede in Naples. I'm sure he'll be able to tell me if I ask. In fact, maybe we can even ask tonight. It's not unusual for Chef Louie to visit once things lighten up in the kitchen." The Inspector glanced at the menu. "So… What will you have, Ms. Lawson? I'm having Cacciucco, a Tuscan stew. Been looking forward to it all day. And if you like lobster, might I suggest Linguine with lobster. It's excellent."

The Churchill sisters split an order of Fritto Misto, a dish of crustaceans, mollusks, shrimp, and squid. Ida managed to convince her sister a second glass of champagne would do no harm, and once our meal was served, just as the Inspector promised, Chef Louie appeared from the kitchen. He was a heavyset man who looked like he enjoyed his own cooking and was dressed in a tall white hat with an apron tied around his waist.

"Buona sera." The chef placed a hand on the Inspector's shoulder. "I hope your meal is satisfactory."

"*Saporito. Superb.*" The Inspector kissed his fingers. Then, wiping his mouth, stood up and gestured to me. "Chef Louie, please allow me to introduce you to our honored guest, Ms. Lawson. We've been bragging about you and your cooking classes for residents. In fact, Ida and Irene have been wondering if you might have suggested a class in Naples for Dede. They're concerned she's disappeared."

"Disappeared? No, that can't be possible. Last week, Dede asked me for some referrals for some cooking classes. She knew we'd be docked in Naples on Friday and wanted some suggestions. There are some good schools outside of Naples. One I know started Saturday. I'm sure she left early. You know Dede, it's hard to pin her down. But I'm sure she'll show up like she always does. I wouldn't worry."

The Inspector clasped his hands together. "See, it's as we suspected. Nothing to worry about. Dede's off to cooking school, and she'll soon return with more recipes for us all to enjoy. Mystery solved. Yes?"

I smiled and put my napkin on the table. Ida and Irene might have accepted that Dede was off to cooking school a day earlier than expected, but I wasn't buying it. No investigator I knew would have been so easily persuaded to accept the sudden disappearance of a wealthy socialite like Dede Drummerhausen, not without further investigation. Yet Inspector Garnier appeared to have dismissed the idea as though it were nothing more than folly.

"Ms. Lawson?" The Inspector addressed me, "Are you planning on attending tonight's lecture?"

Ida slumped back into her chair and waved a hand in front of her face. "Why should she? Waste of time if you ask me."

"Ida!" Irene pressed her shoulder to her sister. "Please…don't do that."

"Why? The man doesn't need my praises. And I don't trust him."

Irene placed her hand on top of Ida's. "You'll have to excuse my sister. Ida taught history and considers herself a historian and the Professor nothing more than a blowhard. The two can't be in the same room without arguing."

"I wish I'd known Ida when I was still working and investigating antiquity fraud. I would have welcomed her opinion. Instead, Professor Brawn was recommended to me, and I used him as my expert witness. His opinion was highly valued. I'm sure it wouldn't have been much different than your own, Ida, but it's a little late for that now. And, charmed as I am with your company, ladies, it's getting late. Camile and I want to attend tonight's lecture." The Inspector nodded to his wife and pushed himself away from the table. "I hope, Ms. Lawson, you'll join us. Professor Braun plans to discuss what we'll see tomorrow when we visit Ischia and, if possible, the ancient underwater city of Aenaria.

Chapter Ten

The Inspector had me at *Underwater City*. I had read about Aenaria, an ancient Roman settlement, thought to be nothing more than a myth until two divers uncovered evidence of a smelting factory below the surface in the late seventies and kept it a secret. It was only now—twenty years later—that it was to be opened to the public, and I was looking forward to hearing more about it. But even more interesting than the findings of a submerged city was the Inspector's casual mention of his investigation into antiquities fraud. It piqued my interest, as did the idea that Inspector Garnier had maintained a close relationship with Professor Braun and, like the Professor, had a luxury suite aboard *Athena*, plus a home in Paris, and based upon his dress and talk of his recent travels, a very luxurious lifestyle.

I followed the Inspector and Camile to the elevator, which took us to the Promenade Deck, where tonight's lecture was scheduled in the conference room. The room was crowded. The drapes had been drawn across the ship's rear windows, and the light was low. Six rows of red padded folding chairs with a dozen seats each had been set in a semi-circle facing a dais, behind which were four large whiteboards with maps of the Mediterranean. The Inspector pointed to the first row with a vacant seat between the Professor's wife and Marco and told me to take it while he and Camile took the last two empty chairs in the back of the room.

As I moved to take the empty seat in the row, I noticed Professor Braun at the podium. He appeared to be engaged in a very animated conversation with a grey-haired man, who I estimated to be about the same age as the Professor but dressed in a tight-fitting, short-sleeved black t-shirt that showed off his more fit physique and muscled arms. In his hand, the muscled man held a small bronze gold cow he had picked up from an exhibit table next to the podium where dozens of books, clay pots, beads, jewelry, and several items beneath glass cake plates were displayed. From where I was sitting, I heard him say something in what sounded like Russian. The Professor backed away, waved him off, and dismissed him. Angered, the man slammed the bronze relic on the table, then turned, rushed past me, and out the conference room doors. My eyes followed him to the back of the room, where I noticed Neil and Captain Byard. Whatever the incident, neither Neil nor Byard appeared phased. I finger-waved to Neil and the Captain, then turned back to watch Professor Braun.

* * *

"Welcome to our tour of the Middle Sea." The Professor stepped out in front of the podium and opened his arms, gesturing to the maps on either side of him. "But first, my good friends and fellow explorers, let me apologize. Due to our late departure from Naples, we've had to adjust our itinerary."

There was an audible sigh among those seated, but before it could grow, the Professor hushed the crowd and said we wouldn't be disappointed.

"Rather than visiting just one of three Poet Islands, we're privileged to visit all three, and in addition to Procida, where we visited today, tomorrow Athena will moor in Ischia's harbor, and I'll be conducting a tour, not only of the island but for those who want to join me the following day, a dive beneath her waters to the lost city of Aenaria."

The audience sighs turned to oos and awes, and several people clapped.

"So, here we are, the Middle Sea. Or perhaps you've heard it called the Mare Nostrum. Mare Internum. The Hinter Sea. The Western Sea. The Great Sea. Or maybe even the White Sea. Whatever its name, this is the Mediterranean connecting three major continents. And here…" the Professor pointed with a laser to one of the whiteboards, "is a map showing what was once the rim of this Great Sea, home to the ancient world. Where cities like Baiae, the ancient seaside Roman resort, Thonis-Heracleion in Egypt, Helike and Pavlopetri in Greece, and Atlit Yam in Israel once thrived, and great ships loaded with their wares would come for trade. But now, these cities and their treasures all rest silently beneath her shores in a watery graveyard of lost civilizations. Their mosaic streets, buried in silt. Their bronze and stone statues that once lined the streets and decorated their homes upended. Their temples crumpled and broken. Destroyed by tsunamis and earthquakes."

Then, moving his pointer to another whiteboard, the Professor outlined a series of seismic fault lines beneath the Mediterranean's ocean bed. "But before the complete destruction of these ancient cities, those that sailed her shores created a network of trade routes connecting three major continents. Asia. Africa. And Europe. Giving birth to new civilizations and three major religions. For fifteen hundred years, from the 2nd century BC until 1453, when the Ottoman conquest of Constantinople closed what we know today as the Silk Highway, this, where we are today, was the center of the ancient world."

The Professor lectured for another twenty minutes, pointing to his whiteboards and highlighting areas of the Mediterranean where the remains of sunken cities had been found, including Aenaria, which we would visit the next day. Then pausing, the Professor returned to the display table and picked up a shiny, silver metallic-looking rock.

"This," the Professor said, "is Galena. It doesn't look like much to the naked eye, but if you know what it is, you know it's an ore used to produce lead and a source of silver and sometimes copper. It was found twenty-five years ago by two recreational divers, and it was our first clue that the mythical city of Aenaria existed beneath the waters where we're sailing."

The Professor handed the rock to one of the residents in the front row, then asked Greta to come up to the table and help those who might like to have a closer look at his collection. Several pieces on the table appeared like those I had seen pictured on the poster in Terra Murata. Greta, wearing a gold wreath crown that looked like something Julius Cesar might have worn, stood guard over the table, carefully handing items to those curious enough to come up and look and warning others the things beneath the glass-covered cake plates were not to be handled.

I squeezed between several residents and asked Greta about the gold wreath on her head. She paused as she handed a silver bracelet to one of the onlookers, then explained the crown had been a funereal wreath found among the graveyard of an ancient Macedonian kingdom.

I was about to pick up one of the coins on the table when Marco pushed me aside and reached for a gold signet ring, much like I had seen the Professor wearing that afternoon and slipped it onto the tip of his pinky finger.

"Nice, don't you think?" Marco held his hand out so I might admire it.

"Excusez-moi." Camile squeezed between Greta and me and took a bronze cuff bracelet from the table.

I put down the coin I had been looking at and stepped back from the table. Then, I took my camera from my bag and clicked off several shots. The table and the crowd around it would be perfect for my story. But before I could get any close-up shots of the table and items on it, Professor Braun stopped me.

"Please, no photographs." The Professor put his hand in front of my lens. "It's fine for our little group on board to see, but I'd prefer you not take pictures. Some of what's on the table is very valuable, and I've been entrusted to transport these items to a museum in Alexandria. I'm sure you understand. Security reasons, you know."

I pulled my camera away from his hand. "Then how about one of you in front of the whiteboards?"

"Happy to oblige." The Professor stepped back behind the podium and, taking his laser pointer, directed it to the map of the Great Sea.

I took several shots and started to put my camera away.

"Will you be going ashore tomorrow? There's a lot to see in Ischia. You're welcome to join my tour, but a word of warning: with this crowd, you could probably cover more ground on your own and spend the afternoon enjoying one of the spas or the mineral baths. But the day after, I've put together a special tour, and I hope you want to join us for our dive to Aenaria."

"I wouldn't miss it." I couldn't believe the words coming out of my mouth.

CHAPTER TEN

I was concerned about a deep-sea dive in a part of the world I didn't know much about, particularly with a group of people I didn't know, and some, like the Inspector, who I felt might be uncomfortable with a reporter in their presence. But I chose to ignore the gnawing feeling in the pit of my stomach in favor of visiting the sunken city. I'm a strong swimmer. Coming from the desert, I had spent my youth on swim teams and told myself the dive couldn't be all that difficult.

"Good. It will be my pleasure to show you. Meet us on the Marina Deck. I've arranged a special tender to take us to our dive spot. Thursday. Two p.m."

Chapter Eleven

As I left the conference room, the man I had seen arguing with the Professor earlier that night pushed past me, bumping my camera from my shoulder as he reentered the room. I felt like I had been hit by a linebacker.

Realizing he had knocked me aside, he stopped and addressed me. His voice was gruff. "Kat Lawson?"

I stepped back and noticed several people exiting the conference room had stopped to watch.

"My name's Oleg Sidorov. You are visiting journalist, correct?"

I nodded. My hand gently massaged my shoulder.

"I saw your name in paper this morning. Please, I need to speak with Professor Braun before he leaves. Is urgent. But we talk. I've stories about *Athena* you need to know. Call me. My number is in the ship directory." Then, patting my hand on my bruised shoulder, he left me standing in the doorway and hurried toward the podium.

Whoever Oleg Sidorov was, I made a mental note to take the Russian up on his offer. If Oleg knew stories about *Athena's* past or had information about some of her residents, I sensed he'd be a good source, and I looked forward to talking with him.

But until then, I planned to visit with as many of *Athena's* residents as possible and headed to the lobby, where a group had gathered to discuss tonight's lecture. I was pleasantly surprised when I noticed Byard standing beneath Athena's statue.

"Are you looking for me?" I repositioned my camera from my bruised

CHAPTER ELEVEN

shoulder and smiled.

"I could be if you wanted me to be." Byard's grin suggested he had been waiting for me despite our canceled dinner.

"You have time for a stroll? I was hoping we might chat."

I led the way through the Promenade doors to the deck and stopped at the railing. The water was smooth, like black glass beneath a full moon, and the evening breeze felt like silk against my skin. I would have welcomed a romantic stroll beneath the stars any other time, but tonight, I needed information. I curled my fingers around the railing.

Byard pointed to the lights beyond Athena's stern. "Peaceful, isn't it?"

"It's like another world."

"The Romans would have agreed with you. They named Procida the first of the Poet Islands. They considered her the stomping ground for poets and writers. Tomorrow, we'll visit Ischia, and after that, Capri."

"You enjoy this, don't you? Being captain of a luxury cruiser? Sailing around the world, charting your own courses. Making your own timeline."

"It's not always easy. There are days when catering to the whims of our residents can get difficult."

"Like herding cats?' I chuckled. "Don't forget, I've met several. Between a few peculiarities and conspiracy theories, you have your hands full."

"I'm not complaining. We have a few oddballs. But most of our residents are quiet retirees. Some are a little grumpy or opinionated. Fact is, they want what they want, but they've earned the right."

"Have they?"

"You don't think so?"

"I would agree that retirees are entitled to their opinions and their proclivities. I live with my grandmother. She's a child from the Depression, and she has a host of habits I disagree with. She still splits a stick of gum in half to save a dime. Which makes me wonder. How can someone like the Professor afford such a luxurious lifestyle?"

Byard bit his lip and shook his head. If he knew anything about the Professor's financing, he wasn't about to say.

"I'm afraid I can't answer that. It's not my job to screen residents. If you're curious about any of them, you should talk to Oleg Sidorov. He handles the sale of Athena's suites, the association dues, and management fees. He's had that job since he first came aboard. Neil calls Oleg Commandant of the Pepsi Navy."

"The Pepsi Navy?"

"Ever hear of it?"

"No. Should I have?"

"Maybe not, but back when the Soviet Union fell apart, their fleet, or a lot of it anyway, was like everything else in Russia, broken, falling apart, and not worth a crap—just a bunch of rusted hulls. Some of it was barely able to float. But Oleg saw an opportunity. Several years before, he had arranged for Pepsi to be distributed in the Soviet Union and introduced the soft drink to Russia. The Russians loved it. But when it came to paying the bill, Russia was strapped. Oleg went back to Pepsi and negotiated for Russia to give Pepsi seventeen rusted Russian subs, along with a frigate, a cruiser, and a destroyer, in exchange for their past due bill."

"You're joking."

"No. Not a bit. In fact, this was also about the time that Oleg was negotiating with Neil for Athena's hull. I think Pepsi got the better deal, but Neil's done okay. Pepsi turned around and sold what they had of the Russian fleet to the Swedes, who used it for scrap metal. I don't imagine Pepsi lost so much as a dime, and it kept the Russians drinking Pepsi. To this day, if the Russians are loyal to anything besides their vodka, it's Pepsi."

"And Oleg? What did he get out of the deal?"

"What do you think? In addition to a cushy job as *Athena's* resident bookkeeper, he negotiated a four-thousand square foot luxury suite directly across from Neil's."

"And family? Does he have any?"

"He's got a daughter in Lucerne and homes in Moscow and London. I don't know much more than that, but rumor is he's one of the wealthiest residents aboard. Anyone else you want to know about?"

"Neil Webster. I get that he's pretty much a closed book when it comes to his personal life, but listening to the Professor talk about Aenaria tonight, I

CHAPTER ELEVEN

couldn't help but wonder if maybe Neil was involved in the discovery."

"Sorry, I don't know. It was way before my time. But I do know Neil's not the type to want a lot of publicity, and if he doesn't want to talk about it, that's fine with me."

Chapter Twelve

I left Byard on the Promenade Deck and returned to Dede's suite. Much as I wanted to think Captain wasn't involved in Dede's disappearance or that he might be a party to bootlegging antiquities across the Mediterranean, I felt something wasn't right. I could understand why Byard would be loyal to Neil. Neil had given Byard a fresh start. But Neil? The more I thought about him, the more doubts I had.

Neil was very closed mouth about his personal life, particularly his financial dealings, and if I was right in suspecting he was involved in the discovery of Aenaria, his explorations as well. As to whether that secrecy might also include a connection to the gold coin I had found in Dede's bag or her whereabouts, I had no idea. But I had to admit, despite all the good things I heard people say about Neil, I was growing ever more suspect that Neil Webster's plans for *Athena* included more than a quiet retirement community for Seniors at Sea.

I'm no financial wizard, but if Byard was right and *Athena* required a guaranteed wealth analysis of five million dollars, then how could a retired history professor and his wife, plus a former private investigator and a young aerialist, afford luxury suites aboard a private ship like *Athena*? The more I thought about it, the more I couldn't let the thought go. The numbers just didn't add up, and I was anxious to return to Dede's cabin, where I could pull my notepad from my backpack and organize my thoughts.

I had barely put my key in the door when Finn poked his head out from behind the Braun's cabin door across the hall.

"Ms. Lawson. I'm glad I caught you. Elli dropped by. She wanted to slip

CHAPTER TWELVE

this under your door, but I told her I'd take it." Finn handed me an envelope. "I had come by to do a turndown for the Professor and his wife. They're still upstairs having a celebratory drink for their anniversary."

"Elli?" I looked at the envelope and wrinkled my brow.

"From the spa. Are you sure you don't want me to turn down your sheets? It's no problem." Finn appeared to be in no hurry to rush off.

"You're working too hard, Finn. I'm quite capable of turning down my own sheets. But I thank you for the offer."

"It's my job. And I do enjoy it." Finn folded his arms and leaned back against the door jam. "To be honest, I miss when Neil and some of my regulars like Dede go ashore and take leave of the ship. Particularly, Dede. She and I have a special relationship. Sometimes, she invites me in for a nightcap. She likes to chat before she turns in."

"Not that I'm judging, but isn't that a little irregular?"

"It is, but with Dede, irregular's the norm. She isn't big on rules."

"You know what, neither am I." I opened the door and nodded for Finn to go in. "And I could use a drink. There's an open bottle of red wine on the bar."

"I'd prefer scotch. Dede keeps a bottle behind the bar. If you don't mind, I'll help myself."

While Finn poured himself a scotch, I grabbed a wineglass from the rack above the bar, filled it from the open bottle, and sat down.

"So, tell me, what do you and Dede like to talk about?"

"What don't we talk about." Finn put his drink on the bar and, adjusting the sleeve of his jacket, pointed to a shiny gold bangle bracelet on his wrist. "Oh, did you notice?"

"Is that new?"

"Greta gave it to me. Quite nice, don't you think?"

I leaned forward to get a better look. The bracelet was similar to several I had seen on the display table at the Professor's lecture earlier that night. "Is it from their collection?"

"I don't know…maybe…probably?" Finn glanced at the bracelet. "I didn't ask. Greta said she wanted me to have it as a thank you for all I've done for them. But not to tell her husband."

I wondered if Greta had given Finn a gold bracelet and if she might also have given Dede the gold coin. I doubted Greta would have given the coin away without her husband's knowledge, but it was worth asking. I pushed the conversation toward the Brauns and continued to ask more about them.

"That's very generous of Greta. Was she as generous with Dede?"

"Not at all. Not that Greta didn't try. She crocheted a handbag for Dede to replace one Dede had recently lost, but Dede didn't like it. I saw her carry it once before leaving for Naples, but it wasn't her style. Whatever, I wouldn't say they were friends. More like socially respectful of each other."

"I find them an interesting couple. Very knowledgeable."

Finn covered the bracelet with the cuff of his sleeve and picked up his drink.

"The Professor is for certain. But Greta?" Finn pointed his finger at me. "Don't quote me."

I waved my hands in front of my face. "We're just friends here. Enjoying a drink. You're not on the record."

"The woman's got fluff for brains. The Professor could talk for hours. He drives Dede nuts. She runs the other way when she sees him. She waits to make sure they've left their apartment before she goes out, just to avoid them."

"And what about Dede? What's she like?"

Finn took a sip of his drink. "Dede's one of a kind. You've heard the expression, an iron fist in a velvet glove? That's Dede. Not in the conventional sense, of course. She's no raving beauty. She's too old and too heavy for that. But she's a delight. Outspoken and ballsy. Whatever you do, don't get in her way. But, between you and me, Dede Drummerhausen is the most stable person onboard. I'd trust her with my life."

"That's quite a description."

"If you really want to know about Dede, ask Neil. He was good friends with her late husband. They were business partners. They spent a lot of time together. Socializing. Entertaining. It wasn't until Dede's husband passed that Dede and I got close. Like I said, we enjoy a nightcap now and again

CHAPTER TWELVE

but don't tell Neil I told you. He would disapprove."

"Your secret's safe with me. But tell me, how is it you came to work onboard, and how did you meet Neil?"

"Ahh, that's easy." Finn got up and went to the glass doors overlooking Dede's private deck. "I fell in love with Neil Webster the minute I saw him. I know that sounds crazy, but I did. I was working aboard a cruise ship when *Athena* pulled in beside us in Porto, Portugal. Neil was on the Sun Deck. A tall, nerdy-looking blond dressed in a suit. He was there on business. I didn't know who he was at the time. All I knew was that I had to meet him. I won't say I stalked him, but I did follow him to a bar in town, and the rest is history. He offered me a job and my own suite aboard Athena. We don't live together for appearance's sake, but we've been together ever since. Except when he's off on business traipsing around the world raising money for one thing or another."

"Leaving you behind to keep things afloat?"

Finn crossed back to the bar and put his drink down. "I've learned not to complain. Being Neil's paramour has advantages, and I have a good life." Finn returned to the bar and finished his drink. "It's late, and I've bent your ear long enough. I should be on my way."

I walked Finn to the door, bid him good night, then checked to make sure Dede's black crocheted bag was still inside the drawer of the entry table. Satisfied it was where I had left it, I closed the drawer and headed to the bedroom, then opened the envelope Finn had given me.

Dear Ms. Lawson,

On behalf of Athena's staff, I would like to welcome you aboard and offer you a complimentary massage and use of the gym during your stay. I look forward to helping to make your visit a healthy, happy experience. Please call for an appointment,

Elli Webster

Extension 1505

I stared at the signature. *Elli Webster?* Her last name wasn't lost on me, nor what I thought was Elli's British accent—not British at all—but South African. A little too much of a coincidence not to be connected to Neil

63

Webster. The Churchill sisters had said Neil was an only child, his only surviving relative an uncle who wanted nothing to do with the boy after his parents died. And yet, here was this girl, younger by at least twenty-five years and on summer break from California. What were the chances? I picked up the cabin phone, dialed her number, and left a message.

"Hi, Elli, it's Kat Lawson. I'd like to take you up on your offer for a massage. If you've time tomorrow afternoon, I should be back on board after my morning visit to the island sometime after 2 p.m. Call me back. Extension 1221."

Chapter Thirteen

I had coffee in my cabin the following morning. Like Dede, I wanted to wait until I was sure the Professor and Greta had left their apartment before I ventured out and risked running into the Professor. As a travel reporter, I needed time on my own to do my job, and I spent the early morning reading through my guidebook about the sights I planned to visit and still be back in time for my massage later that afternoon. Not so much because I needed a massage, but to collect information about some of those on board.

My former boss used to tell me whoever coined the phrase, *Only her hairdresser knows for sure,* would have made a damn good investigative reporter. People talk, he said. You want to know about someone. Talk to everybody who knows them. Priests. Tax Accountants. Best friends. Even their damn hairdresser. And under the circumstances, I hoped I could coax Elli into sharing some of what she knew about Neil Webster and maybe the Professor and Inspector Garnier while she worked out the kinks in my neck.

By nine o'clock, I tossed my guidebook into my backpack and dressed quickly. Taking a pair of shorts and a t-shirt from the closet, I slipped into my tennis shoes, grabbed my coffee, and headed outside to the living room deck for a view of Ischia and the Aragone Castle. The weather was picture-perfect. Small fishing boats bobbed in the harbor, protected from the open sea by a causeway connecting Ischia's island to the Castle, which looked like it rose from the sea like a giant rock. It was hard to imagine, as pristine as everything looked, that somewhere beneath the calm turquoise-blue waters lay the legendary sunken city of Aenaria, dating back to the end of the first century BC, a once great port and center for trade in the Mediterranean.

Anxious for pictures, I snapped several, then, checking my watch, swigged down what was left of my cold coffee. It was 9:25 a.m. I figured I had waited long enough for the Professor and his group to disembark for their tour. I stuffed my camera inside my backpack, then headed downstairs to the Marina Deck to catch one of the morning shuttles to the island.

Unfortunately, the tenders had been running late, and the Professor, Greta, and Camile were waiting with a small group of residents. Upon seeing me, Camile turned her back while Greta left her husband's side and approached.

"Oh, there you are. I was tempted to knock on your door this morning. Will you be joining the tour?"

"I'm sorry, I can't." I feigned disappointment. But after dinner with the Churchill sisters and Inspector Garnier and Camile's chilly reception, I had begun to feel my presence on board, while known to all, was less than welcome and that the observer had become the observed. "My publisher's given me a long list of places to see and photograph. And I have an appointment this afternoon for a massage."

"Such a shame. You'll miss The Atelier delle Dolcezze." Greta put her hand on her stomach and licked her lips.

The Professor took his wife's hand. "Don't let the name mislead you. It's more than a chocolatier. It's an art gallery. Once the meeting place for young arts and cultural types and today, according to my wife—home to the best chocolate in all of Italy."

The midshipman who manned the Marina portal interrupted and held out his hand. "Let's go, people." *Athena's* tender had arrived. Patiently, the young sailor helped those in line ahead of me through the narrow door and down the short rope ladder to the awaiting tender.

I stepped back and told the Professor to go ahead. "Looks like this is going to be a full boat. You have a tour to give. I'll catch the next shuttle."

The Professor squeezed around me. "Whatever you say, Ms. Lawson. But tomorrow, no excuses. I want you with me on the dive to Aenaria. It's like nothing you've ever seen or ever will again. Promise me."

CHAPTER THIRTEEN

"I'll be there." I waved goodbye, relieved I wouldn't be spending the morning in the Professor's company, and found a seat near the pool where I could wait for the following tender to arrive and pulled my guidebook out from my backpack.

"Morning, Kat. You planning to go ashore?" I looked up from my guidebook to see Neil. He stepped back and adjusted his baseball hat. "If you are, I know a good tour guide. That is if you don't mind sitting on the back of a Vespa."

"You driving?" I stood up and stuffed my guidebook back inside my backpack.

"Unless you'd like to. But if you don't know where you're going, I wouldn't advise it. The streets can be challenging, and the locals here don't all speak English. Ischia isn't your typical tourist trap."

I shifted my backpack to my back. "I'm in, but I need to be back onboard by—"

"Two. Yes, I know. You have a massage scheduled."

"Is there anything you and everybody else on this boat doesn't know?"

"Probably not." Neil glanced out the open porthole. The speed boat had arrived. "You coming?"

* * *

The small green Vespa Neil had reserved was barely big enough for two people. But Neil didn't appear concerned and took hold of the handlebars. "Hop on. This'll be fun, you'll see."

I straddled the seat, put my arms around Neil's waist, and held tight as Neil gunned the bike's small engine, and we zipped onto the narrow street.

"We'll start at Mortella Gardens, or as the Italians call it, Giardini La Mortella." I was impressed with Neil's pitch-perfect Italian accent, and as we scooted around small cars and pedestrians with their shopping bags, despite the sudden stops and bumps in the road, I started to relax. Juggling my backpack on my lap, I grabbed my camera and snapped a few photos.

"You might want to wait until we get to the gardens. The view of the bay from there is as good as it gets. You can see the ship from there, and the gardens are the most beautiful in Italy. You'll thank me."

As we got to the top of the mountain, the road narrowed, and Neil pointed the bike onto a smaller dirt path, plush with plant life, the colors like an artist's palate, of green and yellow gold, all melded together with the sounds of birds, and waterfalls. I had never seen a jungle of plant life so radiant or felt the subtle abundance of color and the sunlight so soft against my skin. Neil parked the scooter, got off, and walked ahead of me to the bluff like he had been there a hundred times before.

"To your left is Ischia Porto, and over there," Neil pointed to the Aragones Castle, "is Ischia Ponte, where you can see the Castle. It looks like it's growing straight up from the volcanic rock."

I snapped several pictures, including one of *Athena*, moored in the harbor.

"In her time, before she was destroyed by an earthquake, Ischia was a major trading port. Can you imagine it? Huge trading vessels lined up right below us in the harbor. Offloading gold and silver from what was once the splendor of the ancient world. Their precious icons shipped here to Aenaria's smelting factory to be melted down."

I stepped back and took another shot of Neil on the bluff. Behind him was the causeway between the port and the Castle. I wanted a picture of him for the magazine, looking down on what had once been the legendary city of Aenaria.

I lowered my camera and joined him as he looked out at a causeway below. "So, how did you find her?"

"Find who?" Neil looked at me like he didn't know who or what I was talking about.

"Aenaria. The sunken city. You discovered her, didn't you?" Maybe I was feeling a little overconfident, but I needed to take advantage of the opportunity to push through Neil's barricade to not talk about himself, and if I didn't act now when we were alone, when could I?

"What are you talking about?"

"The Professor's lecture last night. He said it was two divers, twenty-five years ago, who discovered the mythical city. It was you, wasn't it? You and

CHAPTER THIRTEEN

somebody else."

Neil shook his head and started toward the scooter.

"You okay?" I chased after him.

"You're reading too much into the Professor's lecture, Kat." Neil quickened his pace.

"I don't think so. Tell me I'm wrong, and it's not why we're spending an extra day in the Poet Islands? My guess is that's why the Professor knows about Aenaria. You must have told him about it. How else would he know? And he wanted to come back when you were aboard because the Professor knew you'd want to see it again. You both wanted to visit Aenaria before she was opened to the public, and the Professor was still free to do his research. Why do you care that anyone would know it was you?"

Neil stopped. "Because I don't want it to be about me. That's why. I prefer it that way. I won't deny I enjoy coming back here and diving in these waters. But like I told you before, I don't like to talk about my private life. What I did before I bought *Athena*, what I do when I'm not on board, it's nobody's business. Whatever you write, it's not about me. It's about the ship. You got that?"

"Yeah, I got it."

"Good." Neil turned back to the bike and took hold of the Vespa's handlebars. "It's getting late. There's not enough time to cross the causeway and visit Aragonese Castle. Not if you want to return to the ship in time for your massage."

I hopped on the back of the scooter and put my arms around Neil's waist. "We okay?"

"Long as you promise to write a nice story about *Athena*, we're gold."

"Done," I said.

But we both knew I had hit a nerve. Whatever Neil Webster was hiding, I could tell he was anxious that I report nothing more than what he wanted me to see. And the more I saw, the more convinced I was that Neil's presence aboard *Athena* had less to do with celebrating his Aunt Ida's birthday than providing the perfect cover for a modern-day pirate ship with a group of geriatric pirates on a mission to smuggle antiques across the Mediterranean.

* * *

We arrived back at the dock with thirty minutes to spare and found a small portside restaurant with an outside table. Neil ordered an iced coffee—a caffe shakerato—for us both.

"Neil?"

From behind us, a tall, handsome, curly-haired Italian approached with a big smile.

"Antonio?" With his arms wide, Neil put his coffee down and embraced the stranger like an old friend.

The stranger put his hands on Neil's shoulders, stood back, and stared at Neil. "I thought that was you. I saw *Athena* in the harbor and wondered if you might be aboard."

Neil introduced me. His mood was near jovial in the presence of his friend.

"Kat, I'd like you to meet Antonio De Luca." Then, grabbing Antonio's chin and pinching his cheeks, Neil added, "But don't let this pretty face fool you. He's not to be trusted. Not with the ladies, for sure."

Antonio pushed Neil's hand away from his face. "Don't believe a word he says. He's just jealous. I'm a gentleman, particularly around attractive women."

"Let me stop you right there, Pretty Boy. Kat Lawson's a reporter. You don't want to mess with her."

Antonio placed his right hand over his heart and bowed his head. His dark curls fell across his light blue eyes. "My apologies to you if I appeared rude."

"Not at all," I said. It was easy to see why Neil liked Antonio. He was gorgeous. The embodiment of a Greek statue, with an air of confidence.

Neil stepped in between us. "Kat, I'm sorry, you'll have to excuse me. I need to catch up with Antonio. It's been a while. Do you mind taking the tender back by yourself?"

"Not a problem."

"But don't forget, I invited you for dinner tonight. Seven-thirty. I'm cooking, remember?"

"I'm looking forward to it."

Chapter Fourteen

The tender dropped me at *Athena's* portside with just enough time to go upstairs to Dede's suite, change into my robe, and get down to the spa in time for my massage. When I arrived, I noticed Oleg standing by the pool. He was dressed—if one could call it that—in a red G-string Speedo and was toweling himself off. Despite his barely-there swimsuit, I hoped we could schedule a moment to talk later.

"Oleg?

Rubbing the towel against his head, the Russian approached. For a man in his mid-sixties, he was in great shape, tan, muscled, without an ounce of fat.

"Afternoon, Ms. Lawson. Had a nice morning?"

"I did, thank you. Neil gave me a quick tour of the island this morning."

"And you passed up Ischia's world-class mineral baths for a massage on board?" Oleg held the ends of the towel against his chest.

"What can I say? Elli made me an offer I couldn't refuse." I opened my hands and smiled. "Free's hard to beat."

"If you get a chance, try the floatation tank. Total relaxation. Good for whatever ails you and the gym's not busy while we're in port. But we should talk." Oleg pointed a finger at me.

"I agree. I was planning on going back to visit the Castle in the morning, but if you've time, I'd love to chat with you."

After learning about Oleg's past and how he had been instrumental in helping Neil buy *Athena* and Neil's decision to put Oleg in charge as *Athena's* onboard accountant, I was anxious to talk with him and learn whatever he could tell me about some of *Athena's* residents.

"Noon tomorrow. It is important we make time for each other. The Ivy Café." Oleg bunched the towel in his hand and turned to leave.

"I'll be there," I said.

***

I found Elli standing behind the counter outside the spa door, her blonde hair in a ponytail and a clipboard in her hand.

"Good afternoon, Kat. Anything we need to work on?"

I rolled my shoulders and rubbed the side of my neck. "I've got a stiff neck. Can you fix that?"

"I've just the thing. Go in and lie down on the table. I'll only be a minute."

The massage room was small, nothing fancy, with the masseuse's table in the middle, a single white counter on one side, and a hook on the back of the door. I hung my robe up on the hook, slipped beneath a thin cotton sheet on the table, and waited with my face in the cradle.

Elli entered the room talking. "So, Kat, have you been enjoying yourself?"

"It'd be tough not to. It's all so beautiful."

"And Dede's suite?"

"It's awesome. Have you seen it?"

"I'm really not supposed to. But, yes. I have. Neil doesn't like *staff* to socialize with the residents. But with Dede, it's impossible not to. She's a regular, has a massage at least once a week, and likes to talk. She's had me in for dinner several times. You know she loves to cook, right?"

"So I've heard."

Elli placed a warm heating pad on my back. "You know…Dede's the reason you're here."

"Oh?"

"It was Dede's idea to contact the magazine. She thought a story about *Athena* and her residents would make a good feature. And the more she talked about it, the people on board and the places they go, the more I did, too. It seemed like a good idea, and we thought maybe it might help."

"Help? What do you mean?" I hated conducting an interview on my

CHAPTER FOURTEEN

stomach, face down to the floor. But even with nothing but a view of Elli's tennis shoes, I sensed she knew more about Neil, Dede, and the ship than she thought, and whatever she knew, I wanted to know.

"Ugh, forgive me. I've said too much. I—I really shouldn't be talking—"

"Nonsense. This isn't an interview. You don't need to worry. Far as I'm concerned, I'm just here for a massage. And if I can help, I'd be happy to." I tried to allay Elli's fears. I wanted her on my side and to feel it was safe to say whatever she wanted. "Look, it's not like I'm from the board of health or anything. I'm just a travel writer, writing about a group of Seniors at Sea, enjoying their sunset years."

"I suppose you're right. It's just—"

"What? You're worried I might not write a great article?"

Elli took the heating pad off my back and began to massage my shoulders. I could feel the angst in her hard hands as she kneaded the muscles around my neck.

"It's just, I wouldn't want to say anything that would harm *Athena's* reputation."

"I doubt you need to worry. *Athena's* a beautiful ship, and I've heard nothing but good things since I came onboard." I paused and considered how I might open the conversation to what Elli might have heard or known about some of the people on board while she continued to work out the kinks in my back. "Although…to be honest, I have noticed several vacancies on board. Captain Byard said some of the residents have second and third homes. But I got the idea that maybe he didn't want to tell me that some might just be empty."

Elli rubbed some warm oil between her hands and then down my back. "All I know is that Dede's worried. She keeps saying how much better things used to be."

"You know how older people are. Always going on about the past. How perfect it was." I tried to sound uninterested, but my mind was racing. I wanted to lead the conversation without being obvious. "Besides, I suppose if Dede mentioned the number of empty cabins to you, she would have said something to Neil as well."

"Maybe. They are close. Neil and Dede's husband were business partners. I think she worries about Neil, but that's just who she is."

"Old people worry. She probably worries about you, too."

"Hardly." Elli kneaded her knuckles into my shoulders as she spoke. "You know Neil's my cousin."

"I wondered. When I saw your last name on the invitation you sent last night, I thought maybe you might be related."

"Our fathers were brothers. My father's the older. I'm his only child by his third wife. That ought to tell you something about who he is…or who he was anyway. He's quite old now, and we're not in touch. Haven't ever been, really… My mother's American. She met my father while visiting South Africa years ago and, as she tells it—Whoops! Surprise! And I was born six months later. According to Mom, it was a rocky marriage from the start. I can't imagine they ever had anything in common. There's a big age difference, at least forty years. I never really knew my father. He was always traveling. After they separated, my father paid for my mother and me to move back to California and cut us off. Totally. He never sent us so much as a dime. Plus, I never even knew I had a cousin."

"That had to be difficult."

"It wasn't easy. But mom did the best she could."

"So, how did you find Neil?"

"Fate, I suppose. I was working at a gym as a masseuse in West L.A. when a client came in and left a copy of *Investor's Daily* in the lobby. I was about to throw it away when I saw an ad for Webster's International with a picture of Neil. Neil looks a lot like the pictures I've seen of my father. There's a strong family resemblance. Anyway, I was curious and called the number in the ad and left a message with a female receptionist. Said I thought Neil Webster and I might be related and asked if she would relay my message to Neil that I wanted to talk. To tell you the truth, I never expected a callback. He probably had no idea who I was. I could have been some nut, but he called back several weeks later, and we talked on the phone. I told him my story, and he said he had always wondered if he had any family other than my father and that he was delighted I had called. Before we hung up, he had

CHAPTER FOURTEEN

arranged for me to fly to London and to have a summer job aboard *Athena*. I really wish I had grown up knowing Neil. It's not fair my father cut him out of our lives."

"Not that it's any of my business, but if your father cut you and your mother off, do you think he did the same to Neil?"

Elli rested her hands on my shoulders. "I don't know. All I do know is that Neil says they haven't spoken in years."

"Then Webster's International isn't part of your father's business?"

"I never thought about it. And I wouldn't ask. As far as I'm concerned, my father's been dead to me for years. He made my life and my mother's very difficult. When I met Neil, I told him I didn't want to talk about him, and Neil agreed. He'd be upset with me if he knew I had mentioned anything to you about my father or Neil's past. Neil's very private, and I wouldn't want to do anything to unsettle our relationship."

"Well, I'm sure he enjoys getting to know you and having family around. From what I can see, he's loyal to the Churchill sisters."

"He is. And you're right about family. Neil's loyal to those loyal to him. I probably shouldn't have said anything about Neil's past. I hope you won't say anything."

"I'm not here to do a story about Neil Webster. I'm here to do a story about *Athena* and her Seniors at Sea, peacefully sailing into their sunset years. And, as far as Neil goes, he's already told me he didn't want to talk about himself. That his business affairs and personal life were off-limits. So, whatever you've told me, it stays between us."

"Good, 'cause I wouldn't want something like that to get around. There's enough excitement around here already. You heard what happened this morning?"

"No. What happened?"

"Frau Braun accused Marco of stealing her husband's red signet ring last night during his presentation. I was in the café early this morning when she started yelling at him. What a Scene! She attacked him, and security had to come and pull her away."

"That couldn't have been good. How's Marco doing?"

I couldn't believe I had missed the scene. It must have happened before I joined the residents going ashore.

"Strange, like usual. But I'm not sure he took the ring. Between you and me, Marco gets blamed for anything that goes missing. He wouldn't still be here if he was crazy and guilty of things everyone says he is." Elli tapped me lightly on the back. She'd finished my massage. "Anyway, let's hope Chief Sully finds the ring. Frau Braun is frantic. She says the ring is one of a kind. It was used by some Roman dignitary to sign documents. It's probably worth thousands."

Chapter Fifteen

No wonder Neil was so guarded about his past. If Webster's International wasn't as well funded as Neil liked to let on, it shed a different light on *Athena's* Seniors at Sea program. It might explain why Neil didn't want to talk about his personal life or business affairs. I thanked Elli for the massage and suggested we get together again, then headed directly back to Dede's cabin. After learning about the Professor's missing signet ring and that Frau Braun thought that Marco might be responsible, I was anxious to check that the Ides of March coin was still neatly hidden beneath the safe's lining.

Finding everything as I had left it, I closed the safe, pulled my journal from within my bag, and walked barefoot to the living room, where I poured myself a glass of red wine. I then retreated to the outside deck, where I planned to make a few notes about some of *Athena's* more *interesting residents*, starting with Neil Webster. Was he the mega-rich billionaire the world thought him to be or a fraud? And while his relationship with the Churchill sisters appeared to be one of extended family, was that all it was? And then there was Professor Braun, his wife Greta, and Inspector Garnier and his wife, Camile. I put a few dollar signs and question marks behind their names. None of them had the type of money to afford such a luxurious lifestyle. The more I thought about it, the more I began to believe that the picture-perfect *Athena* with her gleaming white hull, sailing through the Mediterranean's turquoise blue waters with her happy Seniors at Sea program was more of a cover for a group of geriatric smugglers than innocent seniors sailing peacefully into their sunset years.

Tap. Tap. Tap. "Hello?" From the entry, I heard Finn enter the apartment. "Anyone home?"

I closed my journal and, holding it against my chest, entered the living room. Finn had let himself in and had a tray of chocolates in his hand.

"Oh, there you are." Finn waltzed by me and put the chocolates on the dining table. "I was hoping you might be in. I brought these. I thought perhaps you might like them. It's lonely with Dede away, and Neil's so busy this week with plans for Ida Churchill's party, I was hoping we might chat."

"I'm so sorry. It's very thoughtful of you, Finn, but I can't, not tonight."

Finn picked a chocolate up from the tray and put it in his mouth. "Forgive me. I should have known. I'm sure you're busy." Finn started for the door, then stopped halfway. "Will you be going out this evening?"

"Yes. Neil invited me for dinner."

"Oh?" Finn looked surprised. "Strange he didn't mention it."

I shrugged and walked to the door. "I don't know why."

"Well, then. I'll not keep you. Have a nice evening."

Finn shut the door behind him, and I stood staring at the door with my notepad against my chest. Finn was close to Neil, and as a butler, he was in and out of the Brauns' and the Garnier's apartments as much as Dede's. I would need to keep Finn close if I hoped to learn what he knew about Neil and some of *Athena's* more interesting residents. I scribbled Finn's name on my pad, then returned to the bedroom, where I decided it might be a good idea to lock my journal inside the closet safe, just in case anyone came looking.

After dressing quickly, I chose a pair of black Palazzo pants and a sleeveless tank top, something that showed off my tan, and headed out of the apartment to the elevator, one floor up to Neil's cabin. Halfway down the hall, I passed Camile. She rushed past me, head bowed, arms wrapped tightly around herself, and said nothing. I watched as she stopped in front of the elevator and pounded the button. She looked as though she were about to cry. Then, giving up on the elevator, ran to the other end of the hall and disappeared behind the door to the stairs. Moments later, the door to Neil's cabin opened, and Professor Braun entered the hall.

CHAPTER FIFTEEN

"Good evening, Ms. Lawson." The Professor shut the door behind him. "I understand you'll be joining Neil for dinner tonight."

"I am." I forced a smile while trying to process Camile's rushed exit and the Professor's unexpected appearance from Neil's apartment. Was there a connection? Fearing my suspicion might suddenly play out on my face, I blurted the first thought that came to mind. "And from what Neil tells me, he's quite the gourmand."

"The best. And I happen to know Neil's planning one of his specialties for tonight. You won't be disappointed." The Professor patted me on the back and started toward the elevator, then stopped suddenly as though a second thought had occurred to him. "You haven't forgotten about tomorrow's dive, I hope. I'm looking forward to showing you."

My throat tightened. If the Professor had any idea that I thought he might be involved in a high-stakes smuggling operation, I might never get off this ship alive. Still, I had a job to do and needed to keep my cover. I could barely get the words out.

"I wouldn't miss it."

"Good. Until tomorrow, then."

I waited until I saw the Professor enter the elevator, then walked further down the hall and tapped lightly on Neil's door. Whatever I was about to walk into, this wasn't going to be a casual, friendly dinner. With everything I had learned about Neil and suspected about the Professor and the Garniers, I felt tonight's dinner was more of a game of chess, and I'd need to keep my concerns hidden well beneath the surface.

Neil answered the door. "Kat, I'm so glad you came. Please, come in."

I stepped inside, and Neil hugged me hello. When he let go, I was dumbfounded. I had never expected such a suite, particularly on a ship. Two-story, glass floor-to-ceiling windows looked out onto a deep wooden deck facing the ship's stern. And directly beyond it, the sun was just beginning to sink slowly into the water like a yellow ball on the horizon. To my left, a dramatic, black-lacquered spiral staircase wound from the great room to the second story. Directly in front of me was a spacious living area with an oversized circular couch facing the windows, a baby grand piano on one side, bookshelves, and a full bar on the other, and further to my right, a formal dining room complete with a crystal chandelier and candelabras.

"Kat, you remember Antonio from this morning. I invited him to join us. I hope you don't mind."

Antonio handed me a glass of red wine and lifted his glass to me. "We've white wine if you prefer, but I figured you to be more of a red wine type of woman."

"I'm not sure I have a type. But thank you." I held the glass up to the light and then took a sip. Smooth. Dry. And dusty. With just the slightest hint of blackberries.

"It's very rare. And quite expensive. You like?"

"It's delicious."

"To friendship." Neil clicked his glass to mine, then to Antonio's. "I asked Antonio to join us for dinner tonight. He's on his way to Sorrento, and I suggested he come with us. He'll be staying on board for a couple of days. We'll drop him on our way up the coast."

I wandered deeper into the great room, stopped at the long buffet, and traced the edge of the table with my finger. On top were several ancient-looking face masks, one stone, the other, a death mask made of gold, and several urns of various sizes.

Antonio followed me to the buffet and picked up one of the urns. "Neil tells me this is your first cruise. Are you enjoying yourself?"

"Very much," I said. "I suppose you've sailed these waters many times."

"A few. It's one of my favorite parts of the world. Neil and I've enjoyed quite a few dives in the area."

"Oh?"

"Don't bore her with ancient history, Antonio." Neil took the urn from him and placed it back on the buffet. "I doubt she's interested."

"No, really. I'd like to know. How did the two of you meet?"

Neil answered. "Alright, but this isn't for public knowledge. It's off the record. But, if you must know, Antonio and I met years ago in Israel. I was going through a difficult time. I had some personal setbacks and had gone on a pilgrimage. I suppose you might say I was looking for answers." I

CHAPTER FIFTEEN

hadn't thought of Neil as a particularly religious man. Still, if by personal setbacks, Neil was referring to his uncle's move to disinherit Neil from the family trust, it lined up with what Elli had shared with me about her cousin's financial situation. "When I was there, I met Antonio. If ever there was a Renaissance man, I believe he's it."

"Neil's very generous." Antonio walked deeper into the room, twisting the stem of his wine glass as he spoke. "I'm hardly a Renaissance man. I'm an archaeologist by trade. In the late 60s, I was just getting started and worked with a group of researchers looking for the lost city of Atlit Yam. Have you ever heard of it?"

I shook my head.

"It's a Neolithic village off the Levantine coast, in the Eastern Med."

"And did you find it?"

"We did. Although the world wouldn't be aware of it for another fifteen years. Atlit Yam was submerged 25 to 30 feet below the sea. The remains of a once vibrant city. It had been there for maybe 8 or 9 thousand years." Antonio picked up one of the face masks, held it against his face, then handed it to me. It was heavy and rough. The facial features were primitive.

"Is this from there?" I held the mask against my face.

"It was."

I picked up the second mask, a thin piece of gold metal placed over an oval-shaped stone. "And this one? Is it from Atlit Yam as well?"

"No," Antonio shook his head. "That's a piece I picked up in Turkey. I gave it to Neil as a gift. It's a death mask. Similar to the Mask of Agamemnon, found in Mycenae in 1876 by Heinrich Schliemann, a German archaeologist. The real mask, sometimes known as the Mona Lisa of prehistory, is now on display in the Pushkin Museum in Moscow."

"Moscow? How did *that* happen?"

"Schliemann got greedy. He smuggled much of what he found out of Turkey and into Germany, where it disappeared after World War 2 and ended up in the hands of the Russians."

"Enough ancient talk." Neil waved us away from the buffet. "I invited you here to gloat over my culinary skills, not my collection of ancient art. If you want to see my piece de resistance, it's in the kitchen. Follow me."

Neil led the way to the kitchen. A large marble center island had been set up with three placemats, enough silverware, and wine goblets for an eight-course meal. In the center of the bar was a long, slim, white dish ornately displayed with olives, cheese, nuts, and prosciutto, enough that by itself could have easily been a meal. Neil filled two of the empty glasses on the table with red wine, then handed one of them to Antonio and the other to me while he sauteed a filet of fresh sea bass with lemon grass and ginger.

I don't remember how many glasses of wine we had or how often Neil refreshed my glass, but when Neil plated our dinner, and we sat down, the conversation flowed as easily as the wine.

When we finished our meal, Neil tempted us with a chocolate souffle he had prepared throughout our dinner. As he stood up from the table and cleared the dishes, there was a long, loud blast from the ship's horn.

Neil immediately went outside to the deck, and we followed. The blast continued. Three long, continuous blasts. A red flare had been launched into the dark sky from the sun deck above us.

"What is it?" I asked.

"Someone's overboard." Neil went back inside and picked up the cabin phone. From the shocked look on his face, I knew the news wasn't good.

Chapter Sixteen

Antonio and I leaned over the railing, our eyes searching for some sign of a body below. From the sun deck above, a spotlight aimed into the inky black water swirling beneath *Athena's* white hull.

Antonio was the first to spot the body. "Look. There beneath the tender ladder."

I strained to see the ladder flapping against the side of the ship, then spotted the body, lifeless in the water, floating face down. Neil came running to join us.

"Do you know who it is?" I looked anxiously at Neil and then back at the water.

"No." Neil put his arm around my shoulder, and we watched as a crew member wearing a life vest climbed out from the open hatch beneath us, threw a life preserver into the water, and then jumped in.

Moments later, a second crewman appeared at the top of the ladder and tossed a rope to his crewmate in the water. The first crewmember grabbed the rope, swam to the body, looped it around the man's chest, and then signaled to the crewmember to pull. Slowly, the body was dragged limp from the water.

"It's Oleg!" Neil put his hand to his mouth.

"Who?" Antonio did a quick head click to Neil.

"The Russian." Neil's eyes snapped to Antonio like he should know who Oleg was, then back to me. "Kat, we should go back inside. Come."

I followed Neil into the cabin while Antonio, ahead of us both, went directly to the bar and poured himself a drink.

Neil closed the drapes behind us. "Kat, I apologize. You shouldn't have to see something like this. It's highly unusual."

Even in a state of shock, I knew better. Captain Byard had replaced the previous captain who had fallen overboard, and if what the Churchill sisters told me about Dede was true, then Oleg was the third person to fall from *Athena's* decks.

"Do you think he fell?" I asked.

"Either that or he jumped. We won't know more until Doctor Jon has had a chance to look at the body. Oleg liked to drink. Might be he slipped." Neil joined Antonio at the bar and poured himself a drink. "Do you think you might need one?"

"No, I need to go. It's getting late. Let's talk tomorrow."

* * *

Exiting the elevator on Dede's floor, I noticed Finn headed toward me. "You're working late. I'm surprised you're still here. It's almost midnight."

"Frau Braun called and ordered something from the pharmacy. Her stomach's upset. She and the Professor were on the Lido Deck enjoying a nightcap when Oleg went overboard. I assume you heard?"

"I watched the crew fish Oleg out of the water from Neil's deck. Did Frau Braun see it happen?"

"I don't think so. The Professor said he and Greta had gone up to have a nightcap on the Lido Deck. They passed Oleg on their way to the bar. They said Oleg was talking to himself, leaning against the railing, and that he looked drunk. After that, they said they heard a splash, and when they looked back, Oleg was gone."

"Did the Professor think Oleg jumped?"

"He must have. It'd be nearly impossible to fall over the railings. They're five feet high. Oleg couldn't have gone over unless he wanted to." Finn started for the elevator. "Forgive me. I should ask, do you think you'll be needing anything?"

"No, I'm fine. Just shaken, that's all."

CHAPTER SIXTEEN

"Well, don't hesitate to call if you need to. By the way, how was dinner?"

"Dinner?" I had almost forgotten. All I could think about was the crew pulling Oleg's limp body from the water and my last conversation with him. If anything, the Russian had appeared anxious to meet, saying he thought it was important we make time for one another. Hardly the ramblings of a depressed or suicidal man.

"Did Neil serve anything special?"

"I'm sorry. What with Oleg falling overboard, I barely remember eating. But, yes, the meal was wonderful, and so was the company."

"Company?" Finn cocked his head curiously.

"Neil had a friend in. Antonio. He's planning to stay for a couple of days. Until we get to Sorrento."

"Humph." The news Neil had a guest was obviously a surprise and not a welcome one. Finn crossed his arms and clenched his jaw.

"You know him?"

"Antonio De Luca? Oh, yes, I know him. Antonio's been aboard a couple times. Not one of my favorite people. I suppose that's why Neil didn't bother to tell me."

"I'm sorry." I could see the news upset Finn. "I'm sure there's nothing to it. But if you don't mind, I need to rest. This has been a tough day."

"Of course. Have a good night, Ms. Lawson."

I bid Finn goodnight and let myself into Dede's apartment, then closed the door behind me and, with my back against it, sank to my heels.

I didn't need to wait for the doctor's report in the morning to know Oleg hadn't had a heart attack and accidentally fallen from the Lido deck. And I was sure the Russian hadn't committed suicide. If he had wanted to take his own life, he could have just as easily jumped from his own deck. No. Someone had pushed Oleg Sidorov overboard. Just like I was beginning to think someone had pushed the previous captain overboard, and possibly Dede as well. Maybe because they knew too much. Or knew as much as I did.

Chapter Seventeen

I spent a restless night in my cabin, my mind like a ping-pong ball going back and forth from the four million dollar Brutus gold coin I had found hidden in Dede's bag to Oleg's death, the Professor's missing ring and back to the very charming Neil Webster, who I was now beginning to suspect was head of an international smuggling operation, using *Athena* as a modern-day pirate ship to ferry stolen artifacts along the Silk Highway for personal gain. No wonder he didn't want me asking personal questions.

By seven a.m. I was dressed and ready to begin my day. I wanted to be up on the top deck early enough to grab a coffee and walk to the spot where Oleg had fallen overboard. But by the time I arrived on the Lido Deck, I wasn't alone. Neil and Finn stood mid-ship next to yellow tape that had been draped by the railing where Oleg had last stood. They appeared to be in a heated argument. Neil had his back to me. Finn shook his head and pointed back to the island. From the looks on their faces, this was a lover's spat. I filled my cup from the coffee urn the Ivy had set aside for residents who wanted to serve themselves and waited for Finn to leave. Once he was gone, I approached Neil.

"I wanted to thank you for dinner last night. I'm sorry I left so abruptly, but—"

"You were upset. I was, too. Awful situation. Oleg was a good friend and a business partner." Neil wrapped his fingers around the railing, inches from where the yellow tape was draped, and looked out at the water. "Unfortunately, Oleg drank too much. Doctor Jon said his alcohol level was extremely high. I suppose we'll never know what happened."

CHAPTER SEVENTEEN

"You think it was an accident?"

"What else could it be?"

I wasn't about to say I knew this was the second body to have fallen overboard, if not maybe the third. I looked out at the water and hoped Neil didn't see the doubt on my face or have any idea about the thoughts running through my mind.

"I hate to ask, but what happens now? Do we return to Naples?"

"No." Neil shook his head. "We have a morgue on board."

"A morgue?"

"Cruise ships all have them. We're required to have a place to store a body, and with an older clientele like we have, we're prepared for such things. Right now, Oleg's body is tucked neatly in a refrigerated section behind our infirmary. But don't you worry about it. I'd hate for any of what's happened to influence the story you're writing. However, I am afraid Oleg's death will affect my ability to go with you on our dive today. I'll need to go back to Naples to file some paperwork. I'll take the helicopter and be back by the end of the day.

"And what about the body?"

"We'll stop in Sorrento. We were going to drop Antonio there anyway, so while it wasn't a scheduled stop, it's not like it's out of the way. They have facilities to handle the body. Meanwhile, Antonio's agreed to dive with you in my place. You don't want to miss seeing Aenaria. It's not just thirty feet under the water. It's more than two thousand years back in time. And one of the reasons we're here. But do me a favor. If you haven't any diving experience, meet with Elli this morning and have her check you out on our scuba gear in the pool before you go. We don't need any more excitement around here."

***

Neil left me on the deck, and I finished my coffee, then decided to go inside the cafe and order a full breakfast. The café was busy, and I found a small table where I could eat and perused the menu. If I were going to dive, I'd need to keep up my energy.

"Kat! I'm so glad you're here. Do you believe what happened?" Ida limped toward me, holding her left arm against her side with her sister Irene close behind.

"Are you okay?" I thought I detected a slight lisp.

"I'm fine." Ida brushed aside my concern with a sweep of her hand. "But Oleg, you can't tell me that's a coincidence. Not after Dede."

"Ida, please." Irene grabbed her sister and started to pull her away from the table. "I'm so sorry, Kat. Please excuse us. Ida's not feeling well. Call us later, will you?"

I promised I would and watched as the two sisters shuffled their way to the door.

"Poor dear. I don't imagine she's long for this world." It was the Inspector who spoke. He and his wife Camile were seated at the table next to me.

I put my elbows on the table and leaned closer. No time like the present to do a little Q&A. "I was thinking the same. How old do you suppose they are?"

"It's Ida's 90th birthday on Saturday. I think Irene's even older. Whatever they are, they aren't in the best shape." The Inspector blotted his mouth with his napkin.

"How long have you known them?"

Camile closed her eyes and shook her head. From the pained look on her face, she wasn't happy being in her husband's presence and couldn't be bothered to discuss such things.

"Four years." The Inspector patted his wife's hand. "Camile and I came aboard about the same time the Professor did."

"Did you two know each other?"

"Some. Over the years, the professor has been helpful to me when we had cases dealing with antiquities and stolen art. He's quite an authority. I have a great deal of respect for him."

"Excusez-moi." The chef interrupted our conversation. In his hands, he held a black backpack. "Your lunch, Inspector. Exactly as you asked."

"Je vous remercie." The Inspector thanked the chef and stood up. "We're

CHAPTER SEVENTEEN

going back to the Castle today. Camile insisted we pack a lunch. Would you like to join us?"

"No, thank you. I was going to try to squeeze it in this morning, but I'm doing the dive to Aenaria this afternoon at two p.m., and Neil suggested I take a scuba lesson."

"Ahh, but of course. Wise idea. The dive's the opportunity of a lifetime. You'll never see anything like Aenaria ever again."

Chapter Eighteen

I said goodbye to the Inspector and Camile and hurried back to Dede's suite, where Finn stood outside my door with a bouquet of red roses.

"Flowers?" I wasn't expecting anything. "For me? Who're they from?"

Finn looked at the card and shrugged. "Card doesn't say. Just, 'Have a good day.'"

"That's odd."

Finn opened the door and waited for me to go inside. "Would you like me to put them in the living room?"

"Put them wherever you like. It doesn't matter." I had an uncomfortable feeling the flowers were from Captain Byard, and if they were, I wished he hadn't sent them.

"Looks like you have a secret admirer."

"I doubt that." I walked Finn to the door, then realized I'd missed an opportunity to ask him about what I had just seen on the Lido Deck. "I noticed you with Neil this morning. It looked like you were arguing. Things okay?"

Finn looked up to the ceiling. "I'm fine. Or I will be once Antonio leaves. He's not a good influence on Neil. Bad things happen when that man's around."

"What do you mean by bad things?" I put my hand on the door handle. I wasn't about to let Finn leave until I knew more. "You can't think Antonio had anything to do with Oleg's death. He was in Neil's apartment when it happened."

"I'm just saying, this isn't the first time Neil wasn't around when—" Finn

CHAPTER EIGHTEEN

put his fist to his mouth.

"When what, Finn? When someone drowns. Like the last captain? Captain McKay? I heard he fell overboard. That he was drunk. Was Antonio onboard when that happened?"

Finn reached for the door handle. "I shouldn't be talking like this. Neil would be furious if he thought I said anything. He already thinks I imagine things. He says I'm a jealous Nellie. Please, don't say anything. I need to go."

Finn opened the door and slid quietly out into the hallway. I waited until I heard the door latch, then locked it behind him. Whatever secrets Finn kept to himself, I had a growing sense of apprehension that I needed to keep my guard up.

* * *

It was almost 11:45 by the time I left the apartment. I had changed into my swimsuit, a simple red tank designed for serious swimming, slipped into my robe, and stuffed a tube of sunscreen and my camera into my backpack. Satisfied I had everything I would need, I set out for the indoor pool on the Marina Deck.

Rather than take the elevator and risk running into any of the residents in my robe and flip-flops, I decided to take the stairs. Poor choice. Captain Byard was coming up the stairs as I was going down.

"Morning, Kat. Off for a dive?" Byard stepped back and put a hand on the rail so I could pass.

"Actually, I'm off for a scuba lesson. I've never done any open-water diving before, and I'm joining the dive team this afternoon to Aenaria. Should be fun." I started back down the stairs, then stopped mid-step. This was awkward. I owed the man an excuse for not following through on our dinner plans, and if Byard had sent the flowers, I should at least address it. "By the way, thank you for the flowers. They're lovely."

"What flowers?"

"The bouquet of roses this morning. You didn't send them?"

"No. Must be another admirer."

"I apologize. We don't seem to be getting off to a good start. You've invited me for dinner at least twice, and I've canceled twice with short notice. I don't mean to be rude. It's just—"

Byard interrupted. "You're not being rude, Kat. When we met, I thought there might have been a connection, but you're here to do a job, and I was out of place. If I made you uncomfortable, I apologize. Have a good day. Enjoy the dive."

Byard skipped past me up the steps. If it wasn't Byard who had sent the flowers, then who was it?"

* * *

I arrived on the Marina Deck and found Antonio and Elli seated on the pool's edge, dangling their legs in the water. Elli was in a tank suit like mine, and Antonio, looking like Michael Angelo's David in board shorts with his broad shoulders and sculpted abs, sat next to a pile of scuba gear, a wetsuit, a tank, several masks, and fins.

"You nervous?" Antonio stood up and handed me a face mask. "I assume you know how to swim?"

"It's not the swimming that worries me." Finn's warning rang in my ears. Bad things happen when Antonio's around. But I didn't let on. As long as I maintained my cover as a travel journalist on assignment, I figured I was safe. "It's the open ocean. I have a fear of being some shark's breakfast."

"Don't worry, we already fed them."

Elli laughed. "He's kidding, Kat. Besides, the water's clear where we're diving, and I'll be with you."

Elli helped me into the wetsuit and once fitted, I joined Antonio in the pool's shallow end.

"The most important thing you need to know is don't hold your breath." I adjusted the facemask, and Antonio handed me the mouthpiece. "Slow and steady. Like a walk in the park."

I can't say Antonio's diving instructions would qualify for any type of underwater certification, but he must have felt I passed his basic test. After swimming beneath the pool's waters twice and feeling at ease with the tank on my back, the mask, and the air regulator, he declared me fit to go.

"We've got two groups of divers today. Neil arranged for a speed boat to tender us out to the dive area. Kat, you and Elli will come with me, along with Professor Braun, Doctor Johansson, and Marco."

"Marco?" Elli rolled her eyes.

"He signed up last minute. He insisted he go with the first group. He said he wanted to be with the Doctor."

Chapter Nineteen

The boat Antonio had arranged for us to tender to our dive spot was unlike any we had used to shuttle back and forth to the islands. Instead of a small speed boat, our dive team of six watched as Carlo, the toy boat's skipper, rolled out an inflatable pontoon from the back of the *Muse*, inflated it, attached an outboard engine, then motored to *Athena's* exit hatch.

Antonio threw the rope ladder down to Carlo and called for me. "Ladies first."

I looked overboard. Carlo held the end of the ladder, trying to keep it steady as the pontoon bobbed in the water below. The wind had picked up, and the sea was choppy. My stomach lurched. The climb down was maybe five and a half feet, much steeper than the day before.

Antonio extended his hand. "Don't worry, Kat. You've got this. Just hang tight to the rope. You'll be fine."

I wasn't about to wuss out. Taking a deep breath, I took hold of the doorway, turned around, and, with a quick nod to Antonio, slipped one foot onto the weightless ladder as it swayed against *Athena's* metal hull. Keeping my eyes level, my hands gripped to the rope ladder. I climbed one foot after the other down onto the pontoon. Elli followed along with Antonio and the rest of our team, Professor Braun, Doctor Johansson, and Marco, who appeared surprisingly nimble despite the climb down the ladder.

The pontoon was roomy enough for six plus our driver, but I worried as we bobbed in the water that we might sink when we loaded it with all our gear. Worst-case scenario, I figured as long as we stayed within sight of the

CHAPTER NINETEEN

bridge connecting Ischia to Aragonese Castle, I could swim to shore.

"Hey, Elli," Chief Sullivan hollered from *Athena's* open portal above us. "Sorry, kid, but I need to change places with you."

"Great," Elli whispered under her breath and stood up. "Sorry, Kat. Rank has its privileges. Have a good dive. We'll catch up later."

Like an obedient midshipman, Elli scampered up the ladder. Then Sully, half-dressed with the top half of his wetsuit hanging loosely around his thick waist, climbed down and sat beside me.

"Sorry to interfere, guys. But this is the only chance I have today to escape, and after last night, I need a break."

"Don't we all." The Professor adjusted his swim mask on the top of his head. "After Oleg's dive off the deck last night, it's going to be a long time before Greta agrees to a drink up on the Lido Deck again."

"Can't say I blame her." Antonio moved the bucket of swim gear he had lugged onboard to the center of the pontoon. "Thing is, I never would have pegged Oleg as suicidal. But then, you never know."

"Maybe you didn't, but I always thought Oleg might be a Russian spy. Probably knew too much about things he shouldn't and decided it was better to take his own life than wait around for someone to do it for him." Sully stretched the sleeves of his wetsuit over his shoulders and pulled the zipper up over his hairy belly.

Antonio handed me my mask. "Did you get a chance to talk with him, Kat?"

"Not really." I dipped my mask over the side of the boat to clean the glass. I didn't want to meet Antonio's eyes for fear he'd see the doubt in my own. Or that I was beginning to harbor thoughts that Oleg's death was no more accidental or suicidal than the previous captain's death might have been and that it might somehow all be tied to Dede's disappearance.

"Strange, I thought I saw the two of you talking the night of the Professor's lecture." Sully bumped his shoulder against my own.

"I wouldn't call it a conversation. Oleg ran into me as I was leaving the Professor's lecture. But we never really spoke."

"That's a shame." Sully checked his waterproof watch as he spoke. "Oleg always had a story to tell. I'm sure you would have found him interesting. He was a big talker. Problem is, the man never knew when to shut up. Know what I mean?"

Antonio reached back into his dive bag and took out his mask. "Hey, let's not speak ill of the dead. It's a beautiful day for a dive. There's no point in filling Kat's head with things that don't matter. Right, Kat?"

I smiled and didn't answer. Carlo started the engine, and the water splashed onto us as the pontoon picked up speed across the cove toward our diving spot.

The Professor put his hand on my knee. I must have looked pale. "You going to be okay?"

"I'm fine. A little motion sickness, that's all." I wrapped my arms around my waist. It wasn't motion sickness, but the sudden realization that I was the only woman onboard and headed out to sea with a group of men I knew nothing about until four days ago. Men who all knew each other. Men who knew Oleg and worried he might have spoken to me. And now, Oleg was dead, and I was alone at sea with six men who might have a lot to lose if they thought Oleg had told me something they didn't want me to know.

I put my hand in the water and splashed my face. I had to think of something to say to keep my cover and move the conversation from Oleg to the dive. I shouted over the sound of the motor to Antonio. "How many times have you made this dive?"

"Half a dozen. July's a great month to dive these waters. You should be able to see quite a bit. Professor, why don't you tell Kat what we'll see today."

The Professor explained we would be diving through ruins dating as far back as 200 BC. We would swim above the silted remains of Aenaria's mosaic streets and through a garden of moss-covered broken statues. He warned us not to touch anything. We would see the remains of a foundry, where ancient bronze and silver statues and idols from the Hellenistic period were melted down and recycled for their material value and made into coins. But all of it, the entire city, now nothing more than a watery graveyard, had been destroyed by a sudden earthquake and swallowed up by a giant tsunami.

Carlo cut the pontoon's engine. "Ready?"

CHAPTER NINETEEN

The Professor stood up and, with the aid of the Doctor, began to assemble his gear onto his back. Chief Sully helped Marco while Antonio secured his own tank, then helped me with mine.

"Don't worry, Kat, you've nothing to fear." Antonio showed me how to hold my mask to my face and roll backward over the side of the pontoon and into the water.

I did exactly as shown. Closed my eyes and did a backward somersault into the sea. When I opened my eyes, I was surrounded by tiny bubbles. Like a fish in a pod, I followed Antonio and my fellow divers through a forest of wavy seagrass. At times, the grass was so thick I would lose sight of my dive team, only to follow the bubbles and find them waiting behind giant fronds with pods of plankton. I could still see the sunlight from the surface above when Antonio paused, nodded to me, and swept the sediment from what once had been a mosaic walkway. I felt as though I had been transported to a silent, watery graveyard laid flat by currents of sand and silt covering the ocean floor.

Antonio swam ahead while a school of colorful fish swam between us, some stopping long enough so that I could touch them before swimming on. The Professor joined me, tapped my arm, and signaled me to follow. I shook my head, hesitant to leave the group. But the Professor was insistent, taking me by the arm, pulling me through the thick seagrass, and pointing ahead as we swam. Seconds later, Marco appeared, swimming frantically toward us with his hands to his throat. Realizing Marco's panic, the Professor let go of my arm and took Marco's hands from his neck. I look around for help. Chief Sully had spotted us, and behind him was Doctor Jon. Both men swam toward Marco and pushed the Professor aside. The Doctor placed his hand on Marco's chest and pantomimed for Marco to slow his breathing. Slowly, with the Doctor on one side and the Chief on the other, they rose to the surface with Marco between them. I followed, and moments later, treading water, Antonio joined us.

"What happened?" Antonio ripped his mask from his face. He looked angry.

"I don't know." I slipped my mask from my face to the top of my head.

"Marco looked like he was in trouble."

Spotting us in the water, Carlo shuttled the pontoon towards Marco, the Doctor, and the Chief while I paddled backward to avoid being hit.

"Marco, you okay?" Antonio hollered from the water as Marco boarded *The Muse*, then, with his back to us, gave us a thumbs up.

I waited until the Professor and Sully were aboard, then swam toward the pontoon and threw my mask inside.

Antonio waited for me to climb onboard, then followed and helped me to unleash the scuba tank from my back and placed it with his own at the rear of the pontoon.

"You sure you're okay?" Antonio handed me a towel.

"I'm fine." I toweled my wet shoulders and tied the towel around my waist.

"I apologize. I should have insisted Marco not join us—"

"It's alright. Is Marco okay?"

"He'll be fine. He panicked, that's all."

The Professor reached into an ice chest for a cola. "Like one? Or perhaps something stronger. With Vodka, perhaps?"

"No, thanks." I hugged myself. I was shaking, not so much from the chill of the air but from what I thought might have been a close call, if not for Marco, then likely for me.

The Professor popped the top off a cola. "I'm sorry you didn't see the foundry, Kat. I wanted to show you the carvings on the wall."

"Is that where you were taking me?"

"Of course. I wanted you to see it for your story."

I didn't feel like that's what the Professor had in mind when he grabbed my arm and tried to pull me from the group. I couldn't help but think he had intended to lose me among the tall, wavy sea fronds where I'd be lost, and he could later claim I'd wandered off and they had searched but couldn't find me. Or perhaps he had planned to yank my breathing tube from my mouth and make my death look like an accidental drowning. But I wasn't about to let on.

"You've nothing to worry about," I said. I pushed my wet hair from my face and met the Professor's eyes straight on. "I've got everything I need."

CHAPTER NINETEEN

"Good. Then I can tell Neil you were pleased, and you will write a nice article."

"Absolutely." I feigned a smile. "And if I have any questions, I know who to ask."

The Professor raised his soda in a mock salute, then sat next to Sully while I found a spot at the end of the boat next to Marco. I closed my eyes and sat back. I wanted to let the warm rays of sunshine drench my body when Marco leaned closer.

"Did you like the flowers I sent?"

Chapter Twenty

"The roses are from you?" I couldn't believe what I had just heard.

Marco smirked, bowed his head to his shoulder, and whispered so only I could hear. "Did you think they were from the captain? Or you hoped they might be?"

I jerked my head. Was it obvious? "Who are you?"

I never would have imagined the flowers might have been from Marco, and I could not wait to hear what he had to say.

"Someone who wants to talk with you. Meet me for High Tea. The Ivy Café at four-fifteen, in the back. Corner table. None of these non-teetotalers will be there. They'll be in the bar, so we can talk." Marco leaned back and closed his eyes, and out of the side of his mouth, whispered, "And you can thank me later. I may have saved your life today."

* * *

Had Marco not said he had saved my life, and if I didn't think there might be an ounce of truth to it, I wouldn't have given his invitation a second thought. I would have dismissed it and convinced myself that his request for tea was nothing more than that of an addle-brained old man who wanted attention. But, if Marco knew I was in danger and had risked his life to save mine, I needed to know what he knew and why. Anxious to learn what he knew, I returned to Dede's apartment and changed quickly into a long, sweeping caftan. Something I thought more appropriate for speaking with a man who had a reputation for being both a klepto and nighttime nudist.

CHAPTER TWENTY

The Ivy Café was nearly empty. It was happy hour, and most residents were enjoying a drink at the bar outside on the Lido Deck. Marco was, as he said he would be, seated at a corner table with a tiered tray of cakes and cookies in front of him.

"You wanted to talk?" I took the chair opposite him and sat down.

"Try the scones. They're excellent." Marco used a pair of silver tongs, selected a lemon scone from the tiered tray, and placed it on a plate before me. "Tea?"

I shook my head. I wanted answers.

"What's going on, Marco? Why the flowers, and what did you mean when you said I could thank you for saving my life today? What do you know?"

"I think you have a pretty good idea." Marco picked up the teapot and, ignoring my objection, was about to fill my cup. I placed my hand over the top.

"I'm not a hundred percent sure I do. Why don't you explain it to me."

"I was sitting here when you had tea with the Churchill sisters on your first day aboard. I heard them tell you about Dede. How they think she went missing."

I removed my hand from above my cup. "Okay, I'm listening."

Marco finished pouring my tea. "I think you, being a reporter and all, must be beginning to wonder if things aboard the *Athena* might be less about Seniors at Sea than something a little more exciting. Perhaps…Senior Smugglers at Sea. Has a nice ring, don't you think? It might explain some of the more unusual things that have happened aboard. Namely, shall we say…murder."

I blinked. "You care to expand?"

"Oleg's death to start with. Some aboard think it might have something to do with you."

"Me?" I put my hand to my heart. I couldn't believe what I was hearing.

"It seems, Ms. Lawson, that some worry Oleg might have said something to you?"

"Like what?"

"I'm not entirely sure," Marco held his cup in both hands, his long, bony

101

fingers tapping the rim as he spoke. "But it's the reason I believe you're in danger. Unless, of course, you choose to believe Oleg's death was, as Chief Sully would like us all to think...accidental."

I exhaled.

"And if Oleg's death hasn't piqued your concern, then you might start with the Professor's missing ring. It's not the first of things that have gone missing around here, and I understand his wife is quite upset about it. The ring would probably fetch a pretty penny on the black market."

I took a sip of my tea. "No offense, but I heard the Chief and Captain Byard searched your cabin."

"They always do. Something goes missing, and my cabin's the first they search. But, between you and me, it takes a thief to know one."

"So, you admit you're a thief?" I put my cup down.

"I prefer to think of myself as more of a Robin Hood. I don't mind stealing from the rich. The rich have more than they need. But I draw the line at looting tombs of the dead and the graveyards of lost civilizations. That's cultural homicide. One does have to have one's values."

"Good to know." I nodded slowly. I wasn't sure where Marco was going with his story, but it felt close enough to what I suspected was going on that I wanted to listen. "So... you're a thief with a moral compass."

"I am, but we're not here to talk about me. I'm here to tell you that you need to be careful. The group you went diving with this afternoon is worried Oleg might have told you that *Athena*'s carrying a bounty of stolen artifacts. It's worth millions. Their biggest yet. And if anyone were to find out...well...let's just say that's why I think you're in danger and why I finagled my way on board your pontoon this afternoon."

"To save me."

"Yes, I told them I had to go on the first dive with the Doctor because I was concerned about diving without medical assistance. You wouldn't have come out of the water if I hadn't been with you."

I swallowed. I was inclined to share that opinion. "And you don't think anyone suspected you?"

"Everyone who knows me thinks I have dementia and am easily riled. They

CHAPTER TWENTY

didn't want to risk me throwing a temper tantrum and not let me onboard the dive boat. Which is lucky for you. If not, you might not be here."

I pushed my cup away. "Let me get this straight. You don't suffer from dementia? And you're not a kleptomaniac? What you're telling me is that this is all an act?"

"Not all. I do enjoy the occasional moon bath now and again."

I rolled my eyes. *Why me?*

"It doesn't matter what you think. What I'm trying to tell you is you're in trouble."

"And that these men, all of whom I was on the dive with this afternoon, the Professor, the Doctor, Chief Sully, Antonio, and Carlo, you believe them to be thieves and murderers?"

"You can add to that list the Inspector and his wife. I believe they're the reason why Oleg was murdered. He uncovered what the Inspector, his wife, and the rest of them were doing, and Oleg wanted in. At the end of the day, it was easier to get rid of Oleg than cut him in."

"How do you know this?"

"Like I said, it takes a thief to know one. And I know the Inspector and the Professor knew each other long before they took up residence aboard *Athena*. It's no coincidence they're here together."

"Explain."

"Years ago, I served time at Fleury-Merogis, a French prison in the suburbs of Paris. While there, a group of thieves were arrested for breaking into a Freeport in Geneva, Switzerland, and stealing rooms full of Greek and Roman antiquities. It was the talk of the prison yard. Perhaps you heard of the break-in?"

I shook my head. So far away, on the other side of the world, news of the break-in hadn't made the nightly news in the US.

"Doesn't matter. Although it was very dramatic. The thieves used an aerialist…but I'll get to that in a moment. What does matter is that Inspector Garnier, who had a reputation for investigating some of the world's largest art thefts, had been called in to investigate, and he asked Professor Braun to work with him to verify the authenticity of the items stolen. Things like gold jewelry. Statues. Coins, and such. All were believed to have been looted from museums and private residences during the 2nd World War and secured away in a Swiss Freeport in Geneva, in what, for all practical purposes, is a warehouse for stolen art and antiquities. There's probably more art hidden away in that Freeport than in some museums. Ultimately, the Inspector was successful in helping the prosecution to obtain a conviction against those charged. But he could never have done it without the help of one attractive young woman he convinced to turn evidence against the thieves she worked with."

"Camile?"

"Mademoiselle Garnier. Yes. And mademoiselle's plea came with a marriage proposal from the Inspector."

"And you know this because—"

"After the trial, one of my cellmates happened to be her ex. And because her ex was French, he was extradited back to France to serve out his sentence."

"Small world."

"Even smaller, considering the Professor and the Inspector bought luxury suites aboard the Athena several years ago."

"And you don't think that's a coincidence."

"Not at all."

"What about Neil? Is he involved?"

"I couldn't tell you what Neil knows. But I do know Neil's been friends with Antonio for years and that it was Antonio who taught the Professor to dive. He worked with the Professor on his underwater research. He got even closer to the Professor when he heard he was advising Inspector Garnier about the break-in at the Geneva Freeport."

"So, you think Antonio saw an opportunity—"

"And jumped all over it. There's no record of what was hidden, or for that matter, stolen from the Geneva Freeport." Marco sat back and stirred his tea slowly. "During the war, the Germans kept records, but afterward? It's anyone's guess what was stolen or where the records might be. As I see it, Antonio learned about the break-in and convinced the Professor and Inspector to siphon off some of what was stolen and work with him to find buyers on the black market."

"And knowing Neil, you think it was Antonio who suggested they take up residence on *Athena*."

"Exactly. And, if I'm right, the antiquities you saw the other night at the Professor's lecture are nothing compared to what I believe they have hidden away and are likely onboard right now."

"I don't get it. If you're right, why would the Professor display any of what they have? Why risk it?"

"Money. And lots of it. Plus, who's to say what's real and what's not? The Professor's not stupid. I'm sure he's got some kind of certificate of authenticity. Easy enough to get…or make. Believe me, I know. A collector takes a picture of his collection, claims he's had *said items* in his collection for years, then fakes a certificate of authenticity to prove its provenance. In some cases, collectors are as bad as the thieves."

"And you know this because—"

"Prison, my dear, what else is there to discuss?"

"I see." I picked up my spoon and tapped it nervously on the table. "And the Doctor and Chief Sullivan? They're all part of this, too?"

"Why not? They're getting on in years. They're bored and probably easily bribed. As I see it, they're a group of senior citizens who've gone rogue. Mutineers who have decided to cash in on a bounty of previously stolen antiquities in hopes of subsidizing their retirement. All they need to do is pirate them across the Med to an awaiting market of black marketeers."

"It's a Gang of Eight, then?" I counted the names on my fingers. "Inspector Garnier, Camile, Professor Braun, Greta. Chief Sully, the Doctor, and the *Muse's* Captain, Carlo."

"That's how I see it?"

"What about Captain Byard?"

"I don't think so. The last captain, maybe. But things didn't work out so well for him. You heard he drowned?"

I nodded.

"Captain Byard's been with the ship less than a year. I doubt the Inspector or the Professor would trust him. He's a recovering alcoholic, and after the last captain got himself drunk and fell overboard, I doubt they'd want to risk pulling Byard into the fold."

Marco's theory aligned with my thinking and explained how Inspector Garnier and Professor Braun could afford such a luxurious lifestyle. Not to mention how it might help Neil plug a big hole with the loss of his inheritance. The sale of a single gold coin, like that in Dede's bag, could go a long way to keeping *Athena* afloat.

"If you know this, why haven't you contacted the police?"

"You're assuming, Ms. Lawson, the police would do something about it and not be bought off and look the other way. I'm not willing to risk that. The fact is, I like my life. But I do have a past, and as it is, I'd rather not get into how I afford such a lifestyle. If I expose those onboard, I'd likely have to disclose my financial assets. Which, by the way, have nothing to do with the sale of stolen antiquities, but still might be…shall we say… touchy?"

"How touchy?"

"I'll only say that I was never into getting my hands dirty. My specialty was more white-collar crime, securities fraud, and such."

"If I understand you correctly, you're telling me all this because—"

"Because you're in a position to help. And, I'll be honest, Ms. Lawson. My motives are not entirely unselfish. You see, I believe if things continue to go as they are, it's not unlikely that I might end up taking the blame for whatever they're doing. I have a record, and as you pointed out, when the Professor's signet ring went missing, the Chief and Captain searched my cabin and no one else's."

"Just what is it you're proposing?"

"I believe if we work together, we can both achieve our goals. I can help protect you, and you can continue with your little charade, pretending to be a reporter while you uncover exactly what the Inspector and his little band of sea wolves are all about. Once you gathered enough evidence to convince the police, I can relax, enjoy my septuagenarian years, and sail into the sunset, which was my plan in the first place."

"And you think this is a win-win?"

"Why not? You get your story. I get rid of some undesirable shipmates,

CHAPTER TWENTY

and everything returns as it should."

"Question."

"Go ahead."

"You said you were here, in this restaurant, when you heard the Churchill sisters tell me about Dede. Do you believe them? Do you think she fell overboard?"

"What I think is that Dede Drummerhausen is missing. And for a good reason. She's a pawn. As I see it, the Inspector and his crew have been using Dede and several other unsuspecting residents to smuggle coins, jewelry, and whatever else without their knowledge off and on *Athena*. More than once, I've heard a resident report a purse snatching or a lost bag when in port. And for a group of smugglers trying to unload high-value collectibles, *Athena's* the perfect cover."

"You didn't answer my question. Do you think Dede Drummerhausen fell overboard?"

"No. Not at all."

"How can you be so sure?"

"Because someone like Dede doesn't go overboard without making a big splash."

Chapter Twenty-One

I left Marco in the café and, as I returned to Dede's apartment, wondered if I was the last rational being on board. As a reporter, I interviewed convicts, murderers and thieves, witnesses, and sources whose identities I had sworn not to reveal. But I had never been in the middle of an investigation—or, for that matter, the middle of the ocean—with a group of aging seniors, who, given the chance to cash in on a pirate's bounty to subsidize their dwindling assets, all had a very plausible motive. Captain Byard would have me think the Churchill sisters and Marco, while showing early signs of dementia, were harmless. But the facts around me, the coin inside Dede's bag, Oleg's murder, and possibly the death of the previous captain, had me thinking that Marco and the Churchill sisters weren't at all delusional—but right. There was something very sinister going on.

A fact that was ever more present when I opened the door to Dede's cabin and realized someone had been inside. I had been so rushed to meet Marco for tea earlier that I hadn't noticed the entry table's partially open drawer as I left the apartment. But now that I had returned and shut the front door behind me, I could see that the drawer hadn't been completely closed. The small black crocheted bag I had left folded over on itself inside had been moved and now lay flat in the drawer. Fearing the worst, I went immediately to the safe in my closet to ensure the Brutus coin was where I had left it, hidden beneath the safe's lining. I had no way of knowing if the safe had been opened, only that the coin had been left undisturbed, along with my notepad.

I knew Finn wasn't to blame. If Finn had wanted to go through Dede's

CHAPTER TWENTY-ONE

things, he had ample opportunity, and I had been very clear I didn't want anyone in the apartment while I was away. I returned to the bedroom to search for clues about who might have been in the apartment. The bedroom looked as messy as I had left it that morning. The bed was unmade. The towel I'd used to dry off from my morning shower was still on the floor. I've never been a neatnik, but as I took inventory, I noticed one thing was out of place or, better yet…missing. The chocolates. Finn had left them on my nightstand my first night aboard, and now, they were gone. And I had a good idea who might have taken them.

The Professor knew I would be gone for the day. It would have been easy for him to ask his wife to search through the apartment while I was out. All Greta had to do was wait until Finn opened Dede's front door to place the mail inside, then call him for a favor. And based upon the gold bracelet Greta had given him, something Finn would likely do. I could picture the scene. Greta asked Finn to fetch her something while she slipped into Dede's apartment and searched for her handbag and the gold coin inside. Not finding the coin, Greta panicked. She tore through the apartment in a desperate search, looked under the bed, tossed the pillows on the floor, and in the closet. If she had seen the safe, it would only have frustrated her. She couldn't have opened it, and being the chocoholic she was, and no doubt stressed by the situation—knowing Finn might be back at any moment—she would have snatched the chocolates off the nightstand and popped them in her mouth as she left the apartment.

I picked a pillow up off the floor. If Greta had found the bag and knew the coin wasn't inside, did she think I had it or that Dede had found it and taken it with her or hidden it somewhere? I tossed the pillow back on the bed and was about to make it when the doorbell rang.

"Hello?" I peered through the peephole and saw Neil Webster holding an ice bucket with a bottle of champagne. "Just a minute."

I opened the door, and Neil went straight to the kitchen as though he had been invited in.

"Oh, good. You're here. I wanted to check in on you. How was the dive today?"

"Fine." I followed Neil to the kitchen. "I'm sorry, did we have—"

"Plans? No. But I was concerned about you. Antonio told me what happened with Marco on the dive this afternoon and thought it might have upset you. Marco really shouldn't be diving. Poor old chap. He knows better. I wanted to check and make sure you were okay."

So this was how Neil planned to discover what was happening with me. I sat down at the kitchen bar while Neil searched around the kitchen for a towel and, finding one beneath the sink, used it to twist the cork from the champagne.

"No need to worry," I said. "It was nothing. Looked like Marco had an anxiety attack, and Doctor Jon took care of him immediately. Not a big deal. I'm fine. I promise you. And if you're worried about the story, don't be. We had a great dive. My readers will be impressed. There's no need for me to mention anything at all about it." I wanted to get off the subject of my dive as quickly as I could and push the conversation away from me and back onto Neil. "More importantly, how was your day?"

"You mean concerning the paperwork for Oleg's death?"

"It can't be easy losing a long-time resident."

"Can't say it is." Neil crossed from the kitchen to the bar and returned with two champagne flutes he rinsed in the sink. "I liked Oleg. We go back a long way. I wouldn't be here if he hadn't convinced Dede's husband and me to buy *Athena*. He was the consummate salesman. Put together a lot of deals. Had a lot of crazy stories. I'm not sure you could believe half of them, but he was entertaining. Did you get a chance to chat with him?"

There it was. Had I talked to Oleg? The same question I had dodged earlier when Sully had asked. And Marco believed the Gang of Eight was so concerned about. I shook my head. I sensed Neil might have been digging.

"No. I never did. We bumped into one another as I was leaving Professor Braun's lecture. He said he wanted to talk, but then—"

"He died." Neil picked up a dish towel and started to dry the glasses. "I'm sorry that happened while you were aboard. Things like this are never easy. When you have a shipboard full of aging seniors, death goes with the territory."

CHAPTER TWENTY-ONE

"Do you know what happened?"

"I know Doctor Jon listed the cause of death as a heart attack. It could be Oleg had too much to drink. Professor Braun and Greta said he looked drunk when they saw him leaning against the railing. But at this point, it doesn't matter. I filled out the forms. Signed a few papers, and that's it. We'll drop Oleg's body in Sorrento on Saturday. If necessary, there'll be an autopsy."

"You think Oleg's death might have been accidental?"

"No. I don't. The railings on the Lido Deck are too high. Doctor Jon said Oleg had a bad heart. He didn't want anyone to know, and there was nothing that could be done about it."

"Then, you think he jumped?"

"Wouldn't surprise me."

"What about family? Was there anyone?"

"Oleg has a daughter somewhere in Switzerland. I called her myself. She'll meet us in Sorrento. After that, it's out of our hands." Neil filled the champagne flutes and handed me one. "How about we talk about something more pleasant. Aside from Marco's panic attack, I trust you enjoyed yourself."

"I did. And I have to thank you for assigning Antonio to look after me." I clicked my glass to Neil's. "Cheers."

Neil took a sip of his drink. "I'm glad to hear it."

"In fact, everyone was fantastic." If Neil was involved with the Gang of Eight, I wanted to dispel any idea I was suspicious of them. "Particularly Professor Braun. The man's a walking encyclopedia. Where did you find him?"

"I didn't find the Professor. He found us. Or maybe it was Antonio who told him about *Athena*. I believe they had worked together. Either way, Professor Braun and his wife have been on board about four years now." Neil verified what Marco had told me. The Professor had used Antonio on a number of dives for research. When Professor Braun and his wife retired, Antonio suggested Professor Braun check out Neil Webster's new Seniors at Sea program.

"And the Brauns, did they know the Inspector and his wife before?" I was curious how much Neil knew about their relationship or if, in Neil's desperation to keep *Athena* afloat, he hadn't bothered to check the source of their finances.

"I wouldn't know. I never handled the sale of individual condos. I wasn't around enough. Oleg took care of all that."

"And now, it falls on you?"

"I thought we were going to talk about your dive."

"You're right." I lifted my glass. "To my dive."

"May it be the first of many." Neil sipped his drink, then put his glass on the counter. "Perhaps you'll come back, and I could accompany you myself next time."

"I'd like that." I picked up the bottle of champagne and suggested we finish it on the deck, where we could watch the sunset. If I couldn't get Neil to open up about his past or personal life, I hoped that somewhere between the champagne, the sunset, and the sound of the water lapping up against *Athena's* hull, I might learn more about his relationship with some of the Gang of Eight. Instead, Neil apologized and said it was getting late.

"We'll be in Capri tomorrow. Unfortunately, only for the day, and much as I'd like to, I've some business to take care of. Things to do for Ida's party. I haven't been much of a host, but I could ask Antonio—"

"No!" The word escaped my anxious lips before I even had a chance to think of an appropriate response.

"I'm sorry. Is there a problem?"

"No. It's just I have a lot to do." I didn't want Neil to think I suspected Antonio might be a problem, but there was no way I wanted to be alone with Antonio, not after today.

"So, you'll be fine on your own."

"Yes, of course. Please, don't worry about it."

Chapter Twenty-Two

I bid Neil good night and shut the door behind him. His visit had made no sense. Neil had no reason to stop by and check in on me—dive or otherwise. With Oleg's death, Neil should have been too busy helicoptering to Naples and back to care about how my day had gone. Unless, of course, the real purpose behind Neil's visit was because the Gang of Eight wanted assurances I hadn't spoken with Oleg. I could only hope that I had convinced Neil I knew nothing. But I had no guarantee.

I returned to the bar and picked up the champagne flutes. I was about to take them back to the kitchen and rinse them out when I stopped. A chocolate from the gift basket Finn had left on the coffee table had rolled onto the floor. I stooped to pick it up, then scanned the living room for more. If Greta had searched Dede's apartment looking for her bag, might there have been something else as well?

Marco believed the artifacts the Professor had displayed the night of his lecture had been stolen and that the Professor and the Gang of Eight were using *Athena* to smuggle them to anxious buyers across the Mediterranean. I had no proof of any of this. Nor that the items I had seen that night had been stolen. For all I knew, Marco was, as both Byard and Sully had told me, suffering from dementia and a bad case of paranoia. But after my dive with the Gang of Eight today, I was beginning to think that for all Marco's malingering, the man was sane. Still, until I knew more about the Brutus coin I found in Dede's bag, I had chosen not to tell Marco about it. But now that I believed Greta had searched Dede's cabin, I was inclined to think the coin I had found in Dede's bag was real and that Dede was, exactly as Marco had said, little more than a pawn for the Gang of Eight.

As for Neil, I was growing ever more suspicious. I found another piece of chocolate on the floor, picked it up, and went to the kitchen. The first time I had met Neil, he had been rummaging through Dede's spice cabinet. He claimed he was restocking the shelf, but what if he had been hiding something? More old coins or maybe diamonds? I wouldn't have been surprised if a diamond merchant's disinherited son had hidden diamonds inside a spice jar. I opened them all, turned their dry powdered contents onto the counter, and found nothing. I then searched through the cabinets and kitchen drawers and was about to give up when I saw a key attached to a round white metal holder marked Storage Locker.

Palming the key, I decided to take the stairs to the Marina Deck. I wanted to avoid running into anyone in the elevators, and when I got to the Marina Deck, I paused long enough outside the door and peered through the round window. I needed to assure myself the gym was empty and the coast clear. It was the dinner hour, and most of the residents had returned to their cabins to clean up after a busy day on shore, and the gym and storage area appeared empty.

I slipped quietly through the gym, bypassing the pool, and stepped through the watertight doorway to the storage area. Ahead of me were two long rows of wire cages, arranged by suite number and marked with identification tags indicating the owner's name. I quickly found Dede's, suite #1122, at the rear of the ship, right beside the Professor's, #1123, and several storage areas down from that, was the Inspector's locker, #1125.

I didn't need a key. I could see through the wires what was inside Dede's locker. A petit-point embroidered footstool, rocking chair, several small lamps, and at least a dozen boxes marked books. I moved to the Professor's locker. It was stacked with boxes marked Christmas ornaments and old clothes. But it was the Inspector's locker across the aisle that caught my attention. An empty black backpack was stacked on boxes along with miscellaneous swim gear. From all appearances, it looked like the same black bag the chef had packed with Garnier's lunch that morning and that the Inspector had carried back on board just hours before. I was about to

CHAPTER TWENTY-TWO

pick the lock on the Inspector's locker when I heard a sound.

"Someone there?"

I recognized the voice.

"Captain Byard? Hi, it's me, Kat."

"Kat?" Byard's voice sounded surprised. "What are you doing down here?"

I wrapped my arms around myself and walked toward the watertight door. I needed an excuse.

"I thought I left my watch in the gym when I came for my scuba lesson this afternoon."

"Did you find it?" Byard rested his hand on the door's handle.

"No." I stepped through the water-tight door and pointed to the back of the ship. "I looked everywhere and thought I heard voices from the storage area. I thought maybe it might be Elli, and I went looking."

"Elli's not around now. The gym closes at eight. I'm sorry, but you can't be here. You can leave a message on the gym's answering machine if you want. Elli comes in early. I'm sure she'll call you first thing in the morning if she has it."

Byard shut the door behind us. "Anything else?"

I hesitated. Glanced back at the closed door. There was no way I was getting back into that storage area by myself. I was going to need some help.

"Yes, I was hoping you'd have dinner with me tomorrow night."

"Sorry. Can't tomorrow."

"Look, I realize we got off on the wrong foot, but—"

"Tomorrow is Ida Churchill's birthday party. I promised her I'd sit at her table. But Saturday night? I'd love to."

Chapter Twenty-Three

Friday morning, four-forty-five a.m. I stared at the bedside clock as *Athena* pulled into Capri's harbor. I could feel her motor slow, a slight shudder of her hull as we came to a stop, followed by the heavy vibration of the anchor chain as it descended into the ocean's water below. I was exhausted.

Part of me wanted nothing more than to dress quickly, take the Brutus coin from the safe, and go ashore to the nearest police station. But after talking with Marco yesterday, I realized how naive I was about the police and theft in this part of the world. At best, I'd be taking a big chance. What could I tell them? I thought Oleg, *Athena's* previous captain, and maybe Dede had been murdered? Or that I was sailing with a group of marauding senior citizens, a Gang of Eight including an anorexic aerialist, who I believed were smuggling antiquities siphoned from a larger cache of stolen artifacts from inside Genevia's Freeport? The more I thought about it, the more bizarre it all sounded. Who would believe these otherwise respectable senior citizens were bootleggers, raiders of sunken and lost treasures? Modern-day pirates on the old Silk Highway?

Other than the coin—which I wasn't even sure was real—I had no proof. Sure, the Professor was toting around a bunch of ancient artifacts, things that looked like they should be in a museum. But, like Marco said, the Professor wasn't stupid. If questioned, he had the necessary documentation, forged or otherwise. And if I were to hand the Brutus Coin over to the police, what then? What assurances did I have that whoever I would be talking to wouldn't recognize the coin as valuable, take it from me, tell me they would

CHAPTER TWENTY-THREE

look into it, and be done with me? Who would believe me?

I sat up and pulled the sheets around me. I could only hope that if Greta had searched Dede's apartment and found her bag and not the coin inside, Greta didn't think I knew anything about the coin or thought I had hidden it. I was pretty sure that Neil believed me when I told him I hadn't spoken with Oleg. And if Neil had convinced the Gang of Eight I didn't know anything, then I had nothing to worry about. At least, I hoped so.

I weighed my options and decided not to leave the ship. I had a travel feature to write, and if I left now, I'd lose the story and my job. Not to mention any chance to cover what, in my mind, was a major smuggling operation by a group of geriatric pirates looking for their last hurrah. I was itching to write the story. Banner headlines flashed across my mind. Seniors at Sea Turned to Piracy. Lunacy or Piracy? Seniors transport stolen antiquities across the Med. Despite the danger to myself, I believed if I continued to maintain my cover, I could convince Neil and the Gang of Eight I was nothing more than a travel journalist doing my job.

I slipped back down beneath the sheets. If I closed my eyes now, I could catch another hour's sleep. Instead, I heard a scratching coming from down the hall. I grabbed my robe off the foot of the bed and followed the sound to the front door. Someone was jiggling the handle.

I placed my hands against the door and peered through the peephole, but all I could see was a fisheye view of an empty hallway. I took hold of the handle.

"Who's there?"

"Kat, it's me." From the other side of the door, I could hear Marco's whispered, raspy voice."

What now? I pulled the door open, and Marco, who was on his knees, shoulder-rolled from the hallway into my foyer. A pair of lockpicks tumbled from his hand onto the floor.

I closed the door behind me and picked the lockpicks up off the floor. *What on earth?* Marco extended a hand, and I helped him struggle to his feet.

"You better have a good excuse for this, Marco? It's not even daylight out yet."

"Don't worry, your neighbors aren't early risers, and Finn won't be along to slip the morning paper under the door for at least another hour. I wanted to be here for breakfast."

"I don't eat breakfast. Least of all with men who try to slip into my apartment at five in the morning." I slapped the lockpicks back into Marco's hand. "Do you carry these with you all the time, or am I just special?"

"I didn't want to ring the bell. Never know who might hear. And the lockpicks are a holdover from my prison days. It's easier to get someone's attention if you come to them rather than the other way around. We need to talk, Kat."

I sighed. "Fine. I'll make coffee. But this had better be good."

I left Marco in the living room and returned to find him staring at the bookcase.

"Place has changed. There used to be a lot of books on these shelves." Marco took a seashell from the shelf. "Can't say I'm surprised. Dede never struck me as much of a reader. Not like Walter. He was the intellect."

I put the two cups of black coffee on the coffee table. "You knew Dede's husband?"

Marco placed the shell back on the shelf and picked up a coffee. "Walter and I had some business dealings together. Neil, Walter, and I had some great ideas. Used to talk 'til late in the night, right here in this room. At least we did until Walter passed."

I sat down on the couch. "Please don't tell me Walter drowned." I couldn't take another inexplicable drowning. I was having enough trouble accepting that Oleg, the previous captain, and possibly Dede had met with such a fate. I didn't want to even think there might have been four drownings.

"Of course not. There was nothing suspicious about Walter's death. If anything killed him, it was Dede's cooking. Walter ate everything she ever put in front of him. Doctor Jon warned him he needed to watch his diet. But he didn't and died of a heart attack, sitting in his rocker, right over—" Marco pointed to the window. "Humph. I guess she moved that, too. It was his favorite."

"It's downstairs."

CHAPTER TWENTY-THREE

"How do you know?"

"Because I went downstairs to Dede's locker last night after Neil left."

"Neil was here?"

"Yes. And so was someone else. While we were out diving yesterday, someone snuck in and rifled through my things, and then Neil came by after he got back from Naples. He said he wanted to check in on me after my dive. But I'm not so sure if his visit was related to whoever snuck in and went through my stuff or if he was more concerned if I had spoken with Oleg."

Marco sat down on the couch and picked up his coffee. "I don't think Neil was here because of Oleg. In fact, I'm not so sure Neil has any idea about the Gang of Eight or what they're doing. It's why I came to talk with you."

"What makes you so sure about that?"

"While you were looking through Dede's locker, I was out, enjoying one of my moonlight strolls on the Lido Deck."

I closed my eyes and shuddered at the thought.

"Don't worry. I wasn't sleepwalking. I was very much awake and, for your information, not that it should matter, fully dressed."

"Good to know. So, what happened?"

"I had stopped short of *Athena's* stern. I wanted a better view of the moonlight on the water, and I had positioned myself next to the railing behind one of the lifeboats. I wasn't there very long before I heard Antonio and Chief Sully. They were unaware of my presence and had stopped for a smoke less than three feet from where I stood. I heard everything they said."

Marco picked up his coffee and paused.

"What did they say?"

"Antonio was upset about a phone call he had received right after *Athena* left Naples. He mentioned Dede. Evidently, she wasn't carrying the bag she was supposed to have, and whoever Antonio was talking to was worried."

"A bag?"

"A handbag of some kind. And whatever was inside must have been extremely valuable because Antonio kept saying he never should have trusted Greta and the Professor to handle it, but—"

"Wait." I put my coffee cup down on the table. "Dede's alive? She didn't drown?"

"Like I said before, I never thought Dede drowned. I think she's a pawn. The Gang of Eight used her just like they have some of *Athena's* other residents to smuggle things off the ship. Dede probably had no idea."

"Then she still might be alive."

"Possibly. I know that Antonio wasn't happy Dede didn't have the bag with her and said the Professor was lucky he made the pick-up he did in Procida. That they could use whatever they picked up from the old shopkeeper to buy themselves some time. But that he better find Dede's bag and soon."

I debated whether or not to tell Marco what I knew. It all tracked with what Marco had told me and what I believed about the Professor. I knew I couldn't stop the Gang of Eight by myself. I stood up, went to the entry table, and tossed Dede's bag from inside the drawer to Marco.

"I suspect this is the bag the Professor's looking for,"

Marco caught the bag with both hands, eyes wide. "You found the bag?"

"It was on top of the entry table when I arrived. Dede must have decided at the last minute not to take it. Although I don't know why, her wallet and diver's license are still inside."

Marco opened Dede's bag and took out her wallet. "She didn't need her driver's license if she had her passport. And if Dede wore her ship ID, she may have stuffed her passport and whatever money she thought she'd need into Walter's old money belt. He used to insist she wear it when they went ashore. He was always fearful of pickpockets, and it was certainly easier than a purse."

"Yes, it would be. But that's not all I found in Dede's bag, and it's why I think Greta searched my room yesterday."

"What did you find?" Marco clutched Dede's bag in his lap.

"Wait here. I'll show you."

I left Marco in the living room while I retrieved the Brutus coin from within the safe. When I returned, I handed him the small, clear plastic baggie with the coin inside.

"If it's real, it's worth four million dollars."

Marco held the baggie up to the light. "You found this inside?"

CHAPTER TWENTY-THREE

"It was sewn into the lining. Dede probably had no idea. But when Greta searched the cabin, I'm pretty sure she found the bag. It looked like it had been moved. But she didn't find the coin. And Neil—"

"Neil?"

I explained that after I had met the Churchill sisters for tea, I returned to Dede's cabin and found Neil in the kitchen. "I'm still not certain why he was here. He said he had stopped by to restock Dede's spice cabinet. Maybe so, but it wasn't until he left that I saw Dede's bag on the table behind the door and wondered if Neil might have been looking for it."

Marco walked to the patio doors and peered through the blinds. Slivers of the morning light pierced the horizon. In another thirty minutes, the sun would be up.

"I don't think Neil has a clue what's going on. He's not on board enough to know. But Antonio? From what I heard last night, as soon as he heard the drop hadn't been made, he took the first flight he could to Ischia. Trust me, it's no accident Antonio's on board. He's here to ensure the shipment's secure and the group has no more problems."

"Then it got to be Antonio who's using *Athena* as a cover and Neil as his excuse to be on board.

"That's how I see it."

"And this shipment? Just, what is it?"

"Probably artifacts like those the Professor picked up in Procida and displayed for his lecture. Antiquities that Antonio managed to transfer from Camile's hidden cache and laundered through various collectors. It's how collectors make their money. They agree to sit on whatever's been smuggled, take pictures of the items and include them as part of their collection, then phony up the docs to make it look like they've had them for a long time."

"Things small enough to bring on and off the ship in a backpack, then?" I thought about the backpack I had seen with the Professor on my first day and the stack of black knapsacks inside Inspector Garnier's storage cage. All of it in plain sight.

"Probably. And once we finish our cruise around the Amalfi Coast, Athena's headed to Alexandria. From the excitement I heard in Antonio's voice, I think the Gang of Eight is planning for a big payday."

Marco looked at his watch. "It's getting late. I should go. I wouldn't want anyone to see me leaving your cabin. But, if I were you, I'd put Dede's bag back in the drawer."

"I was planning on it."

"And the coin?"

"Don't worry. I'll take care of the coin." I wasn't going to put the coin back in the safe. I didn't know where I'd hide it at that moment, but I wasn't about to tell anyone. "And hopefully, since Greta found the bag and not the coin, she'll have convinced the Gang of Eight that Dede must have it and will leave me alone."

"Let's hope so." Marco moved to the door. "What are your plans today?"

"I'm going ashore as soon as possible. There's a lot to see, and if the Gang of Eight is going to believe I'm here to cover a story, I need to continue doing what I can to keep my cover."

Marco reached for the door knob. "Be careful. You may think you've convinced Neil you know nothing, but I'm pretty sure someone from the Gang will be watching you. Stay out where people can see you. Better yet, get back on board as soon as you can. Chef Louie will be teaching a cooking class this afternoon. It might make a nice addition to your story. The class starts at two p.m. And if there are any doubts about your safety, I'll be your taster."

"I'm sure I don't need it. But you're right. It would be a nice addition to my story. Meanwhile, do me a favor. If you need to get back in my cabin, ring the bell."

Chapter Twenty-Four

I had hoped that if I took the first tender to Capri, I might avoid running into any of the Gang of Eight. Unfortunately, it didn't work out that way. Camile, the Inspector, and Carlo were onboard when I arrived. The three of them appeared ill at ease with each other's company. Not that Camile ever looked happy, but she looked more discontented than usual, with a definite scowl on her small face. I had an uneasy feeling the Inspector might have interrupted a tryst and noticed the fingernails of her left hand were digging into the flesh of the Inspector's as they sat side by side at the stern of the small ship while Carlo stood off by himself, near the helm.

The Inspector greeted me. "Off for another day of sightseeing, Ms. Lawson?"

I reached into my backpack, slung casually over one shoulder, and took out my camera. "Just another day in paradise to report on."

"You do seem to enjoy your job." The Inspector dropped Camile's hand, and she snapped it away like a petulant child.

"It's hard not to when there's such beauty everywhere." I put the camera up to my eye and framed a shot of the Isle of Capri, peppered with sprawling villas clinging to her white limestone cliffs. So different from Ischia's black volcanic rock or Procida, Capri's grittier sister island.

"Well, I do hope you enjoy yourself. This is the island to see and be seen. Lots of beautiful scenery and people everywhere. The perfect place for lovers. Wouldn't you say, ma cherie?" The Inspector put his arm around Camile.

I moved toward the rear of the tender and busied myself with my camera, adjusting the focus and light settings, doing my best to avoid conversation while the rest of those going ashore filed in behind me.

"Good morning, Ms. Lawson. I was hoping you'd be going ashore this morning. Mind if I tag along?" Doctor Jon put his hand on my shoulder to steady himself as the tender bobbed in the water. I nearly gagged. The Doctor reeked of cologne and wore a cotton shirt he had buttoned mid-chest, exposing the top of his potbelly and graying chest hair. "If you're unfamiliar with the island, perhaps I might show you around."

"That's a lovely offer, but I have a lot of quick stops planned. I need to be back on board for Chef Louie's cooking class this afternoon."

"Such a shame. Perhaps a quick lunch then or maybe a glass of wine?"

"I'm really sorry. I don't have time."

The Doctor positioned himself directly in front of me, blocking my view of the island. He wasn't going to take no for an answer.

"You know I wanted to be a journalist myself once."

"Did you?" I held my camera between us like a shield, tight to my chest.

"Yes, but it doesn't really pay well, does it." The Doctor stroked the side of my face. "But then, I suppose, an attractive, single woman like yourself must find other ways to pay the bills?"

I put my hand on top of the Doctor's. "I think you have the wrong idea, Doctor. I'm very well compensated for what I do. And what I do is write stories."

"I'll bet you do. And I'm sure I'd like to read a few. Especially the one you're working on right now." The Doctor slid his hand from my cheek to the neck of my tank top, then slightly lower, and pinched my breast.

In one swift motion, I lifted my arm, raised my knee to the appropriate spot, and kneed him between the legs, sending a clear message—hands off!

The Doctor doubled over immediately, and I put my hand on his back.

"Are you alright?"

Some onboard might have thought the boat had lurched, the water choppy, and the Doctor merely lost his balance, but both the Doctor and I knew better.

The Doctor waved me off. "I'm fine."

CHAPTER TWENTY-FOUR

I doubted the doctor was fine. If he was testing me, trying to get close to learn if I was on to the Gang of Eight, or if he thought I'd be an easy target for his company along with a bit of compensation for allowing him to paw me, I had made it very clear I wasn't interested. Either way, Doctor Jon hadn't counted on my martial arts skills and took a seat at the rear of the boat by himself while I turned my attention back to taking photos.

Our tender turned out to be more of a tour boat than a direct shuttle to the island. And, with the doctor now clearly out of my way, I was able to shoot Capri's Blue Grotto, the three giant Faraglioni Rock formations that jutted from the sea, and the Green Grotto with her emerald-green colored water without being hassled.

Once on the island, I did my best to get lost on the Via Camerelle, a pedestrian street jammed with small designer shops. The walkways were so narrow and crowded with tourists that it was easy to blend into the crowd and dart from one area to the next. If anyone from the Gang of Eight had been following me, they would have had trouble keeping up. By the time I took the chairlift to the top of Mount Solaro for a panoramic view of Capri and the Bay of Naples and got back, I'd barely time to race back to the Marina to catch my tender to *Athena* for Chef Louie's class.

* * *

Chef Louie was a wall of a man. Dressed in his double-breasted cook's jacket and tall toque hat, he was almost seven feet tall, and adding to his overwhelming presence was a butcher knife that he wielded like a quick-draw cowboy. Noting that Marco and I had entered late, the Chef twirled his knife in the air and, catching it by its handle, pointed to those already present, asking them to make room for us at the demo table in the front.

I sat across from the Chef, my arms wrapped tightly around myself. Few things make me as nervous as knives, and being close enough to see the perspiration on Chef Louie's brow as he chopped, sliced, and diced a row of carrots caused me to wonder, had he ever missed? Subconsciously, I counted the fingers on Chef Louie's left hand, the knife a hair's breadth from his sausage-like fingers.

I whispered to Marco. "Please tell me this guy's not one of the Gang."

"Hardly. The Inspector's wife's not a fan. If Camile had her say, Chef Louie wouldn't be here. She doesn't like anything on his menu. But then, look at her. I don't think the woman eats."

Louie put the knife down, wiped his hands, and looked at me. "Now you."

"Me?" The last time I took a knife skills class was in the seventh grade, when my grandmother had signed us up for a cooking class, and I nearly sliced my thumb off.

"Yes, you. You are a journalist, right? Maybe you include me in your story and make me famous? No?" Louie slapped a raw carrot down on the table in front of me. "You try."

I sat back and held up my hands. "I'm really more of a baker. I'm better with dough than vegetables. Maybe someone else should try."

"No. I insist." Louie spun the knife around on the table like a roulette wheel, waited for it to stop, and then slid the blade closer to me. "Try."

Marco elbowed me. "Go ahead."

I sighed, picked up the knife, and, positioning the carrot on the table, began to cut. The first slice of carrot rolled off the table and onto the floor.

Louie put his hand on top of mine. "I think is better you leave chopping to me. You write story."

Relieved, I surrendered the knife back to Louie. He holstered it and wiped the table. Then, clapping his hands together, he addressed those who had come to see *Athena's* famous Chef prepare his signature dish, Guazzetto with baby octopus.

"Today, I show how to prepare my specialty. I make for tonight's party. Very fresh. Very good."

I took my camera from my bag and snapped several candid shots of Louie. He played it up for the camera and smiled a big, friendly grin with a pairing knife in one hand and a baby octopus in the other.

Satisfied I had the pictures I needed, I took my notepad from my bag and began to scribble the recipe as Louie explained step-by-step how to prepare.

The ingredients were simple. Baby octopus, tomatoes, white wine, a glass

CHAPTER TWENTY-FOUR

for preparation, and another for the cook. Olive Oil. Parsley. Garlic. Salt and pepper.

"Twenty minutes to prepare and two hours in the oven and…" Louie kissed the tips of his fingers, then extended his hand above his head."Deliziosa. But for now…you must take my word and wait to taste tonight…for Aunt Ida's birthday. It is her favorite. I hope to see you all there."

Chapter Twenty-Five

The Lido Deck was decorated with thousands of little white lights streaming from bow to stern, the pool had been covered with a wooden floor for dancing, and around it, small tables were set with flowers and glass candle lanterns to celebrate Ida's birthday. Overlooking it all was an elevated platform set beneath a canopy for the honoree and her entourage, Ida, her sister, Irene, Captain Byard, and their host, Neil Webster. Neil had spared no expense to make this night special, including fireworks and a string quartet that had come aboard that afternoon as we set sail from Capri.

By the time I arrived, at least a hundred people were milling around the top deck with drinks in hand. The men were all fashionably dressed in Tommy Bahama-style shirts and women in long caftans with dangly earrings and lots of bangles. The bar was crowded, and small groups had begun to pair off. There was a low hum of activity, the casual buzz of voices, and the sound of the string quartet playing a medley of popular music in the background.

I snapped several pictures, all part of my job and cover, and spotted Elli standing at the bar with Antonio.

Antonio looked drunk and, from the wide-eyed-come-help-me expression on Elli's face, he was standing a little too close. As I approached, Antonio turned his back and ordered another drink from the bar.

I pulled Elli a few steps away and whispered. "Do you need rescuing?"

"I'm fine, but Antonio's had too much to drink."

"What's going on?"

"He offered me a job. That's what's going on. I don't get it. Why would

CHAPTER TWENTY-FIVE

Antonio try to steal me away from Neil? I thought they were friends?"

I glanced back at Antonio. I didn't think Antonio had friends, not real friends anyway. Just people he used. I noticed he had both elbows on the bar, and judging from the smile on his face, he was happily engaged with the barmaid.

"Did he say what the job was?"

"Not really. Just that a girl like me could do a lot better than working as a masseuse on an old cruiser like *Athena*. And if I was interested, I should get off the ship in Alexandria. He said he knew people there he'd introduce me to. He kept talking about some big new discovery he was involved in and that I could make a lot of money if I went to work for them."

"Don't turn him down," I said.

"What?" Elli screwed her face up. It wasn't the answer she expected.

"I'll explain later. Keep him guessing. You don't have to answer him yet." Out of the corner of my eye, I could see Antonio headed our way. He was carrying three champagne flutes. I turned to accept one. "Nice turnout," I said.

Antonio nodded to the head table where Neil sat with Ida, Irene, and Captain Byard. "Neil always does it upright, doesn't he? Look at him up there. First class all the way. He never fails."

"Good evening." Neil stood up from the Captain's table. In one hand, he held a champagne flute, and in the other, a spoon he used to tap against the glass. "I want to welcome you all to my Auntie's birthday party. Aunt Ida, as many know, is not my real aunt. But she and her sister, Irene, are like family to me. And tonight, Ida, I wish to celebrate you and wish you the happiest of birthdays. Cheers."

Neil raised his glass to the crowd. They clapped, and the string quartet began to play. Moments later, the elevator doors opened, and a parade of cooks in their chef whites and tall hats strolled onto the deck and took their places behind a long buffet table covered with dozens of silver-domed servers.

Elli and I found a small table for two and sat down. Across from us, at a much larger table, was the Gang of Eight. It was the first time I had seen them all together. Antonio sat at one end of the table, and Carlo was at the other. Between them was the Professor, his wife Greta, Inspector Garnier, a very sullen-looking Camile, Sully, and Doctor Jon. If their body language was any indication, none of them, particularly the doctor who I noticed had glanced in my direction, looked at all like they enjoyed being there. The men all sat with their elbows on the table, hunched over their drinks, while Greta and Camile nursed their drinks.

One of the servers approached Elli and me and asked what he could bring us from the buffet. In addition to the Guazzetto, the various chefs had each prepared their own specialty. Elli and I ordered a sampler plate that arrived with an artistic display of fish, beef, chicken, pasta, and bread. Each plate was more than enough food for one, and between the food and wine—which was non-stop—we were stuffed.

But before Elli or I could push ourselves away from the table, the ship's elevator doors opened again. This time, Chef Louie rolled a giant, tiered birthday cake, six levels high, with sparklers flaring, onto the center deck. With a champagne glass in his hand, Neil stood, nodded to the string quartet, and, together with the crowd, began to play and sing Happy Birthday.

When we finished singing, Byard helped Ida to her feet. Hugging her red scarf around her neck, Ida waved and threw kisses to everyone while Louie cut the first slice of birthday cake and placed it on the table before her. I snapped a couple of candid shots. The type of colorful action pics my editor would love for my Seniors at Sea spread. Then, thinking I might also get some pictures of the Gang of Eight—should I need them to identify its members later—I turned my camera in their direction.

The Eight were huddled together. The men, with their elbows on the table, all leaning in, conversing, while Camile, her chair slightly removed, sat stoically with her arms crossed tightly across her body, tapping her foot, her eyes to the sky. She appeared to be counting the seconds until she could leave. Then Greta stood up. Through the lens of my camera, I noticed a small gift box in her hand. I followed her with my camera's lens as she approached the head table and, taking the lid off the box, placed it in front of Ida. Ida's brow furrowed. Her mouth looked as though she was about to

CHAPTER TWENTY-FIVE

spit. Whatever Greta had placed inside the box angered Ida.

Ida smashed the heel of her hand down on the table. "You really think I'd accept anything from you? What is this, some peace offering to keep my mouth shut? You and your husband are nothing more than thieves! You not only steal from the past but from the future as well!" Then, taking a handful of cake from her plate, Ida shoved it into Greta's face.

"Awe!" An audible gasp rose from the crowd.

Irene screamed. "Ida, please."

Neil pulled Ida away, wrapping his arms around her as Greta retreated back to her table. Then, with his arms around both of his aunties, Neil nodded for Byard's help, and the two men escorted the sisters to the elevator. But from above the hushed murmurs of the crowd, Ida continued to scream like an angry child throwing a temper tantrum, flailing her arms above her head, while Irene tried to soothe his sister's unexpected outburst.

Chapter Twenty-Six

I kept my camera on Greta, snapping pictures as she returned to her table. Grabbing her champagne flute, she tossed back what was left of it, then slapped the glass down. Realizing the situation had grown hostile, the Professor took his wife's hand and led her away from the table. Antonio followed along with the Inspector and Camile, leaving behind plates of half-eaten birthday cake and a table of empty wine glasses.

I nudged Elli. "Do me a favor. Follow them. Tell Antonio you want to talk more about his job offer and call me later. It doesn't matter how late. I'll be up."

It was after two a.m. when the cabin phone rang. Sitting in bed with my notepad in my lap, I had made two lists. One with the names of the Gang of Eight. And the other, a much shorter list, with names of those I felt I could trust. Marco was a yes, at least as long as things went well for him. Captain Byard was a possibility. Finn, as well. And Neil? I wasn't at all sure which list to add his name to, so I scribbled it on a list by itself. As for Elli? I had yet to add her name to the list of those I felt I could trust when the phone rang.

"Hi." I tossed my notepad onto the bed.

"I hope you were serious about my calling." Elli's voice was whispered. "It's late, but—"

"Talk to me. What did Antonio say? Did he mention anything about Ida?"

"Only that he doesn't like either Ida or Irene. He thinks they're sponging off Neil and that Ida's nuts and Neil would be better off if he had them both committed. I was surprised to hear him talk like that. It was a side of him I hadn't seen before, and I didn't like it."

"Did he mention anything else? About the job maybe?"

"He talked around it. We all went to the bar at Romanos. That is, the Professor, Greta, and Monsieur Garnier."

"Camile didn't go?"

"She said she wasn't feeling well. But I suspect she used that as an excuse to sneak off with Carlo. You haven't been on board long enough to know, but Carlo tethers a line between *The Muse* and *Athena* when we've dropped anchor in the harbor. He says it's for security reasons, to ensure smaller boats don't get in between us. But in reality, it's a zip line. And when Camile can, she slips away from her husband and flies like Tinker Bell into her lover's arms."

"It's a five-story drop from *Athena's* stern to *The Muse's* bow. She really does that?"

"She is an aerialist. What do you think? And she's married to the Inspector. Can you blame her?"

I let the subject of Camile go. After seeing Camile on my first day aboard, working the rings above the pool, it wasn't hard to imagine Camile on a zip line. But still, it was the middle of the night, and the water was pitch black.

"What about Antonio? Did he mention anything more about the job?"

"No. I couldn't steer the conversation away from Ida. We were all sitting close together at the bar, and Greta kept going on about what a waste it was to have the Churchill sisters on board, taking up that nice suite, and that Ida was never more than a secondary school teacher. Not at all like her husband, a real Professor. If Neil could have heard them talk, he would have booted the Brauns and the Garniers off *Athena* right then. And good riddance. If you ask me, Greta's nothing but a greedy fat pig. If she could have pushed Ida overboard tonight, she would have. She was that angry, and she didn't stop there. She went on about Irene, and then she started in on Dede."

"Dede? Why?"

"I don't know why. Only that Greta blames Dede for everything."

"What do you mean, blames? What did she say?"

"Professor Braun tried to hush her up, but she was crying and hysterical.

She kept saying how much she hated being stuck on *Athena*. That it's all Dede's fault."

I cradled the phone to my ear and, picking up my notepad, scribbled Elli's name to my list of those I thought I could trust. "Meet me tomorrow. Ten a.m. outside the Ivy. You and I need to talk. There're some things you should know."

Chapter Twenty-Seven

When I got upstairs to the Lido Deck the following morning, Elli was waiting for me with a cup of black coffee.

"I figured you'd want it strong, right?" Elli handed me the cup. "I don't know about you, but I didn't get to bed until after three."

I thanked Elli, and we found an open spot along the railing. A small speed boat had arrived in the blue water below, and Oleg's coffin, nothing more than a plain, pine wooden box, had been loaded onto its deck. We watched as Neil and Antonio boarded the boat, and Neil placed a bouquet of white lilies on Oleg's casket.

Elli took a long-stemmed white rose from a bucket by the railing and tossed it overboard.

"Where did these come from?"

"Neil asked the clean-up crew from Ida's party last night to pick up the flowers and put them in buckets on deck so those that wanted to could toss them overboard as a final goodbye."

I noticed several buckets of flowers along the starboard railing and a few early morning residents who had come to bid their farewells, tossing flowers overboard as the tender headed to shore.

"So, you talked to Neil this morning?"

"He called and woke me up. He said he needed to accompany Oleg's body ashore and expected Oleg's daughter to be there. After meeting with her, he and Antonio were going to visit some ruins. He plans to rejoin the ship in Positano. He asked me to look after you until then."

I stared out at the water and the cliffside view of Sorrento. Another jewel of the Mediterranean. I wished I could have gone ashore and maybe on to Pompeii. It was a short train ride from Sorrento, but as this was an unscheduled stop, there wasn't time, and I had a lot of questions for Elli.

"Shall we walk?"

"That's probably a good idea." Elli kissed the tips of her fingers and blew a kiss. "Goodbye, Oleg."

"You, okay?" I saw a tear slide down the side of Elli's face.

"I'm fine." Elli wiped the side of her face with the back of her hand. "It's just…Oleg was one of my regulars. He came by at least once a week for a massage. He was in great shape. I can't believe he had a heart attack. And I don't for a minute think he jumped."

"You think it might be something else?"

"I don't know. But I don't like Doctor Jon, and I think the Inspector's covering something up."

"So do I."

Elli stopped and grabbed my arm. "Then I'm not imagining it. You really think something happened?"

"Yes. That's why I wanted to talk to you this morning. And it's why I asked you to go with Antonio last night."

"You don't trust him, do you?"

"Do you?"

Elli bit her bottom lip. I could see she was hesitant to say anything.

"Let me ask it another way. Does Antonio know Neil's not as rich as he lets on? "

"I doubt it. I may be wrong, but hey, I'm from Hollywood." Elli shook her head. "I've seen hanger-on-ers. Once they know you don't have money, they vanish. And I'm pretty sure Antonio's not gay, and from what I know, Neil's loyal to Finn, so—"

"Antonio has no idea about Neil's finances."

"Neil certainly wasn't going to tell him."

"I wouldn't think so. But I am curious. Do you know how they met?"

"According to Neil, they've been friends for years, going back to when Neil was just out of college."

CHAPTER TWENTY-SEVEN

"Right after your father cut Neil off."

"Probably. I don't know much about Neil's early life. I only know what my mother told me about him after I discovered I had a brother. She said my father never liked to talk about Neil. Maybe my father felt guilty, or Neil reminded him too much of his brother. Whatever it was, my mother said that after Neil graduated college, he went off on some archaeological expedition in Israel. Neil told me that's where he met Antonio. Antonio was bumming around that part of the world. He didn't have a lot of money. He picked up odd jobs on digs, worked expeditions, and that kind of thing. Enough to get by. They had a mutual interest in archaeology. It was Antonio who taught Neil to dive. It's become a big hobby for them both. In fact, it's one of the reasons Antonio wanted to visit Sorrento. And once Neil's delivered Oleg's body to the authorities, Antonio's convinced Neil to come with him to sift through some ruins outside the city."

"Sounds all a little too convenient, don't you think? Antonio's bumming around the middle east, picking up odd jobs, and accidentally runs into Neil Webster, heir to the Webster fortune, and they become best friends and travel buddies."

"Antonio is, if nothing else, opportunistic."

"I'd agree with that. Despite Neil being your cousin and Antonio's best friend, he's offered you a job. Why would he try to hire you away from Neil, knowing it would upset their relationship? Unless…"

"What?"

"Unless Antonio doesn't think he's going to need Neil anymore."

"What are you saying?"

"I'm saying I think Antonio, Professor Braun, Greta, Inspector Garnier, Camile, Carlo, Doctor Jon, and Chef Sully are all dirty. They're smugglers. Possibly murderers. And they're using *Athena* to transport stolen antiquities across the Mediterranean—"

"No." Elli laughed nervously. "You can't be serious? They couldn't possibly be—"

"Hey! Ladies. I thought that was you." Captain Byard skipped down the metal stairs from the bridge. He had a big smile on his face. "Sorry about the delay getting out of port. Can't be helped. Neil called back after he got ashore and said Tatiana Sidorov, Oleg's daughter, wanted to come on board. Looks like we may be here awhile."

Elli looked at me, eyes wide. Whether she was still processing the idea that we had smugglers—possibly murderers aboard— or that Oleg's daughter would be joining us, she froze in place.

I put my hand on her arm. "Well, then. I suppose if we've time, I'll have to schedule a massage."

Elli looked at her watch. "Yes. That's probably a good idea. You'll have to excuse me. The longer we're stuck here in port, the busier the gym's gonna be. Call me, Kat. I'll save some time for you."

I tossed my coffee cup into one of the empty pails that lined the deck. "So, Captain, will Tatiana be sailing with us, or is she coming aboard to go through her father's cabin?"

"Neil didn't say. But if she wants to stay, she certainly can."

"I'm surprised." I looked back at the shore. "Neil told me that when he first contacted Tatiana and informed her about her father's passing, she planned to meet the ship in Sorrento. I would have thought she wanted to stay with her father's body and accompany it home, or at least stay until an autopsy could be done."

"Evidently not. According to Neil, Tatiana requested she come aboard as soon as possible, and she expects to go directly to her father's cabin. She's asked that we respect her privacy and that she not be disturbed. My orders are to ensure that happens and that she's comfortable."

"Sounds like you're going to have a busy afternoon, Captain."

"It does look that way. But at least I have tonight to look forward to. We're still on for dinner tonight, right? Romano's eight o'clock?"

"I'm looking forward to it."

I left Byard on the deck and returned to Dede's cabin, where I planned to spend the rest of the morning taking in the view and scribbling a few more notes into my notepad. I tried several times to call Elli to schedule a massage, but each time I called, voicemail picked up.

Athena seemed oddly quiet as the afternoon wore on, and we waited for

CHAPTER TWENTY-SEVEN

Tatiana's arrival. Moored in the Med's blue waters, the only sound was the cry of seagulls as they skimmed the water's surface and the waves lapped against her hull. Sometime after four o'clock, I heard a knock on the door.

I answered the door to find Finn holding a tray of hors d'oeuvres. "These are from the kitchen. Chef Louie thought you might like something."

I stepped back and allowed Finn to enter the apartment.

"He wanted me to let you know how much he appreciated you attending his cooking class, and in addition to the cheese board, he's included a souvenir cheese knife."

Finn placed the hors d'oeuvre tray, an assortment of olives, figs, nuts, and cheeses on the dining table. On top of the tray, wrapped in a linen napkin with its blade exposed, was a silver cheese knife with a forked tip that looked more like a weapon than something one might use for shaving cheese and serving delicacies. The coincidence wasn't lost on me. And I couldn't help but think Chef Louie was sending me a warning.

"What's happening, Finn? Anyone around?"

"No."

"What about Marco?"

"He's locked in his cabin. I haven't heard a word."

"What about Professor Braun and Greta? Or the Inspector and Camile?"

"The same. It's hot out. I suppose everyone's napping. I don't expect to see anyone until Tatiana boards and *Athena* leaves the harbor."

I walked Finn to the door. "Have you ever met Tatiana?"

"Several times. She looks like Oleg. Very blonde with sharp features. But unlike her father, she's a woman of few words and cold as ice."

"How long do you suppose she'll be on board?"

"I've no idea. It could be Tatiana's here to go through his apartment, pack things up, and leave when we get to Positano. Or maybe she has ideas of her own and wants to pick up where her father left off."

"You mean assume Oleg's role as *Athena's* resident accountant? Wouldn't that be up to Neil?"

"Not necessarily. It depends on what Tatiana knows, what her father may have told her, and whether or not she can convince Neil to let her stay. Not to speak ill of the dead, but Oleg made Neil's life miserable." Finn opened the door and stepped into the hallway. "I'm not sorry he's gone."

I shut the door behind Finn. *Was Oleg blackmailing Neil?* Was that what Finn meant when he said Oleg made Neil's life miserable? Is that what got Oleg killed? I returned to the dining table, where I could see a small speed boat approaching. Onboard, a lone female sat in the center of the boat, shading her eyes against the sun. Despite the headscarf and dark glasses, I could make out her platinum-blonde hair. I took the cheese knife from the hors d'oeuvres tray and slipped it into my backpack. Whatever Oleg knew had cost him his life, and if Tatiana was aware of what her father knew, then Oleg might not be the last person to die mysteriously onboard.

Chapter Twenty-Eight

By the time *Athena* got underway, I was at dinner with Captain Byard. He had reserved a quiet corner table at Romanos next to a window overlooking the deck. The table was set with a small, simple centerpiece of miniature roses, the sun was low over the horizon, and Byard had ordered a glass of white wine for me and sparkling water for himself. Whether it was the uniform, the way he cocked his head when he looked at me, or the slow smile that crossed his face when I spoke, I had to remind myself this wasn't Eric. I wasn't sitting across the table from my first love. This was Byard, a man I had only recently met and didn't really know.

I have no idea how many doppelgängers there are in the world or if there really are such things, but Byard's look was close enough to that of my first husband that it would have been easy to allow myself to be distracted and fall into a flirtatious comfort zone. But Oleg was dead. I had a $4 million coin I had found in Dede's bag, and the Gang of Eight was looking for it. And if they found it, I was going to have a hard time explaining why I had it. I didn't need a romantic dinner. What I needed was to be one hundred percent certain that Byard didn't know anything at all about *Athena's* hidden cargo or her Gang of Eight. I needed to be sure I could trust him.

I let Byard take the lead. He began by apologizing for *Athena's* late departure. I tried to focus, but my mind was racing, thinking about Tatiana, the Gang of Eight, and whatever treasures Athena had hidden on board.

I listened, but only halfway, as Byard explained how Tatiana's unexpected arrival had required our charted course to be delayed until traffic cleared through the narrow channel between Italy's southern boot and the eastern tip of Sicily. Then, he went on about the ancient methods of maritime travel. Yada...yada...yada. My mind refused to focus.

"Plus, now the fog's rolled in, and the currents are unpredictable." Byard looked uncomfortable.

My eyes must have clouded over. Byard took his napkin from the table and twisted it between his hands. I smiled. This was an awkward dinner.

"Sometimes there's whirlpools, and giant fish are thrown up from the bottom of the sea. Have you heard about the sea monsters of Messina?"

"What?"

"I'm boring you."

"No, not at all." I was doing everything I could to appear interested in the rules of maritime navigation while all the while trying to figure out how I was going to explain that I thought he was piloting a ship with a group of outlaw senior citizens intent on smuggling a pirate's bounty across the Med.

"You're sure. You look like something's troubling you."

I put my elbows on the table and leaned in closer so no one might hear what I was about to say. "Actually, something is bothering me. And I was hoping we might have a chance to talk about it."

"Excuse me, Captain Byard." A ship's mate interrupted us before I could go on. "We have a problem, sir. Captain Rob instructed me to find you. Right away."

"What's the problem, Sailor?"

"I think it would be best if you came with me, Sir."

Byard tossed his napkin on the table and stood up. "I'm sorry, Kat. If you'll excuse me. It appears we have a situation. Please go ahead and order. Enjoy yourself."

From my window seat at the table, I watched as Byard and the young sailor rushed out onto the deck where several residents had huddled by the railing. One of the residents pointed to something in the water. Byard stopped, leaned over the rail for a better look, then ran toward *Athena's* bow.

I got up from the table and went outside to the deck. The group along the railing was now two and three deep.

"What's going on?"

CHAPTER TWENTY-EIGHT

A man in front of me pointed to a speedboat. Like a giant water fountain, rooster tails flew from the rear of the boat as it skipped along the water, weaving in and out in front of Athena's bow. "That," he said. "She's trying to slow us down."

"Who?" I slipped in next to the man and grabbed the railing.

"Don't know." The man shook his head. "Could be pirates. Although it's not usual in this part of the world. More common 'round the Suez."

"Eh, that's no pirate." Marco slipped in beside me, his hand on my shoulder. "You know who that is?"

I leaned over the railing to get a better view. Athena had slowed, and the speedboat had turned around and pulled up along *Athena's* side.

I couldn't believe my eyes. Standing in the center of the small boat, clutching her shopping bags, red hair flying, and full skirt billowing about her legs, was the woman whose driver's license picture I had been staring at just days ago.

"Is that?"

Marco smirked. "Sure is. That, my dear Kat, is Dede Drummerhausen."

I looked to see if anyone else was surprised, but instead, those around me had stepped back from the railing and were laughing. A few even clapped.

From below, Dede motioned for the speed boat pilot to hand her his bullhorn.

"Captain, this is Dede. I need you to turn this ship around. I need to get on board."

Captain Byard grabbed the railing and hollered back. "Sorry, Dede, I can't do that. We're under strict orders to clear the harbor. Go back to Sorrento. Take the train to Positano. You can board there. You know the rules."

"I most certainly will not go back to Sorrento, Captain. Toss me a ladder. I'll climb aboard myself, but believe me, you'll regret this."

Byard looked up at Captain Rob, his second in command, who stood on the bridge awaiting orders. "She wants to board. It's up to her. Cut the engines."

I leaned closer to Marco. "She's not really going to do it, is she?"

"You don't know Dede. If she wants to, she will. The Captain can't turn

143

back. So it's up to her. She either returns to shore or climbs Jacob's Ladder from the speedboat to the Promenade Deck."

"But that must be at least thirty feet."

"Up to her. The Captain has his orders."

Marco nodded toward *Athena's* bow, where Byard stood with an extra-long rope ladder. Above him, Captain Rob stood watch from the bridge. Athena slowed her engine and came to a stop, or as close to a stop as possible, without dropping anchor. The speedboat pulled slowly up next to *Athena's* hull. Byard tossed a rope ladder over the railing. It flailed against *Athena's* side until the boat's pilot could grab it. Then, sidling his small craft up next to *Athena*, offered Dede his hand.

With one hand on the ladder, a large bag, and several smaller shopping bags draped over her shoulder, Dede placed a foot on the ladder's bottom rung and began to climb. From beneath her, the pilot held the ladder as best he could while those watching from the rail around me yelled for her to keep coming.

"Don't look down, Dede! Keep coming! We've got you!"

Dede's skirt swelled with the force of the wind that buffeted the ship's side, blowing it up over her shoulders and nearly blinding her as she clambered up the ladder. I was amazed at her athleticism. Despite the ship's rocking or the shopping bags she hung over her shoulder, she scaled the ladder like a woman on a mission, and a minute later, I knew why.

As Dede reached the railing, Captain Byard offered her his hand. She refused and hoisted herself and her bags over the rail until she came to stand directly before the Captain.

"How dare you not return to the port, Captain! I'll have your job for this!" Then, dropping her bags, she slapped Byard's face. A slap so loud that I could hear it from the bow to where I stood midship. "You louse! I'll be speaking with Neil about this, and believe me, he won't be happy when he hears what happened. You'll not be the first Captain to be replaced!"

Chapter Twenty-Nine

Gobsmacked!

It's not a word I often use, but I could not think of a better term to describe how I felt or the scene I would later enter into my journal as I watched it play out before me.

Dede turned her back on the Captain, picked up her bags, and marched toward the midship lobby doors, pushing aside those residents not fast enough to get out of her way. "Hurry it up, people. Nothing to see here. Move along."

As Dede passed, Marco and I backed up against the railing. Now was not the time to introduce myself, nor did I think it wise to return to the cabin.

"Classic Dede," Marco laughed. "The woman thinks she owns the ship."

"Does she?" I took hold of Marco's arm. "Tell me something. Why would she think that? You've been holding out on me, Marco. Tell me what you know. You said you wanted to work together. You needed my help to uncover what the Gang of Eight was up to. But it's a two-way street. If you want me to keep my mouth shut, I need to know everything you know about Dede Drummerhausen and why she thinks Neil would do whatever she says. Because from what I just saw, Dede believes she can get the Captain fired, and maybe she can. But why, Marco? Why does Dede Drummerhausen think she's so powerful?"

"It has nothing to do with the Gang of Eight."

"How about I be the judge of that. What is it, Marco?"

Marco grabbed the rail with both hands and leaned back, looking in each direction to ensure no one was within earshot.

"I was hoping I wouldn't have to get into everything with you, but I can see now how you might need to know. However, I hope you'll use the utmost discretion with what I am about to tell you."

"If it concerns Neil's wealth or his lack of it, trust me, I already know. I've done my homework." I wasn't about to go any further and tell Marco that I suspected Neil Webster might be broke or that he was a fraud hiding behind the illusion of his name and purported wealth. "I knew before I got on this ship that Neil's uncle had cut Neil off and left him near penniless once he left college."

"Not quite penniless, but certainly without the fortune he should have inherited. I worked for Neil's father. I was the family accountant. After Neil's parents died, I continued to handle what was left of Neil's estate. I can't say it was totally selfless on my part. I benefited greatly and felt a certain sense of responsibility to Neil. Neil's parents had been very good to me, but I've often wondered if their death was other than accidental."

"You think they might have been murdered?"

"I couldn't prove it. But the circumstances always felt suspicious. They had made plans to go away to celebrate their anniversary, and Neil's uncle had offered them his plane. It crashed on take-off. Even worse than the crash was the timing. The brothers were in the middle of restructuring the company when Neil's parents died. Without their signatures on the new documents, the company went to Neil's uncle. Bypassing Neil entirely."

"So, his uncle stole Neil's inheritance from under him? And there was nothing you could have done?"

"Neil was just a boy, and at the time, his uncle did everything he could to make it look like he intended to care for his brother's only child. He continued to pay for Neil's schooling in London. Paid for his education through graduate school. And when Neil completed his studies, his uncle offered him a graduation present. A final payout that absolved Neil of any connection with what was by then his uncle's business. He gave Neil an ultimatum. He could walk away quietly, with a couple hundred thousand in his pocket, and agree to never talk about his uncle's business again or try to fight it and lose everything."

CHAPTER TWENTY-NINE

"I take it he didn't fight."

"Neil was no dummy. He knew there was no love lost between them and that he'd lose every penny to the courts if he tried. Neither Neil nor his uncle wanted a scandal…and in the end, it worked out. Neil agreed to his uncle's terms and never mentioned anything about his disinheritance, which ironically was the best thing that could have happened. Neil had complete independence and the illusion of wealth, which had great power. Banks don't lend money to those who need it. They give it to those who they think can make more of it. And with the Webster name behind him, Neil did just that. He opened an investment firm in London and brought me on board as his adviser. He was doing moderately well when he met Walter Drummerhausen. Walter was just beginning to do business in Europe, and together, they have an impressive portfolio. Neil had the name. Walter had the money."

"It sounds like a good match."

"It was. And it got even better when they attended an international financial seminar in Berlin. That's when Oleg approached them about buying *Athena*. Originally, the idea was to build a fleet of floating condos at sea. Neil loved the idea. He always was an adventurous sort. However, I can't tell you much about what happened after their initial meeting, as I left for other ventures once they got together."

"Other ventures? By that, you mean things that resulted in you going to prison?"

"A few infractions. A minor mix-up of details, that—."

"Landed you behind bars for what…four, maybe five years?" Marco had never said how long he had been in prison. Based on our conversation, I figured his incarceration must have begun sometime after Neil, Walter, and Oleg got together. And since *Athena* had been operating less than ten years, and Marco had been on board at least half that time, it seemed like a reasonably good guess.

"An unfortunate situation, I assure you. But where would we be if it were not for my brief stint in Fleury-Merogis? I wouldn't know of Geneva's Freeport break-in, Camile's ex, nor Inspector Garnier's plan to siphon off a good portion of what was stolen and sell it on the black market. And you, my dear American journalist friend, wouldn't have the story." Marco sounded almost cavalier as he recounted his past.

"Yeah, lucky for me." If the Inspector, the Professor, or any of the Gang of Eight had any idea what I knew, I'd never get off *Athena*, much less have a chance to write my story.

"And afterward, when I got out, I remembered Neil and Walter had been discussing a possible fleet, and I looked Neil up, and well, here I am."

"So, if I understand you correctly, you were in business with them when they first met Oleg and then again after you got out of prison."

"Yes."

"And, just so I know, where were you the night Oleg died?"

"You can't suspect me. I saved your life."

"Humor me. Where were you?"

"In my stateroom. I retired early that night. Now, if you'll excuse me, I think a brisk walk around the deck would do me good. Good night, Kat. We'll talk later."

* * *

Obviously, I wouldn't be going back to the dining room and finishing my dinner with the Captain that night. Byard had disappeared to the bridge, and I returned to Dede's suite, uncertain if I should knock and wait for her to answer the door or just walk in. The decision was made for me when I met Finn as he was about to shut the door to Dede's apartment behind him.

"Kat! You're here, thank goodness. Dede's a mess. I brought her something from the pharmacy to calm her down, but she shouldn't be alone. I assume you must have seen her come aboard?" Finn didn't wait for me to answer. "Would you be a dear and look after her. Everybody's calling for favors, and I'm swamped."

Finn backed up and opened the door wide for me. I bid him goodnight, entered, and then shut the door behind me.

"Dede?" I could hear Dede in the kitchen, slamming cabinets. I called

CHAPTER TWENTY-NINE

again. I didn't want to surprise her. "Dede?"

A cabinet door slammed, and then, as I stood in the center of the living room, she poked her head out from the kitchen and stared at me. "Who are you?"

"I'm Kat Lawson with *Journey International*. The journalist—"

"Ah. Yes. The travel reporter. I remember. " Dede walked to the bar, took one of the crystal decanters filled with what looked like scotch from the shelf, and poured herself a glass. "I spoke with your editor. Sophie, something or other."

"Sophie Brill."

"Yes, that's the name. We agreed you'd stay in my suite." Already a little tipsy from what Finn had given her, Dede held the glass in one hand and pointed an index finger at me. She looked unbalanced. "So, how's it going? Have you had a wonderful time?"

"Awesome," I said.

Dede's eyes fixed on the brown liquor in the bottom of her glass. Until I better understood who Dede Drummerhausen was, I preferred to keep my answers short and let her do all the talking.

"I would hope so. *Athena's* a beautiful ship. The first of many. Or she was supposed to be anyway." Dede picked up the decanter and refilled her drink.

"I don't mean to pry, but are you okay?"

"Of course, I'm okay. Why? Something the matter?"

"It's just Finn thought maybe I should look after you."

"Finn! You can't listen to him, poor boy." Dede swirled the liquor in her glass. "He's always trying to fix things, got his nose in everyone's business."

"He was concerned. You weren't expected until tomorrow when we get to Positano."

"Yes, well, I'm afraid my arrival was a bit of a surprise for me as well." Dede put her glass back down on the bar. "I assume you saw me come aboard?"

"I did. It looked a little touch and go there for a minute."

"I'm sure it did, and believe me, I plan to make my grievances known to Neil first thing in the morning. I'm surprised he's not here already begging my forgiveness."

"Neil's not on board. He got off in Sorrento this morning. He plans to rejoin the cruise in Positano."

"Augh! Just my luck."

"It was my understanding you were off to cooking school—"

"I was. I had planned to spend three days in Tuscany and two in Rome, but unfortunately, as soon as I got off the ship in Naples, some young punk tried to rob me. Knocked me over before I could beat him off with my walking stick."

"You were assaulted?" With everything I had learned about the Gang of Eight and how they operated, I wasn't surprised.

"If that's what you want to call it, yes. Although, I'm not sure who did the assaulting. I beat the young man soundly. I doubt he'll attempt to rough up any tourists anytime soon."

"Did he get anything?"

"Other than my pride?" Dede stared down at the bottom of an empty glass. "No. Absolutely not. Although I should have taken it as a sign. Everything that could go wrong went wrong. I missed my usual morning breakfast with Ida and Irene. And Greta, the Professor's wife, from across the hall? I'm sure you've met. She was convinced I'd miss my train if I didn't leave early enough to grab a cab. Which, due to the assault, I ended up missing. Not that it mattered. My cooking class, which Chef Louie recommended I take with Roberto, was canceled. Roberto came down with the flu, and I wasn't about to bother taking a class from anyone else. So, I went on to Rome and tooled around there for several days. Treated myself to a holiday, visited a spa, and had a wonderful meal at La Pergola. It's a Michelin restaurant, by the way. Three stars. And the view of the city is fabulous. Worth every minute. You really should visit." Dede filled her glass again. "Anyway, while I was there, I got to chatting with the chef, and he recommended a cooking school in Sorrento he thought I might enjoy. I've spent the last day and a half in Sorrento, and then early this afternoon, I decided to do some sightseeing. I stopped at a small café with a wonderful view of the harbor and was enjoying a glass of limoncello when I noticed *Athena* in the bay and took that as a sign it was time to go. I returned to my hotel and packed quickly and was going

CHAPTER TWENTY-NINE

to call on my way to the dock, but—"

"You didn't have your phone."

"Why, yes. How did you know?" Dede put her drink down on the bar.

"Because I found it inside your bag on the table behind the door when I arrived." I went to the cabinet behind the front door and pulled Dede's bag from the drawer. "I wasn't sure if the bag was yours or if someone might have left it behind and decided to check." I placed the crocheted bag on the dining table and backed away. "When I realized it was yours, I put it inside the cabinet for safekeeping. Your phone is inside."

Dede left the bar and, picking up the bag, rifled through it until she found her phone. "Stupid bag. She should have known I'd never carry such a thing."

"Who should have known?"

"Why, Greta, of course. Haven't you been listening? She made it as a gift for me." Keeping the phone in her hand, Dede tossed the bag back onto the table. "She insisted I carry it. Awful thing. Can't ever find anything in them. Nothing but a nuisance. I much prefer my money belt. My husband always insisted I wear one when traveling." Then, with both hands on the hem of her blouse, Dede lifted it above her round stomach, exposing a wide canvas belt with pockets. "No problem with pickpockets, and I can find everything I need. Except, of course, my phone, which I forgot to take with me."

"Well, then, you'll have to tell the Churchill sisters. They were convinced when you didn't answer your phone that you must have fallen overboard. Ida was worried you had drowned."

Dede smoothed her blouse over her stomach. "Ugh! Those silly old goats. I'm as fit as the day I left. I suppose I should call them and tell them, or better yet, I'll go and pay them a visit. You don't mind my leaving you alone?"

"Not at all."

"I'll be back. Make yourself at home." Then, glancing back at her bag on the table, she added, "If you haven't already."

Chapter Thirty

It was after midnight when Dede lumbered back into the suite. I was in bed—the door to my room open—and I could hear her standing in the foyer talking to someone.

"Don't worry. I'm sure it'll be fine. Just don't say anything."

The front door shut, and for a moment, I thought Dede might have returned to her room, but then I could hear her footsteps as she shuffled down the hallway toward my room. From beneath the covers of my bed, I saw her shadow in the doorway.

"Dede?" I sat up. "Everything alright?"

"I'm fine. I just wanted to check to make sure you were okay. There's nothing to worry about, but there are some things I need to share with you. We'll talk in the morning. Go back to sleep."

No way could I go back to sleep. If I was restless before, I was even more so now after Dede had come to check on me. Did she think I might not be here? And what *things* did she have that she wanted to share with me? Had she searched through the bag and not found the coin and wanted to ask me about it? And why use the word *share* and not *tell*?

I got out of bed and decided to pack. This was my last night aboard *Athena*. Tomorrow, we would anchor in Positano, and I planned to take the first tender to the dock and call Sophie as soon as I got there. Hopefully, she would be back from vacation and in the office. If not, I planned to call her cell. This was an emergency. I needed Sophie to know this wasn't the Seniors-at-Sea-Sail-Around-the-Amalfi-Coast-Holiday-Cruise she had described. *Nothing but a little feature writing this time, Kat. A little fun in the sun. Nothing*

CHAPTER THIRTY

covert or undercover, just pure enjoyment. Your biggest risk will be a sunburn. Take plenty of sunscreen.

If *Athena* was being used to pirate stolen antiquities across the Mediterranean, Sophie would know what to do. She was better equipped to know who to call in this part of the world than I could ever hope to be. And now that she was back from her vacation as well, all I needed to do was get off the ship, take the Brutus Coin I had hidden in the bottom of my backpack as evidence, and bid my fellow passengers goodbye.

I planned to make my departure look as normal as possible, and the following morning, I waited until I heard Dede in the kitchen before I got up. I wanted time alone with her before I left the ship so that I might know what it was she wanted to share with me last night.

"Morning," I said. I slipped onto one of the bar stools in front of the kitchen island. "You sleep well?"

Dede stood with her back against the kitchen sink, nursing a cup of coffee. She was dressed in a long caftan, her red hair covered with a bright orange turban. "Like a rock. How about you?"

"Good, thank you. The accommodations are nice, and now that I've my sea legs, I'm going to miss this. It's a nice lifestyle you've got."

"Coffee?"

I nodded. Dede took a cup from the kitchen cabinet and filled it from the brewer on the counter.

"Cream? Sugar?"

"No. Black's fine."

Dede slid the cup in front of me. "I'm glad to hear you'll miss us. That's why I wanted to chat before you left today. It's not that I want to influence your story, but I hope your descriptions of life aboard *Athena* will be…shall I say, generous? And not too judgmental. We're an odd group, but what group of seniors isn't? My point is that I hope your story might encourage those who can, who are financially able, to consider a residency aboard *Athena*. We've a few too many empty cabins. I'm sure you've noticed."

"I don't think you need to worry. While I can't guarantee the sale of any of *Athena's* empty suites, life aboard is certainly enviable, and I'm sure my readers will be favorably impressed. It'd be hard not to be." I took a sip of my coffee. I wasn't about to let on that I had several stories I was itching to write about *Athena's* cruise from Naples to Alexandria and couldn't wait to get to a computer where I could file them. "However, I am curious. Last night, you said you wanted to share some things with me. Anything in particular? Something I might use for my story?"

Dede refreshed her coffee. "It's more about what I hope you won't use in your story. It concerns the Churchill sisters and some vicious gossip on board. Last night, Irene told me about Ida's outburst at her party and how she attacked Greta. Irene was concerned you might have gotten the wrong idea about some of our residents. I hope you won't let the actions of a few influence you. The truth is, much as I adore the Churchill sisters, Ida's a jealous sort. Never approved of the Professor, and she's given into some pretty wild ideas about him. Goodness knows I'm not exactly fond of Greta, but Ida never should have implied that—"

"That the Professor's smuggling stolen antiquities across the Mediterranean?" I raised a brow.

"Oh, for heaven's sake! You can't possibly believe that. Why would the Professor do that? He's a well-respected man. An esteemed professor. A published author. Ida's my friend, but I'm afraid she's been influenced by Oleg, and everybody knows he was full of it! No offense to the Russians, but the man was always looking for a way to blackmail someone. My guess is Oleg had crossed someone he shouldn't have and ended up taking his own life. I never did trust him. And, believe me, if Neil weren't so loyal and Oleg hadn't been with Neil from the beginning, he would have booted Oleg off *Athena* a long time ago." Dede grabbed a rag and ran it over the countertop. "As it is, I'm not sorry to hear of Oleg's death. I never did like him. Eh...there I go, sounding like an old person rambling on." Dede threw the rag in the sink. "Enough of this crazy talk. It's made me hungry. How about you and I go get some breakfast? It's still early. Your shuttle won't be here for several hours, and I haven't had a chocolate croissant since before I left."

* * *

CHAPTER THIRTY

It was ten-fifteen by the time Dede and I arrived at the Ivy Café, and I knew something terrible had happened the minute we walked in the door. The air was heavy, and the clatter of breakfast dishes and the hum of conversation had come to a standstill. It didn't take but a moment to know why.

Across the room, seated in the same booth where I had High Tea my first day aboard with the Churchill sisters, was Irene. She looked to be in a state of shock, her face drawn, her skin as gray as her hair. Seated with her was Captain Byard. His back was to us, and he appeared to be trying to comfort her. He touched her shoulder while Irene dabbed her eyes with a wadded tissue.

Dede went immediately to the table. "What's going on?"

"Ida's missing!" Irene covered the corner of her mouth with her hand, her fingers trembling as she spoke. "She went out last night after you left. She said she wanted to go for a stroll to clear her head. She does that sometimes. I went to bed, and…when Ida wasn't up this morning, I went and checked her room. Her bed was made, and I thought maybe she came here ahead of me. But when I didn't find her at our table…I…I realized she didn't come back last night. What if she fell overboard?"

Captain Byard squeezed Irene's hand. "We're checking now. Chef Louie was here when Irene came in, and he called me right away. I've alerted security, and Sully's begun a search."

Dede scooted into the booth next to Irene. "You mustn't worry. I'm sure they'll find her. You know Ida. She probably decided to take an extra lap around the Promenade Deck. Maybe got a little winded, sat down, and fell asleep in a deck chair. I'm sure Sully will find her."

Dede wasn't wrong. I'd reported on enough missing persons to know that older people sometimes get lost. It's not unusual for seniors to walk away from their familiar surroundings, and they're often found. Maybe sleeping in someone's backyard, or as I hoped, in this case, like Dede said, a deck chair. I scanned the restaurant. Marco stood at the breakfast bar, his plate in his hand. When he caught my eye, he shook his head.

I addressed the Captain. "Did you ask Marco? Maybe he saw her last night."

Byard shook his head. "Marco was with Irene when I came in. He said he didn't see her."

"What about them?" I tilted my head to one of the other tables, where the Professor, Greta, the Inspector, and Camile sat huddled in whispered conversation. "Did you ask them?"

"They came in after I arrived. Said they hadn't seen Ida or Irene since Ida's party."

"You'll excuse me if I say I don't believe that. A ship like this where everybody knows everyone's business."

The Captain didn't respond, and I walked out to the deck and looked over the railing. It was still early. The first tender wasn't scheduled to arrive until eleven. No one could have left the ship without notice. Somebody had to know something.

I went back into the café and was about to take a seat in the booth next to Dede when Chief Sully entered the room.

"Captain." Sully moved anxiously toward the captain. Perspiration stains had begun to form beneath the arms pits of his heavily starched white shirt. The room quieted. Not so much as the sound of a teacup tittered on a saucer. All eyes were on the Chief. "I'm going to need you to come with me."

The color drained from Irene's face as she stood. "I'm coming too."

Captain Byard offered Irene his hand, and Dede and I followed the Chief to the elevator, where we rode silently down to the Marina Deck. When the doors opened, the Chief led the way to the pool area, where we were met by Doctor Jon. Behind him, Elli stood with a towel in her hand. Her head bowed.

"I'm afraid I've bad news." The Doctor went to Irene and, putting his hands on her shoulders, looked her in the eye. "Irene, you should go back upstairs. I don't think you should see this."

Irene pushed the doctor away. "I'll see what I need to see, Doctor. What's happened to my sister?"

The Chief turned to Doctor Jon. "You might as well show her."

Doctor Jon grabbed the towel from Elli and went to the flotation tank.

CHAPTER THIRTY

"Elli called me early this morning. She was setting up when she found the body."

Irene gasped.

"Irene, you're sure you want to stay?" Captain Byard put his arm around her shoulder and pulled her close.

"I need to know what happened to my sister. And don't tell me she came down here voluntarily and climbed into that...that monstrosity." Irene pointed to the floatation tank. "She wouldn't dare."

The Doctor glanced at Sully and waited for approval before lifting the tank's lid. Sully nodded, and slowly, the Doctor opened the tank. When I saw the body inside, I knew this was no accident. The red scarf Ida had worn for her birthday was wrapped tightly around her neck like a garrote.

Captain Byard and Chief Sully exchanged a look. Nobody needed to tell them Ida hadn't climbed into the tank herself. She was too frail. The lid alone would have been too heavy to lift.

Behind us, the elevator doors opened, and the Professor, Greta, the Garniers, and Marco rushed in.

Greta was the first to speak. "What's happened?"

"Someone's murdered Ida. That's what happened." Dede put her fist to her mouth and turned her back to us.

"Oh, my God, no." The Professor put his arm around his wife, and Greta buried her head in his shoulder.

"Camile." Inspector Garnier pulled his wife close, gripped her hand, and laced his fingers through hers. While Camile stood rigid beside him, the fingers on her hand splayed.

"Chief, can you help me?" The doctor reached inside the tank and, with the Chief's help, slowly lifted Ida's body from the water.

I had seen dead bodies pulled from pools before, but this was different. Ida hadn't drowned. The red scarf she had worn loosely wrapped around her neck and shoulders had been drawn tight around her throat like a garrote. She had been strangled and stuffed inside the tank. Her dress clung like wet wallpaper to her limp body, and as Sully and Doctor Jon laid her gently on the towel, Ida's hand fell open, and Professor Braun's gold signet ring rolled out onto the floor.

"Ahh! My husband's ring." Greta stepped forward to pick up the ring, but the doctor grabbed it before she could get it.

"I don't know whose ring this is. But it's the Chief's job from here on in." Doctor Jon handed the ring to Sully. "Now, if you'll excuse me, folks, I've got a job to do."

Marco sidled up next to me. "I know what you're thinking. But I didn't do it."

Chapter Thirty-One

"People!" Chief Sully stepped over Ida's body and raised his hands. "I realize this is a shock, but you all need to remain calm. Right now, this is a crime scene, and until I alert the authorities, nobody leaves the ship or says a word about what you've seen until I say you can."

"So what does that mean? We're all under some sort of suspicion?" Camile yanked her hand from her husband's and crossed her arms.

"It means exactly what I said it means. Nobody leaves to go ashore until I say so. Elli, you take Irene back to her cabin and stay with her, and don't talk to anyone about this. You got that?" Elli stepped forward, slipped her hand behind Irene's elbow, and started toward the elevator. "Captain, I need you to stay with me. Dede, you, and Ms. Lawson return to your cabin and stay there."

"What about me? Can I go with them?" Marco raised his hand. "If there's a killer on board, I don't want to be alone."

"Nobody said anything about a killer—"

"Well, what else would you call it, Chief? Another *accidental* drowning?" The sarcasm in Dede's voice cut thick.

Sully clenched his jaw and, for a second, looked like he might respond, but the Inspector stepped forward.

"Dede, how about we let Sully do his job before we start throwing accusations around? Like it or not, the Chief's right. He needs to investigate, and the best thing you can do right now is get out of his way. Go back to your suite with Ms. Lawson, and I'll get word to you as soon as we know what's happened."

Dede stood her ground, her face red. "Don't for a second think you can patronize me, Inspector. You may be friends with Irene, and maybe you can convince her this was another accidental drowning, but not me. I'm friends with Neil. Ida Churchill was his aunt and one of my best friends. I intend to let Neil know exactly what I think happened here, and believe me," Dede scowled at Camile, "whoever is responsible for Ida's murder will pay for it. No matter who it is."

Camile fisted her hand and looked like she was about to throw a punch in Dede's direction, but the Inspector seized her arm. "That's enough, Dede. You need to leave. Now."

"Oh, don't worry. I'm leaving, but you haven't heard the last from me. Kat, you coming?"

Marco and I followed Dede back to the elevator. Behind us, the Inspector shouted to those remaining.

"Captain, you and I need to go to the Bridge with Sully. The Doc here knows what he needs to do. Professor. Greta. If you don't mind, take Camile with you back to the café. I'll meet you there."

**

Dede, Marco, Irene, Elli, and I shuffled into the elevator and waited in silence for the gold-filagreed mirrored doors to close. As soon as they shut, Dede turned to Irene and apologized.

"I am such a fool. I should have believed Ida, and now I think I might have been the last person to see her alive. Other than the killer, that is."

"Dede, what are you saying?" I couldn't believe what I was hearing, but even as I questioned her, bits and pieces of what I had heard early that morning when Dede returned from visiting the Churchill sisters replayed in my mind. *Don't worry. I'm sure it'll be fine. Just don't say anything.* Was it Ida she had been talking to?

"After I left the Churchill sisters last night, Ida came after me. She followed me back to my cabin. She tried to convince me she thought something was going on. That the Professor and Greta were up to no good and that Oleg's

CHAPTER THIRTY-ONE

death wasn't an accident. Of course, I didn't believe her. Not until I saw her body just now. I should have paid more attention."

Marco stared at our reflection in the mirrored doors. "You better hope they don't try to pin Ida's murder on you, Dede. Believe me, the Inspector is very good at deflecting guilt. I'm the first one they come to when one of their own steals something from them. Like the Professor's signet ring? I didn't take it. But I'd bet that Ida found it, and whoever had it murdered her for it and left before they could take it back."

"Or left it behind deliberately to make Ida look guilty." The words spilled from my mouth as I imagined how the Chief and Inspector might spin Ida's death.

Marco added to my unfinished thought. "It would be easy enough to say Ida was trying to hide the ring inside the tank when her scarf got caught up in the drain and pulled her in."

"But the tank wasn't full. It shouldn't have been, anyway. I make certain it's empty every night." Elli shook her head. "And, there're all kinds of safety features. That couldn't happen."

"You and I both know that. Doesn't mean the Inspector and Sully won't say it happened that way." Marco stared at our reflection in the mirrored doors as the elevator stopped, then motioned with a finger to his lips for us not to say another word.

When the doors slid open, standing directly in front of us were Carlo and Captain Byard's second-in-command, Captain Rob. Both men had holstered sidearms and stood with their hands folded on their belt buckles, forming an impenetrable wall in front of us.

Captain Rob was the first to speak. "Ladies. Marco. The Chief has asked me to escort you to your cabins and to remind you not to talk with anyone about what you've seen. And to make sure, he's asked me to collect your cell phones until his investigation is complete."

Carlo held out a bag. Reluctantly, I tossed my phone in the bag. Marco and Elli did the same. Irene, looking like a deer in headlights, said she didn't have a phone, and Dede said her phone was still in her cabin.

"Not a problem. Carlo can get it when he drops you back at your cabin."

Then, motioning for us to step forward, he instructed Elli and Irene to follow him. "Dede and Ms. Lawson, you go with Carlo—"

"What about me?" Marco asked.

"You can go with them as well. But remember, nobody leaves their cabin or talks to anyone outside until the Chief says so."

Chapter Thirty-Two

Dede didn't wait for Carlo to lead the way to her cabin. She pushed him aside and walked stiffly down the hall with Marco and me behind her. When Dede reached the door, she opened it quickly and nodded for us to enter.

"But not you!" Dede pointed to Carlo. "You can wait here." Then, marching back into her apartment, Dede retrieved her phone, threw it at Carlo's feet, and slammed the door shut.

Marco stumbled ahead of me into the entry, nearly tripping over the rolie bag I had left in the hall. "Looks like you won't be leaving us today, Kat."

"Or anytime soon," I said.

"Nonsense. Neil'll be along shortly. He'll set the Chief straight. We need to wait until he's back." Dede went to the living room blinds, opened them, and slid open the door to the deck. "

"I'm not so sure about that." I took the backpack I had been carrying from my shoulder and put it on the dining table. "If Neil has any idea what's going on, then none of us may be getting off this ship."

"You can't possibly think that Neil's involved. Why would he be?"

"I don't know for sure. But I do know it's not just the Professor and Inspector. Near as I can tell, there's a gang of eight. And I think Ida was on to them. It's what got her killed. And maybe Oleg as well. Like you said, she didn't climb in that tank by herself."

Dede sat down on the couch. "I think you need to tell me what it is you think you know and what's been going on."

"Allow me." Marco went to the bar and poured Dede a glass of scotch.

"The Professor, the Inspector, their wives, Antonio, Carlo, Doctor Jon, and Sully. I call them the Gang of Eight. They've been pirating stolen artifacts from a Geneva Freeport to collectors around the world ever since they came on board." Marco explained that while he was in prison, he had learned of a break-in at the Freeport and later was roommates with Camile's ex. "He didn't have a lot of flattering things to say about her other than she was a petite aerialist and a necessary asset. That is, until she wasn't, and turned against her outlaw crew and married the Inspector."

"And that's how you know the Inspector's involved?"

"The Inspector brought Professor Braun in as an expert witness to verify those items recovered from the heist. They siphoned off what they wanted for their private cache, along with what Camile had already taken for herself. With no public record of what had been stored in the facility or what was stolen, it was an easy move on their part and, I'm sure, very tempting. How else do you think Professor Braun and a public servant like Monsieur Inspector Garnier could afford to retire aboard *Athena*?"

Dede shrugged. "It never occurred to me. Like everyone else aboard, I assumed they had money."

"Because people like you have always had it or managed to marry it." Marco handed Dede the drink he had fixed for her, then returned to the bar.

Dede snapped back, "Well, at least I was honest with what I had."

Marco shook his head. "That was a long time ago, Dede. And you never got the full story. You never wanted to hear it."

"Look," I sat down on the couch, my hands up, ready to referee. "Now is not the time for you to argue about the past. And, Dede, whatever differences you have with Marco, you need to put it behind you. Because what Marco is trying to say may explain why you were attacked in Naples."

"You think it's related?" Dede scowled at Marco.

"I do. And I think if Ida were here right now, she'd agree with me."

Dede looked at me, her eyes narrowed. "What are you saying?"

"The black crocheted bag I found on top of the entry table. The one you left behind that Greta made for you. I believe she gave you the bag because there was a very rare and valuable coin inside."

CHAPTER THIRTY-TWO

"What coin? I never saw a coin."

"You wouldn't have seen it. The coin was hidden in the lining." I stood up, fetched my backpack from the dining room table, and fished inside for my camera. After Greta had searched my apartment, I moved the coin from the safe and hid it inside my camera's battery compartment where nobody would think to look for it. The coin, no bigger than a small round button-sized lithium battery, fit neatly into the slot, and with the camera around my neck or tucked inside my backpack, I felt reasonably sure no one might find it. I opened the battery compartment, slid the coin from inside the camera, and placed it on the coffee table.

"And if I'm right, it's one of three gold coins like it in the world today. It's called the Ides of March coin or the Denarius of Brutus coin, identifiable by the letters E-I- D-M-A-R on the front. It was minted to celebrate the assassination of Julius Caesar. It's estimated to be worth about four million dollars."

"And you found it in the bag Greta gave me?" Dede stared at the coin like she was afraid to touch it.

"At first, I thought it might have been a good luck charm you'd hidden in the bag, and I put it back where I found it. But when I went to visit Procida, I met a shopkeeper who was advertising antique coins and jewelry. One of the coins pictured on a poster outside his shop was exactly like the coin I had found in your bag. The shopkeeper told me there were only three coins like it and that it was very valuable."

"And very unique." Marco picked the coin up and turned it over.

"Yes, and very easy to hide." I took the coin from Marco and slipped it back into the camera. "When I realized how valuable it was, I removed the coin from Dede's bag and hid it in my room safe. And later, after someone had broken into Dede's suite, I transferred it to my camera. I'm almost certain it was Greta who broke in, and I believe she found your bag. But I do know she didn't find the coin, and I've been worried ever since that she and the Gang of Eight might suspect that I have it."

"And you think they may be watching you?"

"I'm not sure. I've done my best to act like I don't know anything, but after

Ida's murder, I'm worried. I don't know what to think."

"Well, I'll tell you what I think." Dede stood up and hobbled toward the kitchen. "I think we need something to eat. Who knows how long we'll be locked up in here. Marco, make yourself useful. Call the kitchen. Use the house phone. Tell Chef Louie to send something up and make sure it includes some chocolate croissants. All this worry has me hungry. I'm starving."

* * *

Thirty minutes later, Finn knocked on Dede's door and rolled a food cart into the living room using his passkey to let himself in. The cart, covered with a white linen tablecloth, was piled high with fresh fruits and cheeses, a basket of rolls with jams and jellies, a chocolate croissant on top, and an elegant silver tea and coffee service. Enough food to last us for several days.

Marco and I stepped aside while Finn took one of Athena's logoed china coffee cups from the cart, filled it with black coffee, and handed it to Dede.

"Dede, what's going on? You never—"

"Ida's dead, Finn." Dede took the cup and sat down on the couch. "You didn't hear?"

"No. No. That can't be. Not Ida." Finn put his left hand to his heart and stepped back as though he had been shot. "What happened?"

I explained how Dede and I had gone for breakfast at the Ivy when we saw Irene sitting with Captain Byard. "She looked worried. Ida hadn't come home last night. Irene was frantic. Sully came in and asked us to come with him to the gym. Irene, Captain Byard, Dede, Marco, and I went downstairs. It was awful. Elli said she was setting up this morning when she found Ida's body inside the immersion tank."

"That's awful." Finn glanced back at the door. "And I thought the guard at your door was because Captain Byard wanted to lock Dede in her room until he could talk with Neil about Dede's arrival last night."

"There's a guard?" I took a cup from the cart and poured myself a coffee.

"Yes, but I can't say I'm surprised. Not after Dede slapped the Captain last

CHAPTER THIRTY-TWO

night. However, when Marco called the kitchen this morning and ordered room service, I did think it was odd. Not so much the room service, but Marco calling for it. No offense, Marco, but you and Dede aren't exactly friends. I couldn't imagine why you'd be here. I told Chef Louie I'd make the delivery right away. What a way to start the day. Poor Ida, what was she doing in the gym?"

I could see Finn hadn't grasped the severity of the situation. The idea Ida had been murdered escaped him.

"Ida didn't just die, Finn. And the guard outside Dede's door isn't there because Dede slapped Captain Byard. It's more serious than that. The Inspector. Camile. The Professor. Greta. Doctor Jon. Sully. Carlo. Antonio. They're all part of a conspiracy to smuggle stolen antiquities across the Mediterranean, and anyone who gets in the way of their Gang of Eight ends up dead."

"What are you saying?" Finn put his hand to his chest.

"I'm saying Ida didn't die of natural causes. She didn't have a heart attack and keel over, Finn. She was strangled. Murdered and stuffed inside the immersion tank. Probably because she knew something or saw something, and one of the Gang of Eight wanted her dead."

Finn jerked his head. "Are you serious?"

"I've never been more serious. And we don't have a lot of time. I need to talk to Captain Byard. Have you seen him this morning?"

"No. But I know he's not on the Bridge. Captain Rob is. He called the kitchen while I was there and asked the chef to send up some fresh fruit."

"What about the rest of the ship, the residents? Anything unusual going on?"

"Not that I can tell. There are a few early risers. But the first tender isn't due for at least another hour. Most people are still inside their cabins."

"So you don't think anyone else knows about Ida?"

"Well, I certainly didn't. Not until I walked in here. After last night, I expected that you might have wanted to sleep in."

Dede answered. "I never sleep in. I was up and about, rummaging around the kitchen for something to eat. I was debating whether or not I should go up to the Café for a chocolate croissant when Kat came in, and I convinced her to join me at the Ivy Café. Other than Irene and Captain Byard, we must have been among the first there."

"Not quite. I was there before you came in." Marco took a banana from the cart and began to peel it. "The Professor and Greta were already there with the Inspector and Camile. They had a table together in the corner."

"Now that is odd," Finn said. "The Brauns usually sleep late. Especially Greta. She's not much of a morning person."

I glanced at Marco. "I think it's safe to say, based on the guard outside Dede's door, that Sully's doing what he can to contain the situation. He doesn't want anybody on board talking about it."

"I would agree, " Marco said, "but I doubt Sully intends to contain the situation as much as he plans to manage it for their benefit. Think about it, Kat. We're locked in here and—"

"The Professor, the Inspector, and the rest of the Gang of Eight are all free to roam about. For all we know, it wasn't Elli who found Ida's body, but the Chief who led her to it."

"Because he knew where the body would be."

I went to the sliding doors and stared at the water. Dede may have surprised us all by coming back so unexpectedly. But with Ida dead and Dede's unexpected return, it didn't take a lot to think that whoever had killed Ida would find Dede a convenient scapegoat.

"They'll blame you for Ida's death, Dede. You admitted you thought you were the last to see Ida alive. And if they think you have the Brutus Coin or know anything about it, they'll threaten you with Ida's murder until you turn the coin over to them."

"And if you don't," Marco made a fist and hit the palm of his hand, "the Inspector will threaten to charge you with murder, and you'll be dragged out of your comfortable quarters here and be the subject of a murder investigation before the sun sets tonight."

"Can the Inspector even do that? He's retired, and this is Italy, not France." I had no idea what rules would apply to a murder on the high seas.

"Doesn't matter. If Camile killed Ida, the Inspector would try anything.

CHAPTER THIRTY-TWO

You saw how Camile reacted when they pulled Ida's body from the tank. She would have fled if the Inspector hadn't held her hand. What's he got to lose? He's done it before. He'll do it again."

Chapter Thirty-Three

Bzzt...bzzt. The wall phone in the kitchen rang, and Dede asked Finn to answer. From the living room, we could hear Finn chatting on the phone. Then poking his head out the kitchen door and with the receiver in his hand, he announced, "Dede, Tatiana's on the phone."

"Oleg's daughter?" Dede's eyes narrowed.

Finn clasped the palm of his hand over the phone's mouthpiece. "Captain Byard gave us all firm instructions we weren't to bother her. But she's on the phone and insists on talking with you."

Dede pushed herself up from the sofa, toddled to the kitchen, and took the phone from Finn. "Tatiana?"

Whatever Tatiana said, Dede responded in a welcome tone. "Of course, dear. You know I'll do whatever I can. I want to speak with you, too, but for reasons I won't get into right now, I have a guard at my door, and I'm not permitted to leave my cabin." Dede paused and whispered to us. "Tatiana wants to see me. What are we going to do?"

"Not to worry. I'll fix it." Finn took the phone back from Dede. "Tatiana, darling, stay where you are. I'll come to get you and explain everything. But do me a favor, luv, don't talk to anyone." Then, hanging up the phone, Finn spun around and waltzed into the living room. "We're going to need more food. Marco, would you mind helping me clear the cart? I'm going to make a second run."

While Marco and Finn cleared the food cart, transferring what we hadn't eaten to the refrigerator, Dede explained how she had come to know Tatiana.

"We met years ago when Oleg was helping Neil and my late husband

CHAPTER THIRTY-THREE

negotiate with the Russians to buy *Athena*. Back then, Oleg and I were friendly. Tatiana was barely out of her teens, a pretty girl, and anxious to see the world. Her father spared no expense to see she was happy. I don't know what kind of education she's had, but she speaks Russian, French, English, and Italian. And she has an apartment in Paris, Milan, and undoubtedly something in Moscow."

"And her mother?" I asked.

"Tatiana never talked about her, and I've never asked. My relationship with Oleg was strained at best. I never trusted him. But early on, I took an interest in Tatiana and taught her to make Sharlotka. It's a Russian dessert, like a sponge cake filled with baked apple pieces, cinnamon, and vanilla. You'd think she might know, but no one ever took the time to show her."

"Did she say what she wanted to talk about?"

"I imagine she wants to talk with me about her father. And if she's willing to risk seeing me, I'm pretty sure it's because she doesn't believe he died of a heart attack."

"Ladies?" Finn rolled the food cart from the living room to the front door. "I'll be back, and when I return, expect the unexpected."

Marco started to open the door.

"Wait." I crossed in front of the cart. "Finn, you need to be careful. If any of the Gang of Eight even think you know about them or might be helping us, you could be in danger."

"Kat, how foolish you are. I'm a steward aboard a ship full of wealthy, self-absorbed residents who scarcely notice when I enter their suite, pick up their laundry, bring them their mail, or deliver their evening chocolates. They only notice when I'm not there. You needn't worry. I know how to be invisible when I need to be."

I stepped back from the cart. "Let's hope so, Finn."

* * *

It was several hours before Finn returned with the food cart. Like before, it was piled high with food, this time with sandwiches, cold cuts, and bottles of water and wine. Finn wheeled the cart into the living room and asked Marco to double-check the lock on the front door. Satisfied we wouldn't be disturbed, Finn unloaded the food from the top of the cart, stepped back, and pulled the tablecloth away like a magician.

"Voila! I bring you, Tatiana Sidorov."

Crouched beneath the top of the cart in a fetal position was Tatiana. Uncoupling her arms and legs, she clambered out from her hiding place. No more than five-one and maybe a hundred and five pounds, I could see a strong, blonde family resemblance to her father. Recognizing Dede, she scanned the room, stood up, crossed her arms, and held her head high.

"What is this, Dede? Why all this secrecy? Is it because my father is dead?"

"No." Dede put her arms around Tatiana. "I'm sorry about your father. But this lock-up isn't about your father. It's Ida Churchill. Do you remember her?"

Tatiana stiffened and stepped back. "The old lady who lives with her sister. Yes, I remember."

"She died last night. Or, more accurately, she was murdered."

"Like my father."

Dede bit her bottom lip, then responded. "You think your father was murdered?"

"I know so. He tells me he fears for his life."

"Why? Why would he say that?" I stepped in front of Dede. If Tatiana thought her father had been murdered, I wanted to know what she knew and why. "Doctor Johansson thought it was a heart attack—"

"Doctor Johansson?" The disdain in Tatiana's voice was palatable. "My father tells me about this doctor. And my father says if anything ever happens to him, I must not believe what this doctor says."

"Your father told you that?" My eyes went from Tatiana to Marco.

"More than once." Tatiana's voice was firm. "My father was a strong man. Very fit. He is never sick. I know *Athena*. I spend many summers here. My father doesn't have a heart attack and fall over the railing. He was pushed. It is why I am here. And why I want to talk to Dede."

Finn looked anxiously at me and handed Tatiana a bottle of water.

CHAPTER THIRTY-THREE

"Please," I pointed to the couch. "Tell me everything your father told you."

Tatiana's eyes darted from me to Dede. "Who is this woman?"

"A friend," Dede said. "She's a reporter, and she's here because I have asked her. You can trust her."

"Maybe I decide that." Tatiana opened the water bottle and took a sip. "Tell me what you know about this doctor."

I began slowly. "I know the doctor is part of a group of people—"

"We call them the Gang of Eight." Marco handed me a water bottle and stepped back to the cart.

"Yes, My father tells me something about these people. I don't know all the names, but I know the Professor and Inspector Garnier are dangerous. My father says they are thieves. That they smuggle stolen art. The types of things you see in museums. Very valuable. He has seen some of their hoard. Greek and Roman antiquities worth hundreds of thousands of Euros. Jewelry, clay pots, gold coins, and what he says is their biggest haul yet, a life-size bronze statue."

Marco and I exchanged a look. Up until now, I had thought the Gang's haul was small items, the type of thing one could easily hide inside a backpack or a bag like that Greta had made for Dede and be carried on and off *Athena* without notice.

Marco interrupted. "Did your father say what the statue looked like?"

Tatiana looked down at her hands. "He said it was a naked bearded warrior and that this man Antonio bragged he found it in these waters almost thirty years ago."

"The Riace Warriors. That has to be what she's talking about." Marco took a water bottle from the cart and sat down. "They were believed to have been cast around 460 to 450 BC and found in the ocean off Calabria in 1972. Buried in the silt beneath the ocean waters. Can you imagine it? Pulling two life-sized bronze statues from the sea? Initially, reports said there were three statues, but the third disappeared after excavating the first two. Many thought the ocean had reclaimed the third. It's never been found, but if Antonio had known of the excavation…maybe even worked it…he could have hidden the third statue. Stashed it in some watery grave until the

173

time was right to transport the bronze across the Mediterranean to potential buyers in the Middle East."

"Did your father say how he learned about all this?"

"My father enjoyed history. He and the Professor were friends. At least, he thought they were. They talked about their travels, and the Professor had shown him some of his collection. Weapons. Pottery. Jewelry. Things from the ancient world the Professor used for his seminars and when he travels to lecture at university. But always, when he returns, my father notices the Professor never brings these things back. Once, my father tells me the Professor has shown him a gold chalice. It is thousands of years old, intricately carved, and the Professor tells him it is one of the few remaining from its time. But now my father says it is gone."

"And how did he learn about this warrior statue, the Raice Bronze?"

"My father tells me, one night, he is in the gym, in the submersion tank. He liked to go there often. But this night, he says the top is open, and he is about to get out when he hears Camile and Carlo talking. They don't know he is there, and they are talking about a golden statue Antonio has snuck aboard. The Professor has told the group they have a buyer in Alexandria, and Camile and Carlo they are very excited. After the Golden Warrior is unloaded, they will have enough money for Camile to leave her husband. Later, my father tells the Professor and Inspector Garnier he knows about the warrior statue and wants in." Tatiana paused and took a sip of her water. "My father is not a perfect man. He makes them an offer and tells me he will be very rich. I begged him not to get involved, and after that, he didn't talk about it again. But I knew something was wrong. And when Neil called and told me my father has died, I knew then that these people had murdered him."

I recapped my water bottle. "Did you try to tell Neil you thought your father had been murdered when you saw him in Sorrento?"

"Ugh! Neil." Tatiana crushed her water bottle in her hand. "I don't trust him. And what could I say? This man Antonio is with him. Instead, I tell Neil I want to visit my father's cabin on *Athena* and that I not be disturbed. I don't tell him I believe I will find evidence to prove my father has been

CHAPTER THIRTY-THREE

murdered. But that is why I am here."

"So, you've been locked in your father's cabin since you came on board?" I asked.

"Yes."

"And you didn't hear Dede come aboard after we left Sorrento or know that Ida had been murdered."

"I told you, I was in the cabin alone. It is only after I call Dede and say I want to talk that Finn comes to my door."

"Did you find anything suspicious in your father's cabin?"

"I find some ledgers. I'll need to spend some time with them."

"It's probably nothing," Finn picked up Tatiana's crushed water bottle and handed her another. "Oleg kept the books. He managed condo sales, leases, and association dues."

"If you like, I could take a look." Marco scratched his head. "If anything is going on, I'll find it. I'm good with numbers."

"Do you hear that?" Dede stood up and went to the balcony. Outside, I could hear the sounds of a motorboat. "Come, you have to see this."

Tatiana and I joined Dede on the deck. Finn and Marco followed. Moving closer to Athena was a small motorboat.

"Look," Dede pointed to the boat, "it's Neil, and Antonio's with him."

I stepped away from the deck and considered what Antonio's return might mean. Neither Neil nor Antonio had been on board when Ida was murdered. Both had gotten off in Sorrento with Oleg's body and as far as I knew, only Neil was due back on board today. We were to have lunch with Dede before I returned to the States. But now, with Ida dead and Dede and I locked away in Dede's stateroom with Marco, what chance did I have of leaving? I didn't know if anyone on board, besides those who had followed Sully to the gym, knew anything of Ida's death or if Captain Byard had notified the coastal authorities. For all I knew, Byard had been replaced by Captain Rob, and the Gang of Eight was now in charge and had no intention of reporting her death. I had anticipated with Ida's murder that *Athena* would be held until the harbor security had cleared us to depart, but I hadn't expected to see Antonio again. And the fact that he was returning sent chills down my back.

I knew I wouldn't be going home anytime soon, if at all.

Chapter Thirty-Four

"Finn? Do you have your cell phone with you?" I didn't trust that Sully or the Inspector had radioed ahead to alert Positano's authorities of Ida's murder. And, if I had any chance of getting help and off *Athena* before Neil and Antonio came on board, I needed to act quickly.

"Sorry, Kat. I forgot to charge it last night. I left it in my suite."

I glanced at Tatiana. "How about you? Do you have your phone with you?"

"No." Tatiana narrowed her eyes. She looked worried. "It's in my father's cabin, why?"

"What's wrong, Kat." Finn looked concerned. "Don't you have yours?"

"No." I explained how Carlo had taken our cell phones when he escorted us to Dede's suite. "And I don't suppose the wall phone is good for ship-to-shore?"

"It would be," Finn said, "except you'd have to go through the operator, and since you've been locked in, I doubt you'd be put through."

I joined Dede and Marco on the balcony and looked overboard as the small motorboat pulled beside us. One of the crewmen threw a short rope ladder from the Marina Deck's open portal to Neil and Antonio below. I watched as they climbed aboard.

"So, what happens now?" I asked.

"We wait." Marco returned to the food cart, grabbed a soda, and sat down. "*Athena*'s scheduled to be here for the day. If Captain Rob doesn't want to call any unnecessary attention to us, he won't do anything unexpected. *Athena* will remain moored out here in the bay. Some residents will come and go as they like, and we'll leave at about nine p.m. As scheduled."

"And what are *we* supposed to do? Wait until the Professor and Inspector Garnier decide what to do with us?" Without a phone or any way of contacting anyone on shore, the best thing I could think of was to dive from Dede's deck and try to swim ashore. But if the dive didn't kill me, Dede's deck was at least three stories above the waterline, the swim might. I'd be lucky to get a hundred yards from the ship before one of the Professor's henchmen would spot me in the water, and then where would I be? Probably right back where I started, or worse, isolated somewhere below deck where I'd be easy enough to dispose of without concern.

"I doubt there's much we can do." Marco popped the tab on his soda can.

"And what about me?" Tatiana started for the door. "I won't be locked in like some prisoner."

Finn grabbed Tatiana by the arm. "Think about it, Tatiana. Right now, nobody but us knows you're here. And if whoever's standing guard outside the door sees you walk out, it might not go so well for you. Don't forget, these people murdered your father. They won't stop there if they think you're on to them."

"So, I'm stuck with you then?" Tatiana ripped her arm from Finn.

"Hey, you wanted to see Dede, and I got you in. But I doubt I'd be as lucky hiding you beneath the cart again, and I'm not willing to risk it. So, if I were you, I'd stay."

Finn's beeper sounded. The color drained from his face as he checked his pager for a message.

"You okay?" I asked.

"I'm being summoned to the Bridge."

"Is that unusual?"

"Not necessarily." Finn tucked his beeper back inside his butler's cummerbund and headed to the door. "I'll be in touch."

* * *

Twenty minutes later, Captain Rob made a shipwide announcement. "Residents. This is Captain Rob. Welcome to Positano. We will begin our tender

CHAPTER THIRTY-FOUR

service shortly. Temperatures today are expected to be in the mid-nineties. Doctor Jon suggests residents take a bottle of water with them when they leave the ship and not forget their sunscreen. Please be advised *Athena* is here for the day only, and we will depart promptly at nine p.m. Enjoy your day."

"Did you hear that?" I looked at Marco. Dede was sitting beside him on the sofa. "Where's Captain Byard? Why isn't he on deck?"

"Good question." Marco got up and went back out on the deck. "And an even better one is, why haven't we seen any sign of the Italian authorities? Unless, of course, Captain Rob hasn't reported Ida's death—"

"And doesn't intend to," I said. I was standing inside the sliding door when the guard outside Dede's cabin entered unannounced. His presence was so sudden and unexpected that Tatiana crouched out of sight behind the chair where she had been sitting. All of us were frightened.

"You!" The guard yelled at me. "Away from the door. And Marco. Inside. Now!" The guard, a midshipman I hadn't seen before, waited for Marco to come inside, then crossed the room, banged the outside door shut, and closed the blinds behind him. "Nobody goes out on the deck until the Chief says so."

Dede stood up. "Excuse me, young man, under whose authority do you barge into my apartment and try to hold me hostage? Do you know who I am?"

"I know Chief Sullivan has placed you under house arrest."

"With what evidence?" Dede demanded.

"According to the Chief, you were the last to see Ida Churchill alive. You're a suspect."

"You think I had something to do with Ida Churchill's death?"

"I'm sorry, ma'am. I'm only following orders."

"And where is Captain Byard?"

"I don't know, ma'am. All I've been told is to make sure you and your friends here remain in your quarters and that no one goes out on the deck."

* * *

I waited until the guard left. Marco took a seat at the bar, and I grabbed a bunch of grapes from the food cart and sat down on one of the small swivel chairs next to the coffee table. Tatiana crawled out from behind the second swivel chair and took a seat. She looked pale, leaned across the table, and took several grapes from my hand.

"So you write story about *Athena*."

"That's why I'm on board."

"Yes, I know. My father tells me about you."

"About me?" I was surprised to hear Tatiana say her father had spoken to her about me, but not totally. Gossip was rampant aboard *Athena*, and I was an anomaly on board, a travel reporter, much younger than the average resident, and unexpected. But still, I wondered why Oleg would bother to mention me to her. "When was this?"

"He calls me when *Athena* is in Ischia. I know he is upset. His voice…it is anxious, and he says he will talk with you that night."

"But we didn't talk. And unfortunately, I don't know what your father might have wanted to tell me. But maybe we can work together. I've got a lot of questions, and I'm sure you do too." I put the grapes on the table and dusted my hands. "The way I see it, there's been three suspicious deaths aboard *Athena*. The previous Captain. Your father. And now Ida. And I know you think Neil had something to do with your father's death. But the thing is, I was with Neil the night your father died. I was having dinner with Neil and Antonio when we heard someone had fallen overboard."

"My father didn't fall." The anger in Tatiana's voice was palpable. "Someone pushed him. I know it."

"But why? Because he knew about the Gang of Eight?"

"No. Is more than that. I told you I found ledgers in my father's cabin." Tatiana explained that her father was *Athena's* bookkeeper. The job, along with a luxury apartment, was part of Oleg's agreement with Neil for helping to broker a deal with the Russians for *Athena's* dilapidated hull. Once *Athena* had been remodeled with upscale condos designed for senior living and christened, Oleg became the resident property manager. It was his job to oversee condo sales and collect association dues. Neil was too busy traveling

CHAPTER THIRTY-FOUR

to concern himself with the responsibility, and Walter, Dede's husband, didn't feel up to the task as his health was beginning to fail.

"And you think the ledgers prove Neil had something to do with your father's death?"

"There are two sets of books. What do you think? One that shows *Athena* is deeply in debt. The other I don't understand, but I believe it proves my father knew too much, and that—"

"Neil needed money and was using *Athena* to pirate stolen antiquities across the Mediterranean to pay the bills."

"And when my father found out and wanted in, Neil arranged for his murder."

Marco stood up from the bar and reached over my shoulder to take a grape from the table.

I put my hand on top of his. "You're an accountant. Did you suspect—"

"No. He didn't." Dede returned from the kitchen with a chocolate croissant in her hand and sat at the end of the couch. "Marco's never had anything to do with *Athena's* financing. He wouldn't know the first thing about it. Neil and my husband, Walter, handled everything until things got too busy, and Neil needed to travel for the business. Tatiana, you may remember Walter from when you first visited us onboard years ago."

"I remember you teaching me to make Sharlotka while Walter sat in the kitchen and watched."

"We had a good time. Back then, Walter and Neil were in business together. But I'm the reason Marco never worked for Neil or Walter after they bought *Athena*. I wasn't about to have an ex-felon handling our financial affairs. In fact—"

"Dede," Marco held his hands up, "you don't need to get into it. It was a long time ago. It doesn't matter."

"Maybe it does. I never told you before, Marco, and maybe it's because we're locked in here, and I've no idea what's going to happen, but lately, since I've become friends with Neil's niece, Elli, I've begun to rethink things. And I can't help but wonder if what you did—what you went to prison for—you did to save what you could of Neil's inheritance. What I'm saying, Marco, is that I'm sorry I've been so rude to you all these years."

Marco put his fist to his mouth. "Thank you, Dede. You didn't have to say that, but thank you."

"But as for Neil, Tatiana, he's always been quiet about his personal life. That alone is enough to make him suspicious, but I know the man and his financial dealings are sound. My name and Neil's are still on the business account, and I know he wouldn't do anything to risk my safety or those he feels responsible for, including becoming part of some high-stakes smuggling operation. I'm sorry to say this, Tatiana, but if your father kept two sets of books, I'm certain Neil had no idea, and I'd be more suspicious of your father."

"Do you feel that?" Marco went to the blinds and swept them aside. "We're moving! Look."

I joined Marco at the sliding door, and together, we watched as small whirlpools formed in the black waters beneath Athena's hull as she pulled from the harbor, and the lights of Positano began to fade into the night sky.

Marco checked his watch. "It's nine p.m. We're right on schedule. They're not wasting any time."

"So much for thinking Chief Sullivan planned to escort Dede ashore and turn her over to the local authorities for Ida's murder."

"That was never going to happen." Marco walked back to the bar and poured himself another drink. "We know too much. Once the Inspector knew we were on to them, they never intended to let us go."

"So what do we do now?" Dede asked.

"Pray," I said.

***

Five hours later, there was a heavy knock on the door, and Chief Sully and Inspector Garnier entered Dede's cabin. Sully held a gun with a long silencer attached, and the Inspector had a sidearm holstered beneath his shoulder.

Tatiana screamed and ducked behind the bar.

"Well, would you look who's here?" Sully walked over to the bar and

CHAPTER THIRTY-FOUR

grabbed Tatiana by the hair. "She's going to make it easy for us, Inspector. We can eliminate this Russian doll when we toss the others overboard. Save us answering a lot of unnecessary questions about her father, and nobody will know the difference once she's gone."

Sully strong-armed Tatiana, tying her hands behind her back with plastic wrist ties, and handed her off to the guard.

"And you, too, Marco. You should be more careful about choosing your friends. It would have been better for you if you hadn't tried to get so close to Ms. Lawson here. We knew she was trouble when she started asking a lot of uncomfortable questions."

"Like what?" I asked. "Questions about the jewelry, like that gold signet ring you found on Ida? Or was it the questions I asked about the antiquities the Professor claims are on loan to him for his lectures? Maybe because I was curious about *Athena's* itinerary, spending so much time in such a small area? That shouldn't have been so upsetting unless you and your group were worried that I thought Ida might know something or that I had talked about it with Oleg. But you murdered him before I had a chance."

"Nobody murdered Oleg. He was drunk and fell overboard." Sully looked at the guard. "Cuff them. We need to get moving."

Inspector Garnier took Dede by the arm. "You too, Dede."

But Dede refused to move. "I'm not going anywhere. Not until I see Neil."

"Oh, you're going to see him, alright, and Captain Byard, too. Now get moving." The Inspector took his gun from his holster, shoved it into the small of Dede's back, and pushed her toward the door. "And you too, Ms. Lawson."

I stood up and slung my backpack over my shoulder.

"Hold on there, Ms. Lawson." The Inspector took hold of the strap over my shoulder. "What do you think you going with that?"

"I'm a reporter. It goes where I go."

"What's inside?"

"What do you think?" I opened the bag. "My camera. A notepad. Pair of shorts and flip-flops. Anyone finds this bag without me, and they'd know I was in trouble."

The Inspector glanced inside. "Fine. Take it with you. We can throw it overboard when we're done with you." Then, nodding to the guard, he told him to cuff me.

The guard cuffed my hands, and I followed Dede out the door. "Where are we going?"

"You'll see when we get there." Garnier poked me in the ribs with his gun. "Just keep moving. End of the hall to the stairs."

Chapter Thirty-Five

The lights on the Marina Deck, where we had been earlier that morning and found Ida's body, had been turned off. The entire gym area was dark. The only light was that that came from a snack machine. And the only sound was the sloshing of water from the indoor pool. Sully went ahead of Marco and Tatiana and, finding a light switch on the wall, flipped the overhead lights on, then pointed with his gun for us to enter.

The four of us shuffled through the doorway.

"There're some towels on the rack by the pool. You can use 'em to sit on if you like. You're going to be here awhile. And don't get any ideas about screaming for help. Nobody will hear you, not over the sound of the engines. Besides, everyone upstairs is sound asleep. Doctor Jon spiked their welcome-back drinks when we left Positano. Between what the Doc put in their drinks and the ship's rocking, nobody will ever know about what happened here tonight."

"What are you going to do?" Dede snapped. "Throw us overboard?"

"That's up to you, Dede. But right now, you're all going to sit down while we wait for your friends to arrive."

"What friends?" Marco twisted his hands in the plastic ties around his wrists.

"Sit down!" Sully pointed his gun at us again, and we struggled to sit cross-legged on the floor.

"As I said, your friends should be here in a minute. I'm surprised Elli and Irene aren't here already, but they'll be along. After that, Antonio will be down with Neil, Captain Byard, and that nosy cabin boy, Finn. Things got a little out of hand upstairs. Captain Byard tried to be a hero, and Neil doesn't look so good, but they'll be fine."

"Why are you doing this?" I asked.

"Why do you think? You know too much. In fact, Ms. Lawson, if you hadn't come on board and gotten so curious about everything, things might have ended happily. Instead, I'm sorry to say we have some rather unpleasant business ahead of us. Your friends can thank you for that."

"So, Ida was right all along," I said.

"Shut up!" Sully stepped forward, raised his hand above his head, and was about to hit me across the face when the elevator doors opened. He stopped with his hand in the air. "What the... Why'd you take the elevator, you fool? I told you, take the stairs. We don't want to alert anyone."

"What do you expect? The old lady can hardly walk." Doctor Jon held Elli and Irene by the elbow, one on either side of him, their hands tied behind their backs, as they got off the elevator and pushed them toward us.

"You really think you're going to get away with this?" I struggled to get comfortable. The camera inside my backpack felt like a rock against my back.

Sully laughed. "You have no idea who you're dealing with, Ms. Lawson. And yes, I do think we'll get away with it. We've been getting away with it for years. And now, we're on our final trip, and nobody, least of all, some hack reporter from a third-rate travel journal and a creepy old battleaxe like Dede here is going to get in our way."

"I beg your pardon." Dede kicked one of the towels on the floor in Sully's direction. "You can say what you want about Kat's magazine, but I am not a creepy old battleaxe."

The Inspector picked the towel up off the floor. "Take it easy, Sully. There's no point in getting them all riled up. It's going to be a long night."

"Well then, chew on this, why don't you?" Dede kicked her legs from under her and crossed her ankles. "I've known what you were up to all along, and I'm steps ahead of you."

"What are you talking about, Dede?" Sully pointed the gun in Dede's

CHAPTER THIRTY-FIVE

direction.

"I'm talking about the gold coin you had Greta hide in my bag. You think I didn't know about it? You fool. Why do you think I came back when I did? Because I got bored with my cooking class? Please… If you think it's just a few of us who know about you, you're in for a big surprise."

I started to squirm. I had no idea what Dede had in mind, but outspoken as she was, I feared she was about to get us all into deeper trouble than we were in already.

"And what kind of surprise is that?"

"The kind that will land you and your little Gang of Eight in jail."

"Gang of Eight?" Sully scoffed. "Is that what you're calling us."

"Has a nice ring to it, don't you think? But don't quote me. It's not me that's going to write about it. You think it's some accident Kat's on board. That she's some…what did you call her, hack journalist?"

"Dede, please." I struggled against my ties.

"Relax, Kat. They already know. Or think they know. She's not just a journalist. She's an investigator, you idiot. An undercover agent working as a travel reporter. Touch one hair on her head, and you'll spend the rest of your life hiding. That is if you're lucky enough to get off this ship before she's boarded by the entire Mediterranean Coast Guard."

"You're bluffing, Dede. Kat Lawson's nothing but a disgraced reporter who couldn't get a decent job with any credible publication unless she paid them to hire her. We checked her out. She was fired from her last job." The Inspector waved his gun in front of Dede's face.

"I've said enough. I'm not saying another word. Not until I talk to Neil."

"Oh, you'll talk to Neil, alright. But he's not going to be able to help you." The Inspector holstered his gun and turned to Sully. "Come, we'll leave the guard at the door. We have some business to take care of upstairs."

I waited until both the Inspector and Sully shut the door.

"Dede, is there something you need to tell me?" There was no way Dede could have known about my previous work as an undercover operative with the FBI. I hadn't mentioned it to anyone nor written a word about it in my notes. How could Dede possibly know?

"I should have listened to Ida long ago. Poor woman. She was right all along. And now she's dead, and here we are handcuffed below deck in *Athena's* bowels at the mercy of a bunch of no-good, thieving pirates."

"I'm sorry."

"Don't be. I never would have known if you hadn't shown me the coin." Dede sounded more angry than frightened.

"Believe me, I was hoping I could keep what's been going on with the Gang of Eight quiet until I got off the ship in Positano and alerted the authorities."

"Well, it's not turned out that way, but it might be a good thing yet. Call it a lucky move that I agreed with Elli to arrange for a travel reporter to sail with us when you did. And if this Gang of Eight was suspicious of you, all the better that I should add to their concerns and let them think I hired a spy to bust up their operation."

"Bravo, Dede." Marco chuckled. "Convince them poor Kat here is some undercover operative, and maybe they'll think twice before dumping our bodies at sea. At least, let's hope so."

Chapter Thirty-Six

Sully had flipped off the lights as he and Inspector Garnier left the gym area, leaving the six of us, Elli, Irene, Dede, Tatiana, Marco, and me, to sit in the dark on the cold floor with our hands tied behind our backs, wondering what was next. An hour later, maybe more, Sully returned and pushed Neil through the door.

The Inspector followed and turned on the light. Neil was cuffed with his hands behind his back. Someone had tied a bloodied bandana around his head. It partially covered his eyes, and Neil struggled to stand.

"What have you done to him?" Dede tried to get to her feet.

"Stay where you are!" Sully pointed his gun in our direction, and Dede sat back. From the crazed look in Sully's eyes, I had no doubt he would shoot first and ask questions later.

"Easy, Sully. You don't have to shoot anyone. Nobody's going anywhere." I leaned back against the wall. There was nothing we could do to defend ourselves. If Sully shot us now and dumped our bodies overboard, no one would ever know what happened.

Sully nodded to the Inspector, then jerked his head toward Neil. "Put him over there."

Garnier grabbed Neil by the arm and dragged him over to us, then let his frail body fall like a rag to the floor. Elli gasped as Neil's body fell over onto her legs.

I whispered. "He'll be okay. Don't say anything."

"Shut up!" Sully grabbed my hair, pulled my face to his, and shoved the gun's muzzle beneath my chin. "You have anything else to say?"

"No." My back arched against my backpack. Another second and I expected he would have pulled the trigger, except—

The stairway door opened.

Sully turned his attention from me. Captain Byard and Finn stumbled through the doorway, their hands tied behind their backs. Antonio followed with a shotgun, then motioned for Finn and Byard to join us against the wall. He waited until they sat down, then stepped back and surveyed us.

"So what have we got now, nine? Counting Neil, Captain Byard, and Finn. What a sorry group. I have to say I didn't expect this when Neil and I returned to the ship this morning. In fact, I wasn't expecting to come back at all. It wasn't until I got a call from Professor Braun telling me there was trouble. Poor Ida. Can't say that was planned. Made for a good excuse for me to return with Neil, though. Still…such a shame."

Antonio paced in front of us, like a drill sergeant, resting his rifle loose over one arm with his hand on the trigger. Our heads were bowed, each of us too afraid to make eye contact. Then he stopped directly in front of me, and I stared down at his shoes.

"And you, Kat, I couldn't understand why Neil would allow a reporter on board. He's a very private person who doesn't like to discuss his affairs. So I knew you weren't here to interview him. In fact, when you and I first met, I wondered if you might be an investigator. But then I dismissed the idea after I checked you out and learned about your chequered past. What a loser. You're not what I'd expect the FBI or the CIA to hire. In fact, I'd say you were lucky to find a job at all. I don't imagine it'll cause much of a concern when you suddenly disappear, and *Athena* issues a statement saying you and your friends here were lost at sea."

"Stop it!" Dede spit on Antonio's shoe. "You don't need to do this."

"No, we don't. Or at least we didn't plan to. But unfortunately, Dede, you and Ms. Lawson present a problem. And, if Kat here hadn't gotten so nosy, things might have remained as they were. But now. I'm afraid we're forced to make a decision.

"You won't get away with this."

"That's where you're wrong, Dede. We will get away with it. I'll admit we

CHAPTER THIRTY-SIX

hadn't planned to end things this way. We're thieves, not murderers—"

"Tell that to Ida!" Dede jutted her jaw at Antonio, and Sully stepped forward.

Antonio held a hand up. "Ida was a mistake."

"And my father, too?" Tatiana screamed. "You're going to tell me you didn't murder him?"

Antonio shook his head. "Why would we kill Oleg? Your father was a dealmaker. Once he found out what we were doing, he wanted in. He said he had a buyer, some Russian thug your father had crossed in the past, who he thought he could use to settle an old score and guarantee a small profit for himself. If anything, your father got worried he had exposed himself and took his own life before the guy killed him. But we didn't kill him."

"I don't believe you!"

The situation was escalating. Whether Antonio considered himself a murderer or not, we were running out of time.

"Maybe we could strike a deal," I said.

"That depends." Antonio rested his weapon on his forearm. "Inspector Garnier tells me that Dede found the EID MAR coin—"

"You mean the one you had Greta hide in my bag?" Dede raged back at Antonio. "The one that punk tried to knock me off for in Naples?"

Antonio smiled and looked at Sully and the Inspector. "What do you think? The coin's worth a lot of money. What do you say, Dede? You give me the Brutus Coin, and we'll consider offering everyone here a handsome reward in return for their silence."

Dede blurted out. "As long as you're not talking dead silence, I think we might have a deal."

Antonio shrugged. "But of course. I'm not an unreasonable man. Tell you what. I'll give you all a little time to discuss what it is you'd like to do." Then, nodding to both Sully and the Inspector, Antonio added, "Gentlemen, I think we need to leave them alone for a bit. Hopefully, we can all come to a more reasonable way to end our differences."

Marco waited until the door closed before he spoke.

"They're not going kill us. They want to negotiate. They want the coin.

You heard Antonio. They're thieves, not murderers."

"You're wrong, Marco." Byard struggled to speak. Like Neil, Byard had been beaten, and his left eye had started to swell. "It's a trick. I heard the Inspector talking to Antonio on the Bridge. They want the coin Dede told him she has. Once they get it, they'll dump us overboard, shoot us in the water, and let the sharks finish us off."

"This is all my fault." Neil groaned as he tried to straighten his body. "I never should have trusted Antonio."

"You didn't know?" I asked. "You had no idea?"

"What? That Antonio was head of a criminal organization and was using *Athena* to smuggle stolen antiquities across the Med? No. Absolutely not. It wasn't until I returned to the Bridge this morning that I realized anything was wrong. It was still early. Captain Rob was at the helm. I had no idea what was about to happen."

"I'm afraid none of us did." Byard explained that after leaving Ida's body with the Doctor and returning to the Bridge with Sully and the Inspector, he expected they would call the authorities to notify them of Ida's death. "Instead, Sully insisted we wait until Neil could join us."

"Soon as I got to the Bridge, I knew something was wrong." Neil arched his back and winced as he spoke. I could see the pain in his face. "Captain Rob was there, and Captain Byard had a look of concern on his face I didn't like. I asked Sully if he had notified the authorities, and he said no. That he had no intention of calling them. I couldn't believe what I was hearing, and I was about to push Sully out of the way when I felt something hit me from behind. I must have passed out. The next thing I knew, Byard, Finn, and I were in cuffs."

Byard filled in the details. Antonio grabbed the fire extinguisher and hit Neil over the head. "I tried to stop him, but Sully and the Inspector got the better of me. He cuffed Neil and me, and it was over by the time Finn arrived."

"There was nothing I could do." Finn looked at Neil apologetically. "I'm so sorry."

"It's not your fault, Finn. *Athena's* my ship. This is on me. If I had any

CHAPTER THIRTY-SIX

idea what was happening, I would never have endangered any of you. And now, we've had a mutiny aboard. I never would have thought it was possible. Antonio and his friends have seized control and put Captain Rob at the helm. The crew will take orders from the Captain. No questions."

"And no one will suspect anything?" I could have answered my own question. No one noticed the Captain's schedule, who was on the Bridge, or why. The residents were only interested in their safe arrival and departure. There was no reason for concern.

Byard grimaced. "Not likely. If anyone were to ask about me, Captain Rob would tell them I was taking some time off. And remember, nobody saw anything. Athena had dropped anchor in Positano's harbor hours before, and Captain Rob, the Inspector, Sully, and I were alone on the Bridge when Neil and Antonio came on board. Chances are, if anyone saw Neil and Antonio arrive, they wouldn't have thought anything about it. And once Antonio knocked Neil out and Sully cuffed us, we were led down the stairs to the gym, and here we are."

"Well, we can't just sit here and wait for them to return." Dede rolled her shoulders, trying to loosen the tension in her neck. "We need to do something. Kat, where did you put that coin?"

"It's hidden. And it'll stay that way until I'm certain it'll buy our freedom."

Marco stretched his long legs out in front of him. "I like your confidence, Kat. But where's the coin?"

I leaned back up against my backpack. It wasn't only the camera that I could feel up against my spine, but the cheese knife the chef had given me as a souvenir that the Inspector had missed when he searched my bag.

"I have a knife in my bag. And I'm going to need your help to get it."

I scooted away from the wall and told Marco to do the same, then turned so my back was to his. "I know you can't see behind you, but if you lean back against me, even with your hands tied, you should be able to unzip my backpack. Get the knife and try to cut me loose. Just make sure you don't cut my wrists, will you?"

Chapter Thirty-Seven

I wasn't sure if Marco could cut the plastic zip ties from my wrists. It would have been hard enough for someone half his age, but for a seventy-eight-year-old senior whose hands were tied behind his back and shook under the best circumstances, I could only hope he didn't accidentally slit my wrists. Once I felt my left hand free, I took the knife from him and cut the remaining tie from my wrist, then cut the others free.

"Neil, is there another way out of here?" My eyes scanned the gym for a possible exit.

"I don't see how. Sully's locked the elevator doors. Nobody's getting on or off, not while we're here. And there's a guard outside the stairway door where we came in. Short of opening the Marina hatch and jumping out into the ocean, I don't see how we get out of here."

We all huddled together in a circle. Neil next to Finn, then Dede, Irene, Elli, Marco, Captain Byard, and me, with Tatiana slightly to herself. Each of us I knew had to be thinking the same thing. We had to find a way out.

"There's a wall ladder beyond the storage lockers." Byard rubbed his wrists as he spoke. "It won't take us up to the deck. It's for the crew to go between floors, but it will take us down to the anchor chain and the—"

"The war room!" I remembered Byard talking to me about it when he gave me a tour of the ship and thinking how strange it was for a passenger vessel to have such a room. "You said it's where *Athena* stores her arsenal. In case of pirates."

"Exactly."

"And Antonio doesn't know about it?" I looked at Neil.

CHAPTER THIRTY-SEVEN

He shook his head. "He's not a crew member. There's no reason for him to know...and even if he did, the guns and ammo are all under lock and key. We couldn't get them if we wanted."

"But we could break the locks." Byard pointed to an ax mounted on the wall.

"And what about the hose?" I nodded to the fire hose beneath the ax. "Is it hooked up? Can we use it?"

"You bet we can." Finn went to the wall and took the hose from its mount. "And you don't want to be in the way when we turn it on. It'll knock you off your feet."

I slipped the cheese knife into my pocket. "Are you all thinking what I'm thinking?"

"That we fight back?" Dede made a fist and stuck her arm out in front of us all.

Marco put his hand on top of hers. "Do we have a choice?"

"I don't think so." I put my hand on top of theirs and looked up at the clock over the pool. It was almost four a.m. The sun and some of *Athena's* residents would be up in a few hours. "Antonio'll give us one chance to turn over the Brutus Coin, and when we do—"

"He'll take advantage of the fact we're miles from any shoreline and start throwing bodies out the Marina hatch. We'll be long gone before anyone upstairs wakes up or begins to ask questions."

"Wait!" Tatiana stepped back, her hands in front of her face. "What are you saying? You think you stand a chance against these people? I'm not part of your group. I'm not taking part in any of this."

Finn reached behind him and took hold of Tatiana's arm. "Are you forgetting these are the people who threw your father overboard? Do you think they won't do the same to you?"

"It's up to you, Tatiana." I took Finn's hand from Tatiana's arm. "You can help us or try to hide and hope they won't find you and kill you."

"Fine!" Tatiana slapped her hand on top of all of ours. "We fight."

* * *

Thirty minutes later, I sat cross-legged in the center of the gym with my backpack on my lap and the Brutus Coin in my hand. Or, what I hoped Antonio would think was the Brutus Coin and not my camera's battery, which, from the distance of the gym's stairway door to where I sat, looked in size and shape very much like the desired coin.

I wanted to be the first and only person Antonio saw when he came through the stairway door. I knew he would be stunned when he saw me sitting alone in the middle of the room. And I was counting on the fact that much as Antonio had said, he and his group weren't murderers but thieves, that he wasn't lying and wouldn't barge through the doors and shoot me.

Initially, Captain Byard and Neil thought it was a crazy idea that I position myself as a sitting duck. But since Dede had told the Inspector that we had discovered the Brutus Coin and she no doubt, based upon her irrational outbursts, wouldn't be the best person to negotiate our release, they agreed to my plan. I reminded myself as I sat on the cold floor and felt my heart racing that we had split the Gang of Eight in two. And that, at the moment, only three of them are out to get us. I imagined the rest of the gang were upstairs, waiting for word we were out of the way and that they could continue their pirate's crossing, looking forward to a big payday.

My job was to lure them into the center of the gym, where…if all went well…we would surprise them.

The operative term being *if*—

Chapter Thirty-Eight

Antonio was first through the door. My eyes froze on him, and I counted the steps I knew he needed to take before I could signal the others from their hiding places. If there was any sense of relief, it was that Antonio wasn't carrying his rifle. But behind him was Sully, who I feared the most and didn't doubt, given the slightest provocation, would shoot me. Third and last to enter was the Inspector.

"Where is everybody?" Antonio stopped short with Sully and Inspector Garnier directly behind him.

I snarled. "You want them, or do you want the Brutus Coin? I have it. Right here, in my hand." I extended the palm of my hand, hoping to draw my three assailants steps closer to me.

Another two steps, and Captain Byard would slip from behind them and shut the door. Finn and Marco would then blast cold water from *Athena's* high-powered fire hoses mounted on the walls, and, with any luck, all three would slip on the floor and drop their weapons. Elli and Irene would pick them up. Neil and Byard, armed with rifles they had freed from *Athena's* arsenal, would stand guard while Tatiana and I secured the rope we would need to tie them up to ensure they wouldn't escape.

"Where is everybody?" Antonio took another step closer, then, hearing something behind him, turned and—

Woosh! Finn and Marco released a high-powered torrent of water from their firehoses. Sully slipped and fell, his weapon sliding across the gym floor, while the Inspector folded to his knees, his glasses falling from his face, leaving him to pat the ground anxiously in search of them.

I pocketed the lithium battery and went quickly for Sully's gun, kicking it out of the way. But not fast enough. Antonio grabbed me, twisted my arm behind my back, and, with his free arm around my neck, dragged me away from the force of the water. "Tell your friends to drop the hoses now, or I'll break your neck."

Whatever survival instincts I had kicked in. With one arm free, I elbowed Antonio in the ribs and jammed the heel of my shoe down hard on Antonio's left sandal. Then, with all the force I could muster, I slammed the back of my head against Antonio's chin. His head snapped back, and he dropped my arm. In an instant, I was free. But not done. To make sure Antonio wasn't going to be a problem, I turned and kneed him. One quick, swift, very well-placed strike to the groin.

Antonio doubled over, groaned, and crumpled to the floor.

"You okay?" Byard trained his weapon on Antonio.

"I will be. How about you?" I reached for a rope, one of several Camile had used for her highwire practice above the water, and tossed it to Elli.

Byard answered. "Better now that we have these three in our custody." With the butt of his rifle aimed at Antonio's kneecap, Byard edged Antonio closer to Sully and the Professor, who sat soaked in the center of the gym.

Neither man had dared to move. Between Neil's position directly in front of them, with his rifle aimed at their heads, and Tatiana, who had picked up Sully's gun with its long deadly silencer, and Dede with the Inspector's pistol in both hands, the two sat silently. Elli and Finn bound their hands behind their backs, then tied their feet.

Byard checked Elli's knots and nodded to the stairway door. "We still have the guard outside."

"Let me take care of that." Neil rested his rifle on his shoulder and went to the door. Seconds later, the young seaman who had stood guard outside walked into the gym with his hands in the air.

"Nice work, Neil." Byard picked up another rope and tossed it to Elli.

"Yes. Well, it helps when you own the ship." Neil shoved the young seaman over to where our three would-be assassins sat tied and bound on the floor and told Elli to tie his hands and feet.

CHAPTER THIRTY-EIGHT

"Now what?" Finn kicked the hoses away from the group. "The others are still upstairs, and Captain Rob has command of the ship. "

"Not for long. Finn, you and Marco stay here and keep watch on these four. Neil and I'll go upstairs." Byard handed his rifle to Finn. "Elli, you and Tatiana take Irene back to her cabin. Kat and Dede, you should do the same."

"Not on your life, Captain." Dede strode toward the door, the inspector's pistol in her hand. "You're not leaving me out of the action. You still have Camile and Carlo to deal with, and if I have any say about it, I want to be the one to take the Professor and Greta down. Kat, get some rope. We're going to need it."

"Whoa." Neil stepped in front of Dede and held out his hand. "Not with a gun, you're not. Give it to me. Nobody needs to get shot. We've got Antonio, Sully, and the Inspector right where we want them. I'm not going to be responsible for another murder on board."

Dede handed Neil the gun. "Alright, but Kat and I aren't going back to my cabin. We're coming with you. I want to see the Professor and Greta's faces when you tell them I still have the Brutus Coin." She glanced back at me and added, "You do have it, right, Kat?"

I strapped my camera around my neck and patted the side of my backpack. "It's not getting out of my sight."

"Okay, but you and Kat, stay behind me. Kat cut some of that rope and put it in your bag. We may need it." Then, taking the gun from Dede, Neil slipped it into the back of his waistband and handed his rifle to Marco. "You think you and Finn can handle watching these four while we take care of whatever awaits us upstairs?"

Marco took Neil's rifle from his hands. "You've nothing to worry about, Neil. I've always had your back. You know that."

* * *

By the time Neil, Captain Byard, Dede, and I got upstairs to the Ivy Café, it was after seven a.m. Some early morning residents were already enjoying their coffee. Camile, the Professor, Greta, and Doctor Jon were seated in a large corner booth as though they were waiting for their friends to join them.

Their faces fell when we entered. Camile's eyes darted to the kitchen exit, and she started to get up, but Byard stepped forward and blocked her escape. Greta grabbed her husband's hand while the Professor leaned back against the booth and, looking up at the ceiling, shook his head.

"Surprised?" Neil stood opposite Byard at the other end of the booth and, placing his hand behind his back, wrapped his fingers around the handle of the pistol he had taken from Dede.

The Professor took his napkin from his lap and wiped his mouth. "Neil, I can explain—"

"I hope you can, Professor." Neil grabbed the napkin from the Professor's hand and tossed it on the table. "I would really like to hear why you murdered my aunt and Oleg. What did they do to you?"

"You've got it all wrong, Neil." The Doctor put his fists on the table. "We never murdered anyone. And if this reporter hadn't come along and gotten us all concerned she was looking into things that weren't any of her business, none of this would have happened. We never intended anyone to get hurt."

"Oh really? It's a little hard to believe that, considering Oleg fell over a five-foot railing, and my aunt's body was found inside of an immersion tank. In fact, it makes me wonder if you and your friends had anything to do with the previous captain's fall overboard. It's all a little too coincidental, don't you think?"

The Doctor squeezed his eyes shut as if trying to control his temper. Then, he opened his eyes and said, "Oleg was standing in front of the gate we use for the gangway when we dock. He was drunk. His blood alcohol level was so high he would have had trouble walking straight. He must have leaned against the gate, and it came loose. Either that or he jumped. Committed suicide. I don't know. He might have been worried about a debt he owed to some Russian thug he had hoped to cut in on a deal. Who knows, but to tell you the truth, I don't care. As for the previous captain, we all knew he was a drunk. We had nothing to do with his death or Oleg's. But I do know I did you a favor and filled out Oleg's death certificate to make it look like he had

CHAPTER THIRTY-EIGHT

a health issue and save *Athena* from inspection.

"Neil." The Professor looked pleadingly into Neil's eyes. "You know me, this is all a big misunderstanding."

"A misunderstanding?" Dede barged between Neil and the end of the booth, shoving Neil behind her. "You mean a misunderstanding over a four million dollar coin that you hid inside that awful bag Greta made? Did you really think I'd carry such a dreadful thing?"

Greta let go of her husband's hand. "You ungrateful oaf—"

"Ladies!" Neil pushed Dede aside. "The point here, Professor, is that we have the coin. You know it. We know it. And we also know about the hidden cache you've smuggled aboard Athena. The Golden Warrior. The priceless hoard of Greek and Roman antiquities you and the Inspector managed to peel off from that Camile and her former cohorts were charged with stealing from Geneva's Freeport. We know all about it and your plans to unload it in Alexandria. The thing is," Neil paused and smiled, "as you might expect, since we're standing here and Antonio, Inspector Garnier, and Sully aren't, it's not going to happen. You see, we've got your friends tied up downstairs, and unless you plan to make things difficult, this ends right now."

The Professor exhaled and, realizing he couldn't fight his way out, clasped his hands in front of him and put them down on the table. "You have to believe me, Neil. This was never my idea."

"I don't care whose idea it was. You used *Athena* to transport stolen goods across international waters and endangered her residents and my ship. There's no excuse, Professor." Neil looked back at me. "Kat, get some of that rope from your bag and tie his hands and Greta and Camile's too."

Camile put her hands behind her back. "No. Not until I see the Brutus Coin. If you've got it, I want to see it. I'm the one who found it in Geneva's Freeport. These jerks took it from me. It belongs to me. I don't care whose idea you think it was. I want to see the Brutus coin. If you've got it, show it to me. I don't believe you."

Dede took the backpack from my shoulder and slammed it on the table. "It's in here. You want to see it, you'll have plenty of opportunity once you're arrested. Now, put your hands out in front of you!"

Camile clenched her jaw. Her eyes searched the room, looking for escape.

Byard stepped closer to the table. "You're not going anywhere. Best you do as she says."

I took several pieces of the rope from my bag, secured the Professor's wrists, and was about to tie Greta up as well when Camile slapped her hands on the table.

I glanced over my shoulder. Captain Rob had entered the café and, seeing the four of us standing in front of the Professor's table, did an about-face. But not before Byard spotted him and gave chase.

With Byard out of her way and her hands-free, Camile grabbed my backpack and, being the athlete she was, jumped up on the table and made for the doorway. Realizing she had my camera, my notes, and most importantly, the Brutus coin hidden inside my camera's battery pack, I sprinted after her.

We got as far as Athena's stern. Camile climbed onto the railing, sat down, and hugged my backpack to her chest.

I doubled over, panting, my hands on my knees while I tried to catch my breath. "Give it up, Camile. It's over." Then, taking a few steps in her direction, I extended my hand.

"Stop! Don't come any further. I'll throw this bag and everything that's in it overboard, and then nobody will have the coin." Camile held her hand out and looked down at the water. Behind us, the Muse sailed quietly. Camile's eyes darted back to me. I could see she was debating whether or not to jump and make a wild swim for her lover's boat.

"Don't you dare," I screamed.

"Leave me alone!"

"It's a five-story drop to the water, Camile. You hit the water, it'll be like concrete."

Camile was breathing hard. The look in her eyes was frenzied. She opened my backpack and searched inside until she found the small, clear plastic baggie with the lithium battery inside. She grabbed it, probably thinking it was the Brutus coin, and stuffed it inside her bra. Then tossed my backpack onto the deck. "This isn't my fault, none of it. I didn't have anything to do with Oleg's murder. And I didn't kill Ida." Camile looked down at the water,

CHAPTER THIRTY-EIGHT

then back at me.

"Camile. Please, we can work this out."

"No." Camile shook her head. "No one would believe me. I took the Professor's signet ring the night of his lecture. It was mine. It belonged to me. Not Greta. She doesn't deserve it. And when my husband found out I had it, he took it from me. He told me I had to give it back. He killed Ida. Not me."

Camile looked back down at the water. Her movements were jerky. I could see the panic in her eyes.

"How did it happen?" I had to keep her talking. My only hope was that I might be able to talk her down.

"We were going to the Professor's cabin to return the ring. Ida was outside Dede's door. We could hear her talking about the Professor. She said he was a thief. That his collection was all stolen. It made Leon angry. He said she knew too much, and someone needed to shut her up."

"But how did Ida know?"

"Ask the Professor. Everyone thinks it was professional jealousy, but Ida knew the Professor couldn't have the things he had unless they had been stolen. Ida was the real historian. Not the Professor."

"So he killed her?"

"That's what I'm saying. We waited in the hallway until Dede had closed her door. When Ida saw us, she panicked. My husband tried to calm her and suggested we walk her back to her cabin. When we got to the elevator, he strangled her with her scarf, and when the doors opened, he dragged her body into the gym and stuffed her inside the isolation chamber. He threw the ring inside to make it look like she had found it. And then he tried to frame Marco for it."

I put both my hands out in front of me. "I believe you, Camile. The Inspector. The Professor. Antonio. They used you. I get it."

"How could you? You have no idea. After I was arrested for Geneva's robbery, Leon, my husband, that double-crossing conniving inspector, convinced me to betray my friends in exchange for his defense. He took my share of what I had hidden away, and now I'm his prisoner. But with this coin, I can buy my freedom." Camile patted her chest, then put her hand on the railing and started to stand.

"Wait! The coin." I had to keep her talking. "Why hide it in Dede's bag?"

"It was supposed to be proof of *Athena's* shipment. But when Dede didn't show up with the coin in Naples, the buyers got worried and called Antonio. Why do you think he's on board? He wasn't supposed to be. He came on in Ischia to make sure everything was okay, and when he met you, he worried you might be an investigator. So now you know." Camile turned her back to me, put her hands over her head, and did a swan dive off the railing."

"Camile, don't!"

Chapter Thirty-Nine

I raced to the railing. I don't know how long I stood there, staring out at the water, wondering if it were possible that Camile might have made the dive and not died trying. No matter how hard my eyes strained, searching the white churning waves behind us, I didn't see a body. Nor did I see her swimming.

"Kat." It was Neil. He put his hands on my shoulders, and I turned to him.

"She jumped." I covered my mouth with my hand. She couldn't possibly have survived.

"There was nothing you could do."

"Do you think she made it?"

"Maybe. Camile's made high dives like that before. She knew what she was doing. She's a strong swimmer."

I put my hands to my forehead and closed my eyes. I had never seen anyone jump to their death before. I wanted to erase the vision. Camile standing on the railing. Looking desperate. Holding my backpack in her hand, then tossing it onto the deck. I opened my eyes. The bag lay at my feet. The last thing she had touched. I picked it up, held it against my chest, and stared at the water. *The Muse* that had sailed behind us had slowed, and the distance between us grew until Athena's toy boat turned and headed in another direction.

"It's Carlo, he's getting away."

"He won't get far. We've got a tracker on board. Come with me. Professor Braun and Greta have been locked in their cabin, Captain Rob's been relieved of his duties, and Byard's back on the bridge where he belongs. Let's head back to Dede's cabin."

Residents had already begun their morning stroll along the Lido deck. A few had stopped to chat with each other, and as we passed, I noticed a few nervous looks. Judging from their whispers, they were aware something unusual had happened.

Neil put his arm around my shoulder and hustled me to the mid-deck elevator. "Don't worry, Kat. It'll all be fine. As soon as we get back to Dede's cabin, I'll make a ship-wide announcement to settle any rumors circulating. People are going to need to be reassured."

I didn't know what I expected to find when Neil and I arrived outside Dede's door. Across the hall, an armed guard stood outside the Brauns' cabin and nodded curtly to Neil as we passed. Neil returned the nod, didn't say anything, and knocked lightly on Dede's door. Elli answered. She looked relieved, kissed her cousin on the cheek, and stepped back so we could enter.

Irene was seated on the couch in the living room. Tatiana was on one of the small swivel chairs opposite her. On the bar was an open bottle of red wine, and from the kitchen, I could smell the warm scent of garlic bread and roasted tomatoes. Dede was cooking.

Dede came as far as the kitchen door, clutching a potholder. "I hope you're hungry. I called Chef Louie and had him send up what I needed to make lasagna. All this stress. We need to eat something. Give me a few minutes, and we can sit and discuss. Help yourself to a glass of wine or something harder if you like. We deserve it."

Neil excused himself, said he needed to take care of something, and went to Dede's house phone and called the Bridge. Moments later, he was patched into the ship's public address system.

"Ladies and Gentlemen, this is Neil Webster. I'm sorry to report that we've had an unfortunate incident aboard that requires Athena's immediate return to Naples. I apologize for the inconvenience. I'm sure you've heard some pretty wild rumors by now. News travels fast on a ship like this, but you have nothing to worry about. In fact, we actually have something to celebrate. Several residents, Dede Drummerhausen, Marco Marcopoulos, and our visiting travel writer, Kat Lawson, have been instrumental in uncovering

CHAPTER THIRTY-NINE

a smuggling operation aboard *Athena*. And, because of their bravery and personal sacrifice, I'm happy to say we're returning to Naples with those responsible and a cache of stolen antiquities. I want to thank them and each of you for your patience. We expect to reach Naples no later than five p.m., and we plan to resume our previously scheduled itinerary as soon as possible. In the meantime, to make up for this sudden change in our travel schedule, please visit any of *Athena's* restaurants. Her movie theater. The spa. Enjoy a swim in the pool. A massage, or if you like, a workout in the gym. It's on us, folks."

Neil hung up the phone, and I handed him a red wine. "The gym? I thought we left Antonio, Inspector Garnier, and Chief Sully tied up in the gym."

"We did. But Marco and Finn moved them to a more secure lock-up. They emptied several of the caged storage units and created a makeshift brig. Looks pretty good. And after Byard caught up with Captain Rob, I relieved him of his duties and sent Captain Rob and Doctor Jon to the Brig as well."

"So there's five of them downstairs. Four of the Gang of Eight, plus Captain Rob."

"That's right. And with Professor Braun and Greta confined to their cabin, we've got all but two. Carlo and Camile are on the run. That is if Camile's still alive. But we'll find out soon enough. *The Muse* can't pull into any port in the Med and not be noticed, and when she does, we'll have them as well."

"And Captain Rob? Do you think he was part of this all along?"

"I have trouble believing Captain Rob knew what was happening. But put enough money in front of someone, and you never know. Once Camile murdered Ida, and the Gang realized that Captain Byard might be suspicious of them, they made Captain Rob an offer he couldn't refuse."

"Maybe so, but it wasn't Camile who murdered Ida. It was her husband."

"Camile told you that?" Neil sounded surprised.

"Right before she jumped." I explained that Camile had confessed to me she had stolen the Professor's signet ring the night of his lecture and that when her husband found out, he had insisted she return it. "They were on their way to the Braun's apartment when they ran into Ida outside Dede's door and overheard Ida talking about some secret cache she thought the

Professor was smuggling."

"So, Inspector Garnier murdered Ida to shut her up."

"It looks that way. After taking the ring from Camile and strangling Ida, the Inspector threw the ring into the isolation tank. And when Sully found the Professor's signet ring in the tank, the Inspector told Camile not to worry. Everyone on board would think Ida had found Marco with the ring and that the two of them had argued, and Marco killed her. But however it happened, I don't believe Ida's murder was planned. And much as I don't like to agree with Antonio, I believe him when he says they're thieves and not murderers. I don't think he knows that it was the Inspector who killed Ida. None of them would have wanted to risk an investigation or being stuck in Positano. And when Captain Byard refused to leave Positano until investigators had come on board—"

"Antonio got worried." Neil touched his brow. It had started to swell. "The Gang couldn't risk any of their cache being uncovered, so Antonio organized a mutiny. He cut a deal with Captain Rob and put him in command. Once Rob was in command, I was called to the Bridge. And by the time I arrived, Captain Byard had been overpowered. His hands were tied behind his back, and someone knocked me over the head. Next thing I know, I'm sitting on the gym floor."

"Neil?" Dede's voice echoed from the kitchen. "I need a word, please. Could you come here?"

"If you'll excuse me. I'm being summoned." Neil headed to the kitchen. I followed, stopping at the dining table to grab a couple of grapes, then leaned against the archway between the kitchen and dining area, where I was close enough to eavesdrop on their conversation. I still had a lot of questions about Neil Webster and Dede Drummerhausen.

"Does this mean it's over?" Dede closed the oven door and wiped her hands on her apron.

"I think so, but we'll know more when we get to Naples and the investigators have had a chance to go through *Athena's* hold."

"Then I think you should take these now." Dede took the salt grinder off the counter, unscrewed the bottom, and emptied its contents into her hand.

CHAPTER THIRTY-NINE

"Here, just in case."

Neil slipped what looked like a handful of white diamonds into his pocket, then looked over his shoulder and, seeing me, took a step back and exhaled.

"Damn it, Kat. It's not what you think."

"I'm not sure what to think."

Neil reached back into his pocket and held out a small mound of diamonds. "If you think they're stolen, you'd be right. They're part of what Marco took from my father's safe before my uncle claimed my inheritance."

"And…Dede has your diamonds because?"

"It's complicated."

I was about to ask how complicated when Marco and Finn entered the apartment. Neil put the diamonds back in his pocket. Finn went immediately to Neil and hugged him.

"You okay?" Finn touched Neil's head and looked into his eyes.

"It's nothing. I'll be fine. What's happening below?" Neil took Finn's hands from his head. "Your makeshift brig okay? No possibility of a breakout?"

"Not a chance. Captain Byard sent a couple of armed midshipmen down to relieve us. There's no way any of them are getting away."

I left Neil and Finn and joined Marco at the bar. "I owe you. I don't think I'd be here if it weren't for you."

"Probably not." Marco filled a glass of wine and tipped it to me. "But then, if Inspector Garnier had had his way, Dede and I might be the ones investigators would want to talk to regarding Ida's murder. But I trust you've determined I had nothing to do with it by now."

"Camile confirmed it. Right before she took a swan dive off the Lido Deck."

Marco laughed.

I punched his shoulder. "How can you be so cavalier?"

"I've seen her take that dive before. I wouldn't worry. Right now, she's probably sipping champagne with Carlo. And good for her. The Gang used her. The woman was nothing but a tool for them. And before them, it was somebody else who used her. I never thought she was a bad sort. Just unhappy."

I glanced over my shoulder at Irene. She was sitting alone on the couch and caught my eye. She motioned for me to tap Marco on the shoulder.

"Marco, I think Irene wants to talk to you."

Marco and I sat on the sofa with Irene in between us. She looked tired and rested her hand on Marco's knee as she spoke.

"I want you to know, Marco, I never thought you had anything to do with stealing Professor Braun's ring."

"Well, thank you. But to be honest, I do happen to have the ring." Marco reached into his pocket, took out the gold signet ring, and held it between his thumb and index finger. "I didn't take it the night of the Professor's lecture. I'll admit I was tempted, but Camile got it. Looked better on her small hand anyway. But after Finn and I tied Sully and others up, I realized Sully had taken the ring off Ida's body and, given the chance, probably would have kept it. I found it in his pocket and took it back to give it to Neil."

"Is this the ring?" Tatiana stood up from the swivel chair where she had been sitting and plucked the ring from Marco's hand. "Doesn't look like much to me."

"It's not," Irene said. "At least it's not as valuable as the Professor would have you think. In fact, it's not a man's ring at all. It's why Professor Braun wore it on his pinky finger. He liked to tell everyone the ring belonged to some wealthy noble Roman senator. Thought it made him more important than the rest of us. But my sister knew better."

"Why?" I asked. "Is it a fake?"

"No, it's real. Signet rings have been around for thousands of years. The ancient Egyptians, Greeks, and Romans all had them. They were used as seals and dipped into wax to secure important documents. Look, the intaglio or the design of each ring was unique." Irene pointed to the delicate gold filigree on the face of the ring in Tatiana's hand. "And when the wearer died, the ring was destroyed. The Romans started using gemstones instead of metal to carve their designs into the ring, and at one point, every Roman senator wore one to signify his status. But Professor Braun's ring never belonged to some Roman senator. It was a woman's ring. Ida knew because of the design. Senator's rings depicted their rank and status. The design on

CHAPTER THIRTY-NINE

the Professor's ring is of a bunch of grapes. A ring a wife might wear to seal jars of oil or wine. A common custom back then to ensure the household help wasn't stealing."

"Speaking of which," Neil approached Tatiana from the kitchen and held out his hand. "I'll need the Professor's ring to give to the authorities when we get to Naples."

Tatiana took one last look at the ring, then placed it in Neil's palm. "Here. You can have it back. But there's something else you should see. I believe it's connected to my father's death, and I should maybe show it to you before I show it to the police and they charge you with my father's murder."

Chapter Forty

"Tatiana," I stepped between Neil and Tatiana. "I told you before, I was with Neil the night your father died. He couldn't have—"

"You need to look at *Athena's* ledgers." Tatiana interrupted. "Every time I bring it up, someone changes the subject. I don't believe any of you. I've looked at the numbers. They don't lie." Tatiana sat down and pulled one of the two large ledger books she had brought from her father's apartment off the coffee table onto her lap.

Neil took the chair beside her. "Where did you get these?"

They were in my father's cabin. You appointed him as *Athena's* bookkeeper. You can't be surprised I'd find them. But maybe you don't know he mentions to me you have financial trouble. But until I see the books, I didn't know to what extent."

Neil took the book from Tatiana's lap. "This was a private matter, Tatiana. It has nothing to do with your father's death."

"I'm not so sure. Two sets of books? Is odd to me. One shows healthy profit. The other shows *Athena* is bleeding money. I'm sure I don't need to tell you these books could be evidence *Athena* is in trouble. Which investigators might consider motive. If not for smuggling, then maybe my father's murder."

"Tatiana, please." Neil tapped his fingers anxiously on top of the ledger. "I didn't kill your father. But you're right, the books don't lie, money is tight. It always has been. I've had to be creative about financing to keep *Athena* afloat. But your father understood that. He was a master at it himself. You mustn't forget he was the one who helped facilitate the Pepsi Navy. Without

CHAPTER FORTY

him, there would be no *Athena*."

"Don't lie to me."

"I'm not lying, Tatiana. You're right about the books. One shows *Athena* clearly in the black. Making money. An investor's dream. But the truth is, *Athena* is a high-risk proposition. She's losing money every quarter and much more so lately. The second set of books shows a business drowning in debt. And I've had to subsidize those losses with assets from The Webster Group. But it doesn't prove I killed your father or had him murdered."

"I think I'll let police decide that." Tatiana stood up and, with both hands, yanked the book from Neil.

"No!" Finn crossed from the bar behind them and took hold of the ledger. "You won't do anything of the kind. There's no need. Neil didn't have anything to do with your father's death. I did. I killed Oleg!"

"Finn! What are you saying? Why would you do such a thing?" Neil was on his feet.

"Because Oleg was blackmailing you. I heard him. I was in his apartment to drop off some dry cleaning, and I saw him with the ledgers on his desk and heard him yelling on the phone. I thought it was you he was talking to. I didn't know anything about the Gang of Eight, what they were doing, or any Russian thug from his past. All I knew was that Oleg sounded angry. He was arguing about money. Said that he needed more to keep his mouth shut and that if he didn't get it, he'd expose everything, and you'd be ruined. I thought it was you Oleg was talking to. So, the next time I came in the cabin, I went looking for the ledgers, and from what I could see, Oleg could do real damage if he wanted." Finn tore the book from Tatiana's hand and threw it on the floor. "I did it for you, Neil. I knew Oleg was up to something, and the night of the Professor's lecture, he was acting strangely. And when I heard him outside the lecture hall tell Kat he had stories she wouldn't believe, I figured it was you he was talking about. All I could think was that I needed to protect you. So I lured him up to the gangway gate on the Lido Deck the night of your dinner party with Kat and Antonio. I told him I had a bottle of Stoli and invited him to share it with me. Oleg loved his vodka, and I knew he wouldn't turn me down. It was after Happy Hour by the time he

213

got upstairs, and he had already had a couple of drinks. I had used my key to unlock the gangway gate where we planned to meet, so the railing was already loose. It was all so easy. We had a couple of drinks. Oleg finished a cigarette, then leaned against the railing, and over he went. I closed the gate, locked it, and went downstairs to finish my evening rounds."

"You killed him!" Tatiana screamed and lunged at Finn.

Marco lept over the coffee table and grabbed Tatiana's hands from Finn's neck. "Stop it! We've had enough murders aboard *Athena* for now."

Finn reeled around, his hands on his throat, and pleaded with Neil. "I did it for you. I thought I was protecting you."

Neil took Finn by the shoulder. "Why didn't you come to me?"

"How could I come to you? Antonio's been on board all week, and you're seldom around anymore. Always off somewhere trying to raise money. I thought I was helping you and we'd have time together again when Antonio left. And without Oleg's threats, you could relax, and we'd be fine."

"I'm sorry, Finn." Neil pulled Finn close to him and kissed his ear. "I should have realized how difficult this was for you. I came back for Ida's birthday. I really thought we'd have time, but when Antonio showed up…" Neil shook his head. "I had no idea why he was really here. And I was happy to welcome him aboard for a few days."

Finn brushed his eyes. "I screwed up. I'm sorry."

"I'm sorry too, Finn. I never wanted it to end this way." Neil took a deep breath and asked Marco to take Finn back to his cabin. "Make sure he stays there and that no one bothers him. I'll deal with him later."

Neil excused himself and went outside to Dede's deck. I was tempted to follow, but Dede called me to the kitchen, where she had busied herself rinsing utensils in the sink.

"You heard?" I asked.

"Finn's confession to Oleg's murder? Unfortunately, yes. Although, I can't say I'm surprised." Dede grabbed a towel and mopped the countertops as she spoke. "Finn was dogged in his determination to look after Neil, and once Antonio came on board, Finn wasn't thinking straight. I'm sure Finn thought Oleg was blackmailing Neil. I'm surprised, nosy as Finn is, that he

CHAPTER FORTY

didn't know what was happening with the Gang of Eight. But then, why didn't I? I could kick myself. I suppose I'm getting old. At least Finn has an excuse. Poor man, who of us hasn't been blinded by love."

"Do you think Neil will turn him in?"

"I do." Dede tossed the dish towel into the sink. "Much as it will pain him to do so, Neil won't let his emotions get in the way. If there is one thing I know about Neil Webster, he'll do what's right. As for you, Kat Lawson, I can't help but wonder what you will do. We should be in Naples within the hour, and soon, if not today, you'll be off. I don't know what'll happen when the authorities come on board, but I hope you'll …. ugh! I don't know what I hope you'll do. It wasn't my plan for you to experience a mutiny on board. We're ordinarily such a quiet group. Some are a little peculiar. But, all in all, I thought we were content to sail peacefully into our sunset years. I certainly never suspected any piracy. And I had hoped your article might convince other retirees to join us and help fill the vacancies on board. But now? I don't know what you'll do or what to tell you, but I do hope you'll talk to Neil before writing about what you've seen."

I thanked Dede and joined Neil on the deck. He stared at the Naples port ahead, buzzing with the sights and sounds of a busy harbor. Ships' horns. Seagulls. The jarring noise of tall tower cranes loading and unloading containers from various vessels. I grabbed the railing and looked down at the water. Small black whirlpools formed around *Athena's* hull as she maneuvered toward her birth beneath a sky of thin white clouds. Ahead, a dock had been cleared for our arrival. Longshoremen stood ready to grab ropes from *Athena's* crew while police and plain-clothed investigators stood directly behind them, waiting.

"You got a moment?" I let go of the rail and rubbed my hands together.

"Yeah. I know. We have to talk. You've got questions."

"The diamonds Dede gave you? What's that all about? Why did she have them?"

"I told you, it's complicated. But it's not illegal. The diamonds are mine. They were in my father's safe when my parents died. Marco had been working for my uncle and my father. He was their chief financial officer. I don't know all the details. I was very young, but I do know that Marco told me my uncle and father had been arguing over restructuring the company. Their relationship was very acrimonious, and Marco was suspicious of my uncle. When my parents' plane crashed, Marco arranged to have some diamonds he had found in my father's safe smuggled out of the country while he was still working for my uncle. It wasn't until I graduated college, and my uncle cut me off, that Marco flew to London and gave them to me, explaining they were part of what should have been my inheritance. When my uncle realized what Marco had done, he fired him. He claimed Marco had stolen the diamonds and had fled to France, where he was caught trying to sell diamonds on the black market. The police arrested Marco, and he was found guilty and ended up in Fleury-Mérogis. The thing is, Marco never would have spent a day behind bars if it weren't for me. The only reason he was caught was because he was trying to liquidate the diamonds he found in my father's safe so that I'd have enough cash to set up Webster Investment. The few diamonds left I've used as security."

"Which explains why Marco's here."

"And why Dede has always been suspicious of Marco. Even after I went into business with Walter and used the diamonds to secure our partnership, she was uneasy about him. She's never trusted him."

"I don't suppose the fact that he sleepwalks naked or has a reputation as a kleptomaniac helps."

"I've never been sure about any of that. I certainly never saw signs of it growing up or heard a word about it from my parents. It wasn't until Dede forbade Walter or me from hiring Marco after he was out of prison that he started acting out. And to be honest, I think he enjoys the notoriety it affords him. It allows him his privacy."

"And what about the diamonds? Why did Dede have them hidden in a saltshaker?"

"Like I told you, they were security. They've been hidden there since day one. I have full access to Dede's account. Walter set it up that way. He knew I'd take care of her, and when I needed cash to keep things afloat, I transferred it from one account to the other. The diamonds are Dede's security. There's

CHAPTER FORTY

more than enough value in what's in my pocket than I've ever borrowed from her account. But it would look suspicious if the diamonds were found. Particularly right now."

I looked down at the dock. One of *Athena's* crew had tossed a mooring line to a longshoreman, and he had secured it to a bollard on the deck. The gate on *Athena's* Promenade Deck would open in a few minutes, and a portable ramp would be put in place.

Neil tapped the railing with his fist. "I need to be at the gate when Captain Byard welcomes the Port Authority on board. They'll have a lot of questions. Come with me."

I grabbed my backpack, more importantly, I took my camera from inside my bag and strung it around my neck. I wanted to ensure I had the Brutus Coin I had hidden inside my camera's battery pack with me when I met with the authorities.

Chapter Forty-One

Within minutes of *Athena's* gangplank being put in place, Captain Byard welcomed the Port Authority and three uniformed officers, all heavily armed and dressed in blue military attire, complete with berets. Following them up the ramp were several plainclothed detectives and members of Italy's Carabinieri, responsible for protecting Italy's cultural heritage.

Upon spotting Neil and me on the Promenade Deck, Byard waved us over to the gangway where the head of the Port Authority stood with a clipboard. Neil signed several forms, then asked for the Carabinieri to follow him to *Athena's* makeshift brig while four members of the Port Authority took up position at the gate, two at the base of the bridge and two on top. It was clear to anyone watching that this was not a casual tourist stop.

Residents were advised via a ship-wide announcement that due to the unusual nature of our arrival at the Port of Naples, no one would be allowed to leave *Athena* until she had been officially cleared. Which meant I wasn't getting off the ship anytime soon. With Captain Byard busy talking with investigators and Neil on his way downstairs to collect Antonio and his crew of henchmen, I headed to the grand lobby.

Despite the unexpected activity on board, the lobby was empty. Residents, suddenly aware *Athena* had been boarded by police and investigators, were understandably quiet, and most had locked themselves in their cabins while investigators roamed the ship, checking for stolen artifacts. I sat on the side of the reflecting pool surrounding the giant Athena statue and took my phone from my backpack.

CHAPTER FORTY-ONE

For the first time in more than a week, I had a good signal. I decided now would be a smart time to check in with my publisher and let her know that this little pleasure cruise she had sent me on as a reward for my previous undercover assignments had been anything but the R&R she had promised.

Sophie answered like she was expecting me.

"So, how's the R&R going, Kat? Ready to get back to work?"

"Actually, I was calling to tell you this wasn't the rest and relaxation cruise you described."

Sophie chuckled. "What happened? You get sunburned?"

"No. "I snapped. "Hijacked. Or maybe the more correct term would be mutinied. *Athena* was taken over by smugglers—a group of greedy seniors—who pirated a previously stolen cache of old-world antiquities from a Geneva Freeport. They were planning to sell it on the black market."

I paused and waited for Sophie's response. There was nothing.

"Sophie?"

"You do seem to find trouble, Kat."

I choked back a laugh. "Me? Yeah, well, this time, it found me. I didn't go looking for it."

The elevator doors chimed, and I told Sophie I would have to call her back. Neil, along with several midshipmen, all pushing hand trucks loaded with boxes, exited the elevator. I stuffed my phone back inside my bag.

"What are those?"

"What do you think?" Neil stopped and wiped his brow. "Boxes of stolen artifacts. Brass plates. Coins. Jewelry. And there's more to come."

"Where were they?"

"Inside the storage lockers. Marco and Finn found them when they cleared out the cages to create a makeshift brig. There's a lot. Boxes marked books, Christmas decorations, old clothes, and the like, all stuffed in different cages. Together, there are probably close to a hundred boxes. Going through them will take a while, but I think we've got the Gang of Eight's cache."

"What about the Golden Warrior?" None of the boxes were big enough to carry a life-sized bronze statue.

"We haven't found it yet. But we'll keep looking."

The elevator doors opened again, and Antonio, Inspector Garnier, Sully, Doctor Jon, and Captain Rob, handcuffed and tethered together, were shuffled into the lobby with the Carabinieri at their sides. I stood rigid as the group passed in front of me. Their eyes, all except for Sully's, were cast downward. It was just a flicker, but enough that I felt it might be a tell. I followed his upward glance to the Athena statue. Like a transparent silk screen, her waterfall of glass beads draped from the ceiling to the floor, the perfect barrier, had prevented anyone from getting too close.

I stepped out in front of the group. "Stop!"

The Carabinieri halted, and for a moment, I thought they might draw their guns. But Neil was quick to act and, taking me by the elbow, pulled me back toward him.

"Kat, what are you doing?"

"Whoa!" Captain Byard entered the lobby and, seeing what looked like a standoff with Neil pulling me away from the handcuffed suspects and the Carabinieri with their hands on their guns, stepped in between us. "What's going on here?"

"It's Sully," I said. "He knows where the Gold Warrior statue's hidden."

Sully sneered. "I don't know what she's talking about."

"Oh yes, you do." I reminded Byard of my first day on board when we stood on the Promenade Deck, and Sully approached. He explained that our delayed departure from Naples the night before was due to the late arrival of the Athena statue. "It was you who told me Neil liked to have the ship decorated with art representative of the area where we sail, and for whatever reason, the Athena statue had arrived late."

Byard's eyes went to the statue. "And you think the Golden Warrior's hidden inside?"

"I'd bet on it. In fact, I can do better than that. I can prove it." I reached for my backpack and took out the cheese knife the Chef had given me. If the statue was marble, my knife wouldn't make a scratch. But if it was a cheap copy, made of Plaster of Paris, I'd know in seconds.

Neil took the knife from my hand. "Oh no, you don't. If that's real, I'm not paying for it." Then, addressing the armed guards, he nodded to the statue.

CHAPTER FORTY-ONE

"You're the Carabinieri. You're responsible for protecting Italy's antiquities. That thing look real to you?"

"That?" The guard closest to me pointed his gun at the statue. "That's a plaster cast, probably made somewhere around Rome. You can find it anywhere. This stuff here in the boxes, it's real. But that statue, it's a cheap copy."

Neil walked closer to the statue and yanked a section of the beaded curtain from the ceiling.

"You think the Golden Warrior might be hiding inside the Athena statue?"

"I'm sure of it." I went to the wall where a fire ax was mounted, but before I could remove it, Neil put his hands on top of mine and stopped me.

"If you're going to do this, Kat, I think Dede, Elli, and Tatiana should be here."

I let go of the ax.

"And Marco, as well," I said. "In fact, I think everyone on board should see what treasures were hidden in *Athena's* hull and destined to be sold on the black market. And I want pictures and lots of them. I want to document everything." I focused my camera on the giant statue.

Neil folded his arms across his chest. For a moment, I thought he would deny my request and remind me that I had crossed a line. That I knew too much about Neil and his past. His uncle's scheme to disinherit him from the family business. The stolen diamonds Neil had used to leverage his investments. Neil Webster wasn't one of the world's wealthiest men but a venture capitalist, running a high-stakes investment firm, shuffling his finances to balance his books to keep his investors happy. The story I would write would expose not only a cache of stolen antiquities but also the truth about Neil.

But then he nodded.

"Captain Byard, get a couple of midshipmen to help the Carabinieri. Tell them to bring up all the boxes from below and stack them here where we can see them. And make a ship-wide announcement. I want everyone on board in the lobby, including Captain Rob, Finn, and the entire Gang of Eight, to see this."

221

***

While waiting for the lobby to fill with more boxes from *Athena*'s storage lockers, I slipped the Brutus Coin from inside my camera's battery compartment into my pocket and began to shoot pictures of those boxes that had been opened. Exposed were ancient red clay pots, once used to store wine and olive oil, elaborate stone and bronze death masks, like that I had seen in Neil's apartment, a gift from Antonio. Gold wreaths, like Greta had worn the night of her husband's lecture. Beaded necklaces. Several bronze shields, daggers, and small stone and bronze figures that I wondered if might once have been a child's toy or maybe ancient idols. Enough artifacts to fill a museum.

When the lobby had filled with boxes and residents, and those handcuffed few the Carabinieri had arrested, I went back to the wall and took the ax from its mount. I felt like Geraldo Rivera, about to expose Al Capone's Vault. Fifteen years ago, I had watched Geraldo's live broadcast from the basement of a walled-off room beneath the Lexington Hotel in Chicago that was once owned by the famous gangster. The show had been hyped, anticipation was high, and Geraldo's reward was disappointing. There was nothing inside the vault save for a couple of empty bottles of moonshine. Like Geraldo, I had gathered a live audience, convinced them all I knew where the Golden Warrior was hidden, and hoped I wouldn't be as equally disappointed.

I glanced back at Dede. She stood toward the front of the group, with Elli, Irene, and Tatiana at her side. Dede gave me a thumbs up.

With the ax firmly in my hands, I stepped into the small reflecting pool beneath Athena, took a deep breath, and aimed for the shield Athena held in her left hand. The ax smashed through her arm and severed the plaster mold from her statuesque pose, revealing a hollow infrastructure that quickly caved as I hacked away at her lower skirt. It didn't take, but a few strokes before we could all see that hidden within the folds of Athena's skirt was a second statue wrapped tightly in muslin.

"How about you take it from here." I handed the ax to Neil, who quickly destroyed Athena's plaster mold while I snapped several shots for my story.

CHAPTER FORTY-ONE

When it was apparent there was nothing more to destroy, Neil stepped from the shallow water well and invited the Carabinieri to finish the job. Slowly, they chipped away Athena's remains until they could lift the muslin-clad statue free. Then, cutting the protective cloth away, they set the life-sized, naked warrior statue up for us all to see.

I had never seen such a statue. The strength that emanated from the bronze was more powerful than the metal itself. The warrior's stance. His muscled torso. The craftsmanship was jaw-dropping.

Neil put his arm around my shoulder. "And that, Kat, is why I want you to tell your story. The third Riace Bronze. Until today, I never believed it really existed. Antonio used to tell me he was with the group that found the first two. He said it was the most important discovery he had ever made."

"How did he find it?"

"He said he had been snorkeling with friends off of the coast of Riace in Southern Italy, back in the early 70s, when they thought they spotted a body. It was the left arm of one of the two Riace Warrior statues. Antonio hinted there was a third statue, but only two were found when dive teams were dispatched to recover them. The third had magically disappeared. It's believed that twenty-five hundred years ago, the statues were transported aboard a ship that had sunk and remained submerged for thousands of years. Ironically, that may have saved them. Bronze statues were frequently melted down for their metals in factories like you saw in Aenaria."

"And you think Antonio hid it all these years?"

"It was his security. Inspector Garnier had his cache of stolen artifacts from the Geneva Freeport. And Antonio had the third Riace Bronze. Together, they could make millions. All they needed was the right buyer."

"And the right opportunity to get it there." Dede bumped my shoulder and held out the palm of her hand. "I think it's time, Kat, we gave up the coin to the Carabinieri. That is unless you were planning on keeping it as a souvenir."

Chapter Forty-Two

"You didn't really think I'd keep it, did you?" I reached into my pocket and handed the coin to Dede.

"No. But I'd just as soon give it the Carabinieri and be done with it."

Dede closed her hand around the coin, turned her back to me, and strode over to one of the Carabinieri, whom I assumed had to be the ranking officer, and handed him the coin. He looked at it, then at Dede as though he couldn't believe what he had been given, and frowned. There was a mumbled exchange. Dede shrugged, gave him one of her sweet little old lady grins, and then returned to where I stood.

"That's it?" I asked. "You just gave him the coin?"

"Why not? I told him I'd found it in my bag and wanted to return it."

"And he didn't ask anything else?"

"What could he ask. He's got a shipload of stolen goods and a group of thieves to deal with. Seems to me he has his hands full. Besides, I told him I had a lasagna in the oven, and if he wants to join us for dinner, he was welcome. Aside from that, I'm tired of all the stress and worry this Gang of Eight—"

"Nine," I said. "Captain Rob appears to have been a part."

"Whatever. I'm tired of their antics and thievery and want it behind me. I didn't sign on for such. And you, Neil Webster," Dede poked her index finger into Neil's chest, "you need to start spending more time onboard. Irene's going to need you, and it looks to me like we'll have a few more empty cabins. You'll have to get busy training someone to take Oleg's place.

CHAPTER FORTY-TWO

Elli perhaps. The girl's bright, and I think she'd do fine. As for that Seniors at Sea story, Kat, hopefully, you'll write a nice travel feature about *Athena's* spectacular amenities. Something that might help us find some well-to-do retired couples who might like to join us. No more of this highfalutin arrogant riff-faff, if you will. Now, if you'll excuse me, I have a table to set and a lasagna in the oven, and I don't plan to let it burn. I hate when it's crispy."

Dede left the lobby with Elli and Tatiana. Neil, Captain Byard, and I stayed behind while the Carabinieri supervised loading boxes from the lobby floor and down the gangway to their awaiting vans on the dock. When the lobby floor had been cleared of all the boxes, and special care had been taken to rewrap the Golden Warrior statue and place it in a van all by itself, the police turned their attention back to their handcuffed charges. Antonio. Sully. Inspector Garnier. Captain Rob and Doctor Jon. All sat defiantly on the floor next to Professor Braun and Greta. I snapped a dozen more shots. Not one of them looked in my direction. Then, getting them to their feet, with their hands behind their backs and their feet bound, the police duckwalked them through the lobby, out onto the deck, and down the gangplank, where they were loaded into a special bus with barred windows and flashing white lights.

Neil picked the ax up off the floor and handed it to Byard. "I'll need to go with them. But first, there's one last thing I need to do. Have you seen Marco?"

"He's with Finn." Byard nodded to the port side exit door where the two men stood. "They're waiting for you."

"If you'll excuse me. I've some business to take care of." Neil started to walk away, then stopped. "Before I go...Kat, there's something I want to say. I know I've been secretive about my past, but I want to thank you. I don't know when I'll be back on board or if you'll still be here when I return. But I appreciate the risks you took. We might not have caught this group if it hadn't been for you. And I know you'll write whatever story you want about what happened here, and if you still want to interview me for a business feature, I'm all yours. I can't think of another reporter I'd trust with what you know. So, call me when you're ready, and we'll talk. I'll give you an exclusive. You deserve it."

Neil hugged me goodbye, and I wiped a tear away as he let go. My throat was so tight I could barely say thank you.

I watched as Neil approached Finn. It was an emotional greeting and parting. Finn was crying. Neil reached into his pocket for a handkerchief and, handing it to Finn, whispered something into his ear. Then, nodding to Marco, Neil gestured to the doorway where two plain-clothed detectives were waiting.

I swallowed hard. I had covered homicides before and, at times, been surprised when I discovered the victim's assailant. I had no idea Finn had killed Oleg. Not until Finn had confessed did I wonder that if I had known what Finn was thinking, I might have been able to say something to stop him.

"What's going to happen to him?"

"I don't know." Byard shook his head. "There's not much Neil can do about it. Finn will turn himself in, and then it'll be up to the courts."

"*Athena* won't be the same without him."

"You okay?" Byard raised a brow.

"I will be."

"Good. I'll be up on the Bridge if you need anything."

I took one last look at the lobby, its sweeping two-story staircase now empty. The water fountain where the giant gold Athena statue had reigned over the room was in shambles. Bits and pieces of broken plaster lay on the floor, scuffed with the black markings of police boots and trolleys loaded with items removed from *Athena's* storage lockers. Outside the lobby's double doors, beyond the Promenade Deck, I could hear the sounds of seagulls and the blast of horns from ships coming into Naples' harbor. It was over. The Gang of Eight had failed. Antonio, Inspector Garnier, Sully, Doctor Jon, Professor Braun, Greta, and Captain Rob had all been arrested. Finn was off to be prosecuted for Oleg's murder. And with any luck, Carlo and Camile wouldn't get far before the Carabinieri would pick them up.

I walked out onto the deck. I needed to call Sophie back. I checked my

CHAPTER FORTY-TWO

phone. The signal was strong. I wanted to finish our conversation, but not before I took one final, swift walk around the Promenade Deck to clear my head. Sophie said I had a way of finding trouble. She wasn't wrong. But I like to think that maybe trouble had found me and that I had turned it into an opportunity. I had come for one story, and now I had three: a feature about *Athena's* Seniors at Sea program, a story about an organized group of seniors who were smuggling a hot horde of stolen antiquities across the Mediterranean, and a third story I never dreamed I'd get, an exclusive feature about Neil Webster.

I took a deep breath and quickened my pace. I wanted to do at least three laps around the deck before I went back to Dede's suite. I was into my second lap when I heard Byard call my name.

"Kat! Hold up a minute."

I stopped midship and looked behind me. Byard stood outside the small staff-only stairway door that led to the Bridge. He looked winded, like he had raced down the thin inside metal stairway to catch me.

"What's up?" I took several steps in his direction.

Byard jogged toward me, then stopped to catch his breath. "I thought you'd want to know. The carabinieri picked up Carlo and Camile a few minutes ago."

"Where?"

"Sicily. They were in Marsala when the police found them."

"I suppose in some ways that's good news. At least Camile didn't die, and the carabinieri got them all."

"All that we know about. There's bound to be more. Those who Antonio worked with who promised connections to a network of collectors and ready cash from black market investors." Byard nodded toward *Athena's* stern, and we walked slowly until we came to the railing.

"It's such a waste," I said. I crossed my arms and stared out at the water.

"What's that?"

"Smuggling. Stealing from the past. Robbing from the future. Marco calls it a cultural homicide. Look around. We're floating above ancient civilizations and sunken ships with treasures dating back thousands of years.

Things we could learn so much from, but for those who would rob us of our history for the sake of greed."

"You're sounding very philosophical, Kat."

"I'm going to miss this." I wrapped my fingers around the railing and stared out at the Med's lapis blue water.

"Why don't you stay on awhile? I've convinced Neil we should bypass Alexandria for the time being and head for the Greek Isles. It won't be as exciting as what you've experienced so far. But then, I don't think that's what you want, and if you haven't seen the islands, you should reward yourself with a little R&R."

I laughed. "A little R&R is what got me into this in the first place."

A breeze picked up and blew my hair into my eyes. Byard swept it from my face, and for a split second, when I looked at him, I thought I saw my first husband.

"I promise you, no hijackings. No pirates. No hidden treasures in *Athena's* hull. Just a nice… restful…maybe…romantic week?"

"Romantic?" Could I really do this again? Was it Byard, or was it the uniform? The somewhat familiar smile? My stomach filled with butterflies.

Byard put my hand on his chest. "If you like."

I kissed him lightly on the lips, and he kissed me back. I could have lost myself in his arms for the moment and forgotten everything. Except when I opened my eyes, it wasn't Byard's face I saw, but Eric's. The husband I had lost to a senseless war. Forever MIA. A hot shot Air Force pilot. Shot down over Hanoi four weeks before the end of a war that forever changed my life.

My phone rang.

"Excuse me. I'm going to have to take this. It's my publisher."

Byard stepped back. "You're not going to stay on, are you?"

I raised my brows. "I want to, but—"

"It's okay." Byard tilted his head and smiled. Eric's smile. The same familiar smile I missed so much. "Consider it an open invitation."

I watched as Byard turned and walked away. Part of me wanted to stop him, but I knew I couldn't.

I put the phone to my ear. "Hi, Sophie?"

CHAPTER FORTY-TWO

"Kat, I need you to take the next flight back to New York. We've got another assignment. Southeast Asia. And this one is dangerous. Get yourself home. We've got work to do."

A Note from the Author

I was on a family vacation aboard the *Queen Mary 2*, doing a crossing from New York to South Hampton when the idea hit me that murder aboard a cruise ship was too good of an idea to pass up. It's not a particularly original idea, I'll admit. But…what if the cruise ship was a group of seniors who lived aboard and could chart their own destinations?

What fun would that be!

My muse had captured my attention, and the next thing I knew, I was interviewing the captain, the ship's mates, and security. I had researched the ship from the bridge to her bowels, and my mind was percolating with ideas.

I jotted a few character sketches down on my notepad, and as soon as I got home, I headed for the library. Thus began my research. My background is in news and talk radio, and I know firsthand the best stories are those you can't make up. I needed a hook, some historical event I could pull from to make *Murder on the Med* significant to my readers.

And the more I researched, the more excited I got. The Kat Lawson mysteries take place in the late '90s and early 2000s, ten years after the fall of the Soviet Union. The Russian Navy, or much of what was left of it, was in shambles. And there began my story. The Pepsi Navy. A joint venture between the Soviets, Pepsi, and a Norwegian company for the trade of the rusted hulls of soviet ships in exchange for past due payments due to Pepsi. Suddenly, I had my ship, the *Athena*, or her hull anyway. Now, I just needed to blend the lines of history with my fictional characters. And where better to do it than to trace the Silk Highway across the Mediterranean?

The Med, or the Middle Sea, as my fictional character Professor Braun likes to say, was the passageway, the primary trading route from Asia to

Europe, connecting three great continents: the Far East, Africa, and Europe. And beneath her shores lie lost cities and sunken treasures, rich in historical significance and prized artifacts – targeted items for modern-day pirates like those greedy seniors aboard *Athena*.

The Riace Bronzes, or the Naked Bearded Warriors, were believed to have been cast around 460-450 BC and were found off the shores of Calabria in southern Italy in 1972 but did not emerge until 1981. During that time, it was suspected that a third bronze statue had disappeared. As to where it's gone, we may never know. Today, two of the warrior statues are on display in the Museo Nazionale della Magna Grecia in the city of Reggio, Calabria.

The more I researched, the more excited I got as *Murder on the Med* started to take shape on the page. It's my goal as a writer to revisit history, to wrap my stories around facts that keep historical events alive, and to preserve artifacts that belong not just to the past but to the future. To lose them is a cultural homicide we cannot afford.

About the Author

Nancy Cole Silverman spent nearly twenty-five years in news and talk radio before retiring to write fiction. Silverman's award-winning short stories and crime-focused novels, the Carol Childs and Misty Dawn Mysteries (Henry Press), are based in Los Angeles, while her newest series, the Kat Lawson Mysteries (Level Best Books), takes a more international approach. Kat Lawson, a former investigative reporter has gone undercover for the FBI as a feature writer for a travel publication. Expect lots of international intrigue, vivid descriptions of small European villages, great food, lost archives, and non-stop action. Silverman lives in Los Angeles with her husband and thoroughly pampered standard poodle, Paris.

AUTHOR WEBSITE:
   www.nancycolesilverman.com

Also by Nancy Cole Silverman

The Kat Lawson Mysteries:
The Navigator's Daughter
Passport to Spy

The Carol Childs Mysteries:
Shadow of Doubt
Beyond a Doubt
Without a Doubt
Room for Doubt
Reason to Doubt

The Misty Dawn Mysteries:
The House on Hallowed Ground
The House that Vanity Built
The House of the Setting Son.